All in God's

Time

(revised)

By

Deborah Lynne

Copyright

Dedication

The original version of this book, *All in God's Time*, was dedicated to my husband, Scott, and my three grown children, Rachael, Molly, and Chris. They encouraged me over the years to follow my passion.

My revised version is still dedicated to my kids, with much appreciation for their continued encouragement. Scott went on to be with the Lord in 2014. Although he is greatly missed, I know he's happy. I'm still missing him, while I'm blessed to continue to doing what I love…writing.

Thank You, Lord for your peace and direction in my life, Lord.

Scripture

Psalm 46:10a (NLT) - "Be still, and know that I am God!

Chapter 1

With elbows resting on her desktop, Meagan rubbed her hands together as she released a long sigh. "I have to do it," she said aloud, "one more time."

Opening the drawer of her desk, she pulled out her large checkbook and began writing checks to pay her monthly bills for April. Subtracting the amounts of each check she realized she needed a job soon…before her money ran out.

After stuffing each check with its corresponding statement into its respective envelope, Meagan made them ready for the mail and stacked them in a pile on her desk. In her accounting ledger, she marked all her bills paid. Most people paid their bills on line, but she was a little old fashioned in that way. All her payments went via snail mail. She had tried it long ago, but due to some monies removed from her account afterward, money she had not okayed to be taken, she refused to purchase things on line or pay any bills that way again, at least for the time being.

Of course, this was the least of her worries today.

She shook her head in despair. "I'm not trying to be ungrateful, Lord. You have blessed me so much with these wonderful travel jobs. I've managed to put a good bit away, but if a job doesn't come soon, I'm going to have to dip into my savings. Again, thank you, Lord, for my savings…but please don't make me go there. My house, as nice as it is, needs so many upgrades and repairs. I started on a few during this time off period, using some of my savings, but that's what they are for. The time I've been off lasted longer than I'd planned. Now I need to get back to work. I need another job. Thank you for listening." Closing her eyes, she leaned back in her chair, placed her fingertips over her temples, and made small circular motions. A headache attempted to surface, but she would not permit it.

Sighing, she snatched up the stamped and sealed envelopes, rose to her feet, and headed to the front of the house. Turning off the light, her mind nagged at her. Quit traveling. Stay home. Take a local job.

She groaned. "I don't want to! I love traveling." She made her way to the front door. Turning the knob, she opened it and then stuck the envelopes on the bottom hooks of her mailbox to be picked up by the postman later that same day.

The late March winds blew her straight brown hair across her face. She cast a glance at the beautiful white clouds hanging in the bright blue sky.

"Maybe it's not about what I want. Maybe it's about what I should do." She murmured to herself. She knew her family would be pleased to have her home all the time. This past Thanksgiving and Christmas was her first time home in over ten years. That had been her plan. Take six months off. Enjoy the holidays. Get some repairs made as well as a few upgrades, and then get back to work. She should already be lined up to leave this week. April starts in a few days and she should be under contract for three months at her next job site, wherever it was to take her.

"Is that You telling me to stay home? Am I supposed to get a steady job around here? Am I to quit traveling?"

Meagan loved seeing different parts of America. The fact that she didn't have to spend much money doing it was a plus. In fact, she made good money as she traveled and saw the sights. Her job as a radiologic technologist allowed her this lucrative income that afforded her a modest but nice, three-bedroom, two-bath home in one of the older, well established neighborhoods in the Baton Rouge area. Louisiana was home to her. She'd lived there all of her life. When she bought the house the first of last year, she knew she would have to make a few repairs and those repairs cost money.

Meagan had committed herself to that fact and was determined to save enough to pay cash for the expenses as she had the repairs and upgrades made. The money she made was enough to pay the notes on her home, the monthly car payment for her new dark grey Honda SUV, and the rest of the monthly bills yet still tuck away a little over one thousand dollars a month.

In the ten years she'd been traveling she had managed to save a nice nest egg. Of course a good bit was used when she purchased the home. After saving nine more months and building the savings substantially, she was determined to start the repairs. That she did, but along with it came a new roof. That was unexpected. Of course insurance paid part of it due to it being damaged by one of the hurricanes that Louisiana was so famous for.

Thank God for insurance.

When she bought this house she made sure her home was covered for flood damage as well as strong winds, hale, and other acts of nature. Still she didn't want to have to start dipping into the savings to pay her monthly bills. If she were off for another three months, she would have to do just that. Of course, she was blessed to have it, but she also knew if she started dipping into savings to pay bills, she would drain it within a few months, now that it was so low. And that she wasn't prepared to do.

She needed to get back to work! Hopefully it was the traveling work she'd come to love.

The perks of the job were great, but the down side slipped in occasionally…the downside being off too long between jobs. By taking those six months off, she missed a couple of great opportunities and now the jobs didn't seem so readily available. Her handler told her things have seemed to slow down this year, for some reason.

Meagan had enjoyed the time off. She spent a great deal of it with her mom and dad; some with her sister, Shelly, and her family; a little bit with her brother, Troy, and caught up with her friends at church. Most of all, she spent quality time with her niece, Mandy, and nephew, Kirk. Of course, that meant she and her sister did a lot of bonding. In the last few years, they had grown quite close. And this six-month renewal bonded them even more.

Walking through the dining room toward the kitchen, she glanced at her aquarium. "I'd better feed you guys." The only pets she allowed herself were the fish, because as long as they were fed and the motor worked purifying the tank constantly, the little creatures seemed happy. A dog or a cat would take more to maintain, and then she would have to place them somewhere every time she traveled.

That, according to her family, would be okay, but she already asked more than she dared. Shelly had a husband, Brandon, and two wonderful children who took most of her time. Her baby brother, Troy, led a busy single life...no time to care for pets of his own should he even think about getting one, let alone someone else's. Mom and Pops, she thought as a light chuckle rose from within, she wouldn't think of asking them. They had raised three children, two dogs, and a cat. They worked many long hours to care for them all. Now they were enjoying the life of retirement. The kids were grown and the pets had died off, one by one. If they had wanted more animals, they would have gotten them by now.

Dropping a pinch of food into the tank, she said, "Are you guys seeing too much of me lately?" Prince Charming, the slender black fish swam to the surface to nibble on the food, ignoring her question. All he cared about was getting fed. Right behind him the orange fish with black and white striping rushed to the surface to join Prince in the food fest. She too paid no never mind to Meagan.

"Neither one of you really cares, as long as you get fed. Right, Gwenivere?" She smiled down at them both. Latecomers wiggled their way to the surface grabbing bites of food before it was all gone. "Hey, you guys. There's enough for all of you. Lancelot, King Arthur, don't be so greedy."

She closed the cover and then headed toward the kitchen. "They may not care, but I do. I am so ready to go back to work." But I can't worry about that...and I won't. She knew down deep everything happened, or didn't happen, for a reason. He was in charge.

After hand washing a couple of glasses and a saucer, Meagan paced the floor. She had to do something to keep from going crazy. The only sound in her home came from the living room, the motor of the aquarium and the television. Pandora streamed through the around-sound speakers. She paced from the kitchen to the living room, and back again. Her eyes glanced occasionally at the phone on the wall in the kitchen and then at the one on the end table in the living room. Her cell phone was on the counter charging.

"Ring!" she shouted. "Please one of you, ring. I've got to hear from you soon."

Raising a brow she looked at the phone and reminded herself. "A watched pot never boils. Right? I've got to get out of here." She shook her head. Looking up she lifted her shoulders. "I don't mean to be so wishy-washy, worried then not worried...but when, Lord?"

As soon as she said those words out loud, she heard a voice in her head saying, "All in My time. Trust Me."
A smile touched her lips.

She knew. Peace slipped around her like a warm comforter. Why worry? She knew it would be okay. God always met her needs and then some. A job always came before her money ran out. Meagan learned a long time ago in her walk with the Lord that everything happened for a reason and it all happened in God's time. He saw the big picture, and He was in control.

It was the human talking, or her flesh talking. Sometimes Meagan needed to be reminded it was out of her hands.
Picking up the phone, she called her sister.

After two rings she heard, "Don't tell me. You've run out of things to do again and you're so bored you want to come over and spend time with me and the baby." Shelly's laugh bubbled in her ear.

"Hello to you, too. I forget you have caller ID and always check it before you answer your phone. I admit part of what you said is right. I want to come over and visit, but not because I'm bored. I don't want to sit here and watch the phone anymore. I'm going nuts. I'm talking to the phone, the walls, the fish...you name it." Meagan twisted the cord around her finger as she spoke.

"What do you mean 'going'?" her sister joked playfully.

"Ha. Ha. You're funny. But really. My house is clean...well clean for me, and I don't have any errands to run today. I need to stay busy and I couldn't think of a better way to do that than to come over and play with the Kirkster. Who knows? Maybe I'll stay long enough to see Mandy, too. She gets out of school at two-thirty, right?"

Meagan loved her niece and nephew more than she could express. Never having met Mr. Right and settling down herself, she believed this would be as close as she would ever come to having children of her own to love. Meagan had accepted the fact that God wanted her to remain single. She had given up on finding the right man and she wouldn't settle for "Mr. Right Now."

The phone made a crackling sound and then a clunk as Meagan heard Shelly yell, "Hold on. Kirk yanked the phone out of my hand. I'm trying—"

"I wanna talk," the baby said. He was apparently trying to get the phone. Meagan heard his heavy breathing. The noise quieted and she heard, "Mommy, I talk." He smacked his lips.

Meagan saw him in her mind's eye. Meagan couldn't help but laugh. He was such a cutie. Three going on ten. "Hey, my little man. Is that you? Aunt Meggie is coming over to see you."

He squealed with delight. "Aunt Meg—" She heard more clanking and squealing.

"Yes, Aunt Meggie." Shelly obviously had at last won control over the phone. "Come on over. We just baked a batch of brownies. I'll leave the front door unlocked for you. Just let yourself in."

After hanging up the phone, Meagan took a minute to brush back her long hair and bind it with a coated ponytail band. She then splashed some cool water on her face. Dabbing it dry with a hand towel, she looked at her reflection in the mirror. Her light chocolate brown eyes twinkled.

God was in control and things would be fine. She wasn't going to worry about it anymore…at least not today.

Chapter 2

On the drive to Shelly's, Meagan started thinking about her sister and their relationship. She loved Shelly and her family very much. Brandon Bates, Shelly's husband, was business minded, a good family man, and a kind brother-in-law. Her kids, Mandy and Kirk could do no wrong in their aunt's eyes. The sweet family of four always made Meagan feel like a part of them. Meagan was blessed and she knew it. Sure, she had a mother and father whom she loved and they loved her dearly. She also loved her baby brother and knew it was reciprocated, but Shelly was less than a year younger than Meagan and they had a connection almost like twins. In high school they had strayed slightly, but in the last ten years their relationship had grown closer than ever.

The two sisters didn't live far from one another, so Meagan arrived in less than five minutes. "I'm here!" Meagan called out as she entered the front door. "Mmm…chocolate. Your house smells wonderful." The sweet scent played havoc with her taste buds immediately. Her mouth watered, longing for a scrumptious taste of something chocolate. Knowing her sister, the brownies would be ready soon.

A quick glance around the room showed Shelly's tendency for neatness. The sisters were as different as night and day. Everything was in its place at Shelly's home. No clutter gathered on any surface. The light shining through the sheers reflected on the tabletops with their freshly polished surface. How Shelly did it with the Kirkster running around, Meagan never knew?

If her sister wasn't cleaning or playing with the kids, Shelly was cooking something. She would bake from scratch cookies or brownies for the fun of it.

For nighttime meals something like a roast or chicken would be baking in the oven. The scent of something lusciously delicious always filled the air in Shelly's home…something mouth watering that no one could resist. The food always smelled so good it made Meagan hungry even when she wasn't.

She could gain ten pounds just walking into Shelly's house.

"Aunt Meggie," Kirk yelled as he rounded the corner and made a mad dash toward Meagan.

When he got close, Kirk jumped up into her arms. The sweet smell of baby invaded her nostrils as she caught him in her arms and spun him around while he squealed with delight.

"Hey, Little Man. How are you?" She hugged him and then tickled his tummy while he laughed and laughed.

The sound of dishes clanking came from the other room. "Come in the kitchen. I'm fixing us a coke to go with the brownies."

Meagan lifted her nephew high up in the air, and then chunked him across her shoulder like a sack of potatoes.

Laughter peeled from his lips.

"I've got to take the trash out first, Shelly. Then I'll be right with you. Where is that garbage can?" Meagan asked as she twirled the two of them around as if looking for it.

Her nephew shrieked between giggles.

"Come on, Meagan. Don't get him too wound up. He'll never settle down for his afternoon nap." Shelly slipped into a chair at the head of the table.

Meagan strolled into the room with her nephew still draped over her shoulder.

Shelly had set two glasses on the table next to a plate of brownies. "Look what I have for you…if you'll settle down with him," her sister pleaded.

The sisters, although born eleven months apart, looked almost like twins.

Their coloring was the same with hazelnut brown eyes and mocha brown hair, only Shelly's hair curled and twisted like Little Orphan Annie's while Meagan's was as straight as a two by four. Even their size and shapes were similar. Meagan, at five foot three inches, stood one inch shorter than her baby sister.

No matter how much they looked alike, or how sweet and kind they both were their personalities were complete opposites. Meagan, who was quiet and kept to herself a good deal of the time, loved playing sports, strumming the guitar, and singing. Shelly, who never met a stranger, would cheer every game on but don't ask her to get out there and roll around on the ground. She might get dirty or break a nail or something. And she'd rather die than sing in front of a stranger.

"Sit," Shelly said. "Give me an update. What kind of jobs are they offering you now? Where are you about to fly off to? My sister the world traveler…well in the U.S. anyway. Who would have believed it? You who didn't even like to go spend the night away from home when we were kids."

"Time changes people."

Kirk held tightly onto Meagan's ponytail as she walked over to the table. She heaved him up off her shoulder, and he pulled the band with him. It released Meagan's hair as it cascaded over her shoulders and down her back. Kirk laughed watching his aunt's face as she set him down on the floor. Her hair covered his entire face and then some. He giggled some more.

Meagan chuckled and then snatched the band from him. "You little monster," she chided as she slipped the band around her wrist like a bracelet for safekeeping. "I'll get you for that, Little Man." She stretched out her hands wiggling her fingers getting ready to snatch him back up, but he jumped out of her reach.

"Okay. Okay. You win for now," she said as she flicked her brows. "I'll get you later," she pledged.

He practically rolled on the floor in laughter.

"Kirk," his mother said. "Go get your new truck and show Aunt Meggie what you can do with it."

On that, Kirk jumped to his feet and raced down the hall toward his bedroom.

"Please settle down. He's getting too wound up. I mean it."

"Spoil sport!" Megan scrunched her face in displeasure, but only for a quick second.

"Take your coke and grab a brownie or two. Come on. Sit down and settle down. Tell me." With him out of the room, Shelly begged for details, the curiosity apparently about to kill her. "What's up? Where are you going? Give me the low down on your next job."

"There's not one…yet, but I'm not going to think about it anymore today. At least I'm not going to worry about it."

"I thought you had an offer? In fact two. One in Texas and one in Hawaii." Her sister's eyes opened wide in shock. "What happened to them?"

"Things didn't work out on those. I guess I do need to give you an update." Sitting to the right of her sister, Meagan said, "There were three possibilities. The Arizona job fell through. The Texas job got taken. And the one in Hawaii expects me to pay my room and board…forget that! I told them I wouldn't make any money if I did that. Besides, you know I hate beaches. The company said they wouldn't make much money on it either."

"Wow. Sorry to hear that." Shelly's eyes reflected a pitiful look as her lips puckered in a pouty face.

Taking a moment, Meagan bit into the brownie. "Mmm. This is good," Meagan mumbled through partially closed lips, then sipped on her coke. She sighed. "And now, there are no jobs to be had. At least not yet. You'd think with all the travel companies I'm listed with, I'd hear from one of them soon."

"Why don't you start looking around here? I know they don't pay as well, but we would love to have you home all the time."

Meagan smiled. The same thought had just crossed her mind. "I don't think so. Besides, you wouldn't be as thrilled as you think. It's only because I'm gone a lot that you all enjoy me when I come home. I guarantee you if I was here all the time, my appearance would lose its pizzazz." With a sweet smile plastered on her face, she waved her hands beside her face, like the Joker. "Ha-ha!"

"Psh." Shelly slapped her hand in the air as air whistled through her lips. "Get out of here. Don't be so ridiculous."

"I need to get back to work, Shelly. I don't want to run out of money. I still have debts to pay. My house needs a few more things done to it. Besides, bills don't stop just because I'm not working. I may have to take a job around here, but I hope not yet. The truth is I don't really want to stop traveling yet."

"Don't you worry! That's why you make the big bucks, sister. So you can sit for a few weeks or a few months and not—"

The ringing of Meagan's cell phone interrupted what Shelly was saying.

Meagan's heart skipped a beat. Please Lord; let it be about a job. She prayed that silent prayer before tapping the green dot on her phone, accepting the call. "Hello," she said, and then held her breath.

"Hey, sweetie. What are you doing? I called your house but you weren't home. I wanted to see if you wanted to kill some time playing backgammon or acey-deucy or maybe cards or something."

Quickly, she released the pent up air. "Hey, Mom." She was slightly disappointed. She hoped the disappointment didn't sound in her voice. "I'm over at Shelly's. We're sitting at the table eating brownies." She glanced at her sister, lifting a brow, as if to say do you care if Mom comes over?

Shelly appeared to read her sister's thoughts because she nodded and whispered, "Tell her to come on over."

"Do you want to come over here, Mom? Maybe we'll play a little cards or just gab."

"I'm on my way."

After they hung up, Meagan said, "Mom will be here in a couple of minutes. She asked about backgammon. She's in her game mode. Maybe we could play some cards. Like Spades or Hearts...just not three handed Bridge," she groaned as she pleaded with her sister.

Shelly made a face and shook her head. "I thought you loved Bridge?"

"I do. But I don't want to have to think hard right now." Meagan explained, then munched on her brownie some more.

"Sounds good to me...to play anything. But me playing any game at all depends on Kirk. No thanks to his aunt, he still might take a nap, and then I know I could play some cards."

She scratched her head as if thinking. "Now where were we? Oh yeah. About your next job. Have you prayed about it?"

"You know I have."

"Then the best thing you can do is—"

Meagan's cell started ringing again, interrupting Shelly one more time. Meagan shrugged her shoulders. She glanced at the screen this time, before answering the phone.

In her heart and mind she was hoping again it was about a job.

TAA in bold letters, showed on her screen. Her eyes widened as her heart lifted.

"Hello."

"Meagan. It's me, Lauren Woods with Techs Across America. We have a job we would like to submit you for, but it's a little different than most."

Relief spread through her as she heard those words. But after a mere second, the ending of Lauren's sentence gave Meagan pause. Her brows cringed at the thought of what Lauren might have meant when she called it "different."

It must have shown in Meagan's demeanor, because when she glanced at her sister she could tell by the look on Shelly's face, her sister wished she were on a connecting phone listening to the conversation that was taking place.

"You've got my attention. I definitely am ready for my next job. Tell me all about it," Meagan said.

Shelly tapped on the table and whispered, "Tell me too. What's she saying? Tell me."

Kirk ran into the room and rolled his toy truck up on the table by Meagan.

Shelly reached down and scooped him up into her arms. Holding him on her lap, she whispered, "Ssshh, baby. Auntie Meggie's on the phone. Important call." Shelly pressed her fingers against her lips and made the shushing sound again, encouraging silence in her son but her eyes spoke clearly. She wanted to know what was being said.

"It's a small hospital in South Carolina. A doctor owns it. He is requesting a rad-tech, but not just any rad-tech. He wants a woman who has a good moral background. She would be living in a wing of his home. It's separated from the rest of the house by a door with a dead bolt. It has its own private entrance. Anyway, she would spend some time with his children. Three girls. At meals and such…time enough to be an influence in their lives."

"A glorified baby-sitter? No thanks. I didn't get a degree to baby-sit. I do that for my sister for free." Meagan felt a slap on her hand and her brown eyes flashed in her sister's direction. "Besides, I'm not much of a cook."

Shelly stared at her. A frown etched on her face. The lack of knowledge burned in her eyes.

About that time, there was a knock on the side door, and their mom stuck her head in. "I'm here. I'm coming in."

Shelly signaled her to keep on coming, but then she pushed her fingers to her lips motioning for her mother not to say anything. Then she pointed to Meagan on her cell phone.

Meagan waggled her fingers in a small wave at her mom and noticed a slight pout cover her lips. It was probably because she was told to be quiet when she hadn't said hardly anything. But Kirk changed that quickly. He jumped off his mother's lap and hollered, "Ganny! Ganny!" And he went running to her.

"Granny's here. Come give me a kiss," she said softly as she leaned down ready to catch the little boy as he made a mad dash toward his grandmother.

A smile quickly covered her mom's face as Meagan continued to listen to Lauren.

"No," Lauren said. "You wouldn't cook. The girls have a housekeeper to cook and clean for them. Listen. How much time you would spend with them would depend on you, but he wants a woman that could share meals with them occasionally. Talk a little girl talk with them now and then."

Lauren paused only briefly. "His daughters are twelve, sixteen, and seventeen. His wife died seven years ago, and he feels he has neglected them. The housekeeper watches out for them. He just wants the girls to be around a female who can show them…I don't know…I guess how to be feminine…How to make good choices as a female. He says they need a woman's input. Before you say no again, think about it."

It was like Lauren could see through the air waves, because Meagan had touched the tip of her tongue to the roof of her mouth with the intent of the next word coming out of her mouth to be no with a capital N.

However, Lauren didn't give her time to refuse yet. She continued with more details on the job description. "The pay is almost double from what you got on that last job, plus the usual per diem, rental car, and a place to live. I hear it's a mansion with an ocean view." It was like Lauren paused for those details to sink in.

Meagan felt overwhelmed, but it was sounding better and better. She kept that thought to herself for the time being.

"It's a three-month contract. Dr. Richardson said if the girl doesn't work out within a month, he'd let her back out of the contract without any penalties. But if she does work out, there is an option for an additional three months. So that's a possibility of a six-month job. At higher than top pay," she added.

Meagan slowly released the breath she had been holding and said, "Let me consider this for a few minutes before I make a decision. I'll call you back shortly." Meagan had to think on this one for probably more than a few minutes, but she definitely had to think before answering. She didn't want to rush and give the wrong answer…then again; she didn't know what the right answer was either.

"No problem. There are other girls we could offer this to. I just thought of you first. You would be perfect because you have strong beliefs and convictions. I think that is the kind of thing the doctor is looking for."

As she disconnected the line, Meagan thought that was exactly why she wasn't interested in taking the job. She wasn't a mother or anything like it. She has no experience in that field. Besides, how could she teach his girls morals? That was something parents trained their children in as they reared them.

Before she laid down her cell phone, Shelly exploded. "Tell me all about it. It's a job offer, right? Where? When? Tell us. Tell us." The words rushed out of her sister's mouth.

Meagan's mom looked on in curiosity, but she seemed to see the frustration and confusion in her oldest daughter's eyes, so she said nothing to Meagan at that moment. "Give your sister a minute, Shelly. She looks like she just took in a lot of information." Turning her gaze back on Meagan she quietly added, "If you want to talk about it, dear, we'll gladly listen. We can be your sounding board."

"Thanks, Mom. Hold your horses, Shelly!"

Shelly crossed her eyes and stuck out her tongue.

With her elbows on the table, Meagan laid her face in her hands, pressed her fingertips to her forehead between her brows, and then slowly traced her brows. Applying pressure, she tried to push the onset of a headache away. "I don't know. I just don't know."

This was a big decision. Could she handle the job? Three girls?

And living in the doctor's home…that was too strange. Lacing her fingers together she rested her chin on top of them. Her gaze darted from her mom to her sister and back again.

"A sounding board. That's just what I need. Y'all listen and help me make the right decision." Resting her hands back on the table, she relayed some of what Lauren had told her to them. When the details were out of the way, she said, "And I don't know what to do. I wanted to say an outright no. But I didn't."

Shelly's brows furrowed as she shook her head looking confused. With both her hands outstretched and palms up, she said, "You were just saying you needed a job. What's there to decide?"

"But this one is so different. Didn't you hear me?" She tapped the top of the table with her fingertips as she spoke.

"I did, sweetie," her mother said. "Did you say the doctor owned the hospital?"

"Yes. And that I'd work at his hospital. That part is okay. But after work I'd go home at night—to his home. To his kids. At his house." She said these statements strong and in a steady rhythm and then repeated, "His home. His kids. His house." It was worth repeating over and over. That was what made her feel so unsure about this job. "I don't need to be responsible for some rich old man's spoiled brats. I'm not good with kids anyway. I'm thirty-five, never been married; never even baby-sat till you had yours, Shelly."

"Meagan, you are wonderful with the kids."

Her mother agreed.

"But that's because they're my niece and nephew."

"Meagan Phillips. You stop that talk right now. First off, you're not thirty-five…yet," Shelly reminded her. "That's not till August. And that's five months away. Second, you need a job. What else did she say? Like, where is it? How much does it pay? How long will it last?" Shelly was all excited for Meagan.

Meagan heard it in her sister's voice. She wished she could be as excited.

"Have you been praying for the right job, Meagan?" her mother asked. "And hasn't it always been your practice or belief that if the job is the right one, it will be the first one that works out for you because God opens the door."

"Yes," Shelly answered for Meagan. "That's true. That's what she has always said. God's in control…not her. If it's not the one He has for her, He'll close the door."

Meagan had. Her sister was right. Today she was begging God to send her almost any job. Rubbing her face in frustration and then dragging her fingers through her long silky strands of hair, Meagan sighed. "Shelly makes it sound like I should take the job. What do you think, Mom?" She tipped her head slightly to the side as she raised a hand in question.

"That's something you'll have to answer for yourself. But I have a suggestion. Think of the pros and cons. Pray some more…in fact we can pray together. The power of two or more…you know."

"Yes, I do. But I don't know that this is God's answer to my prayers. Think about what I'm saying. I don't know the man. I would be living in his home. Did you two hear me say that? How not right is that?" She was waving her hands all over the place as she tried to make them see the gravity of the whole situation.

Shelly looked at her with a curious look on her face. "Huh?"

Her mom said, "But wouldn't you have your own place? I didn't hear any of the details there."

"I don't know." Meagan shook her head as she was trying to think things through. "Lauren talked like it was a safe situation. She said he lives in a mansion, and whoever takes the job would live in one of the wings. There was a deadbolt to lock your wing off from the rest of the house, so I guess it's like your own little apartment. It does have a separate entrance. And the pay is double of what I made on my last job. Plus it could be as long as six months. That's always something I love to hear. In fact, I'd love to work all the way through November and then come home before Christmas, but then they would have to extend it a second time, well a couple more months the second time."

In her years of traveling, a couple of places she worked had extended over and over until she stayed a year or better. Then Meagan would say no and finally go back home. "I'd love to be home for Christmas again. I really enjoyed that."

"That would be wonderful, two years in a row," her mom said. She patted Meagan's hand gently as it lay on top of the table.

"Wait!" Shelly demanded waving her hands in the air in short little motions as her head was shaking.

What was going on? Meagan saw the doubt in her eyes…and the questions.

"I'm still back on the wing thing. Back up. Back up." She directed Meagan with her hands signaling the back up. "You'd live in a mansion?" She threw both arms out in front of her as her face lit up. "How cool is that? Would you have a maid? And did you say the pay is doubled? How can you even hesitate?" She turned the palms of her hands up and thrust them forward shrugging her shoulders at the same time. "I don't get you. I think you'd have to be nuts to refuse!"

Meagan squeezed her eyes closed as she clasped her hands together on the top of the table in front of her. "I don't know. I just want to be sure."

"I'm glad you're not rushing to any snap decision," her mom

said gently. "Your safety comes first."

"Okay." Shelly jumped right back in the middle of that conversation. With the side of her hand pounding the table as she spoke, she said, "Think. Have you or have you not been praying for the right job? Asking God to send you work?" Shelly paused a brief moment. When no answer came, she said sharply, "Yes?"

Meagan nodded in agreement.

"Well, sister dear, don't you think if it's the wrong job, God will stop it before it goes all the way?"

Meagan glanced at Shelly and then her mom. "I never thought of that." Scratching the top of her head, she realized Shelly was right, but her mom's eyes were wide as saucers, so she probably didn't agree. She was a mom. Moms wouldn't want their daughter staying in some strange man's home, no matter how fancy or how secure people claimed it to be. But Meagan agreed with Shelly. A half smile touched Meagan's lips.

"You've got a point, Sis." She picked up her cell, pressed a couple of buttons, and then held it to her ear.

"Techs Across America. This is Lauren Woods. May I help you?"

"Hey, Lauren. It's me. Meagan Phillips. Go ahead and submit me." She peeked at her sister and thought, what am I getting myself into? Only God knows.

Chapter 3

Three days later, standing in the airport, watching the various suitcases bump along on the ever slow-moving conveyor belt at baggage claim as flights were announced departing and arriving in Charleston, South Carolina, Meagan watched for her two blue cases with the three inch strips of red tape wrapped around the handle. She learned this trick a long time ago to make her luggage stand out from all the rest. So many suitcases looked identical today, and at a moving glance it was hard to read the small numbers to match your ticket when you have over a hundred people at a time trying to find their own luggage. The bold red tape wrapped around her handle stood out like a neon sign making it very easy for Meagan to find her suitcase quickly.

The noise level was high in the airport with people milling around, but Meagan blanked out the sounds around her by focusing on the next step she was about to make. Her mind wouldn't slow down.

Questions raced.

Was she crazy? Meagan was moving in with complete strangers.

Was she nuts? She was supposed to influence three girls she had never met before.

Who did she think she was? Why had she taken this job? There had to be another job coming soon with fewer entanglements, less complications. And it had to be better than this one. She couldn't be an influence to three strange girls. They probably wouldn't even like her. A chill swept through her body as she gasped.

What if she didn't like them? They were rich…that usually meant spoiled. Meagan wasn't one who typically prejudged, or even judged in general, but given the situation she was about to become involved in, what else could she think?

She remembered being in high school even if it had been over fifteen years ago. There were so many different cliques and they all acted out-of-the-ordinary…even standoffish. They each had their own rules and regulations. Girls with a lot of money in the family usually looked down their noses at those without.

She sighed. One month. How hard could that be? If it didn't work out, she could leave without penalty…and with double the pay. That would be like working two months. A smile touched her lips at that thought. Meagan could handle any job for one month. Besides, she knew God had wanted her there or He would have closed the door…but He hadn't.

When she had collected her bags, she walked over to the car rental counter to get the vehicle that awaited her. In the past ten years, the travel companies she worked for had taken very good care of her. Meagan learned to depend on them doing their job well.

After giving her name and confirmation number to the receptionist at Budget Car Rental, she was handed the keys to a fairly new Honda Accord. Nice. Usually the companies rented Dodge Neon or a Ford Focus, a small economy car. This was a nice change. Her personal choice was Honda. In fact, when time allowed, she drove her own car to her new assignment location. That way she brought more of her own personal belongings…like her guitar, some CDs and some DVDs. She loved music. This job, although close in mileage, didn't leave time enough for the drive. She barely had time to pack once she was accepted.

While gone, when she flew, her family took turns driving her car occasionally so the battery wouldn't run down. This kept it in better running condition. Mandy fed her fish, and Auntie Meagan paid her niece nicely for the great job she did. This gave Meagan a special connection with Mandy.

"Your car is the light blue one out front. Bill just gassed it up. He'll take you to it," the agent said.

Bill a tall slender young man eagerly stepped up and reached for Meagan's larger suitcase. "Here, let me help you."

"Thanks."

"Follow me," the young man said.

Meagan pulled her smaller suitcase behind her and tightened her grip on the strap over her shoulder that held her laptop as she followed Bill to the end of the counter and out the front door and to the car.

"Allow me," he said, as he opened the driver's door and pulled a lever to pop the trunk open, and then he quickly slipped the big suitcase into the trunk, followed by the smaller one. "Do you want me to put that back here?" he asked pointing to her carry on.

She shook her head. "That's okay. It's my laptop. I'll put it up front with me."

"Here's the check sheet to go over the car," Bill said as he handed her a clipboard with a form attached.

Meagan placed her laptop on the passenger seat in the front and grabbed the clipboard. "Thanks again for your help."

He smiled, pulled his pen out of his top pocket and gave it to her to use.

"You think of everything," she said sweetly. With quick steps, she worked her way around the car inspecting for any nicks or dings. The automobile was like new. She checked off different areas on the form but failed to find anything to make a special note about, not even with the interior. The car looked to be in great shape.

After writing the odometer reading down, she signed the completed form and then asked Bill, "Do you by chance know how to get to Jennifer Lane Memorial? It's the hospital near the bridge to cross over to get to Lighthouse Isle?"

"I think I know. Is that the hospital the doctor built in memory of his late wife?"

"I guess. I know a doctor owns it. Dr. Richardson."

"Yeah. That's the one," he said. He went on to give her directions that sounded easy enough.

She thanked him as she returned the pen and clipboard. She just wanted an idea of the direction she would be leaving the airport in.

It was on the way to the home she would be staying at. Lauren had faxed a map showing directions from the airport to the house, plus Meagan had the GPS on her cell, so she shouldn't have any problems finding her temporary home, but she wanted to drop by the hospital first.

Her stomach churned a little at the thought of a new job. Although she was competent, she always felt a little nervous going to new surroundings.

Some hospitals had newer equipment than others, and she found people all across the country had different ways of doing some of the same things...at least the main parts of her job never changed.

Meagan found most places she went, the people liked her accent, that Southern inflection, right away. In South Carolina her accent shouldn't stand out as it had in many other places. She never noticed her accent...at least not until she landed in places like Bar

Harbor, Maine, and Boston, Massachusetts. On her last trip, which was Fairbanks, Alaska, her accent was very different from everyone else.

Over time, she had gotten used to being picked on about her Southern drawl. It was always a good icebreaker, but there shouldn't be a major difference here.

As she pulled into the lot, her gaze took in the size of the hospital: not too big, but not too small, three stories high. She guessed the hospital housed possibly forty to fifty patients when filled to capacity.

The hospital on the island in Maine had been about the same size. She remembered enjoying that one because she got to know almost everyone who worked there. She hoped this one proved to be as friendly.

Meagan parked and made her way in. The clean, quietness enveloped her as she heard the tap of her shoes echoing in the massive openness of the entrance. Glancing at the direction signs placed in easy view, she took the elevator to the second floor where the imaging department was set.

The first person she wanted to find was the supervisor of x-ray.

"May I help you?" asked the receptionist who was sitting behind the front desk. Her name tag read 'Catherine.'

"Hi. I'm Meagan Phillips. I'm the x-ray tech who starts tomorrow. I just got in and thought I'd stop by and introduce myself...familiarize me to where I'll be working for the next three months."

"Yes. We're expecting you...tomorrow. Never has anyone dropped by a day early before." Extending her hand, she said, almost with an air of question in the tone of her voice, "Hi. I'm Catherine Tollberry." Her gaze covered Meagan from head to toe as they shook hands.

Catherine had short bright red hair, slightly spiked on top, framing her heart shaped face that was covered with a mass of freckles.

"You don't look so special," she mumbled under her breath as she slightly turned away from Meagan to punch a couple of buttons on the phone.

"Excuse me?" Meagan asked, thinking the girl was speaking to her.

Catherine shrugged her shoulders and then said, "Nothing."

So much for friendly people. "Is the supervisor around today? Would she have a minute for me to introduce myself?"

"I just beeped him." She emphasized that it was a he not a she. "His name is Thomas Gladstone." Within a minute, maybe two, her line rang. Picking it up, she said, "Tom, the new x-ray tech is here."

Silence filled the space for a few short seconds, and then she said, "Yes. I know. That's what I said. She just flew in and stopped by to meet you."

Another few seconds of silence, then Catherine said, "I'll let her know." After replacing the receiver, she said, "Tom will be with you in a few minutes. He said to ask you to have a seat."

"Thanks." Before the word was out of Meagan's mouth, Catherine had already turned her back on Meagan. She moved to the waiting area and sat down hoping all the while she hadn't made a mistake taking this job. If her place to stay was going to be difficult, she had hoped at least the hospital would be a great escape to get her through the month.

So much for hoping. She sighed.

A short time later, a fairly handsome young man with blonde hair and a big smile swept into the room. He couldn't have been much older than Meagan. "Meagan Phillips, I presume," he said, his voice almost melodic, as he reached his hand out to shake hers.

A pleasant person and he was her boss. Things were looking up.

She shook his extended hand and said, "Mr. Gladstone. Nice to meet you. I thought I'd stop by for a moment and see where I'd be working. I hope you don't mind."

"Mind? I like your initiative. And the name is Tom. You'll find this a wonderful place to work," he motioned all around the area with his hand, encompassing the whole hospital. "I came down here as a travel tech myself. But in no time I fell in love with the town, the people, the ambiance of the setting, and I never left. I've been here over five years. Now, I'm in charge of the department." A crooked smile crept over his well-tanned face. He took in a big breath and let it out quickly. An expression of satisfaction showed in his eyes. "And I love it more every day."

Meagan liked the man's enthusiasm. She doubted she would feel the same way after her short stay, but she could only hope. A beach setting was the last place in which she would ever settle, but for a few months she could handle it. Sand and sun was never a favorite of Meagan's.

The first thing she noticed about Tom was the way he talked with his hands. He was very expressive, just like Shelly. She liked that. At least Catherine wasn't the only type person they had here. And maybe the woman was just having a bad day…she hoped.

"I'm sure you'll love it. Would you like a ten cent tour now?"

She shook her head. "I'll wait and take that tour tomorrow morning, if that's okay with you. I still need to find where I'll be staying and get settled in, but I'm looking forward to tomorrow. Thanks for taking a moment with me now."

"My pleasure." Tom gave a small salute and bowed slightly as he moved back, giving Meagan room to head toward the exit. "We'll see you tomorrow morning at seven a.m."

Meagan reached her hand out to shake his again before departing. "Thank you."

As she walked past him and moved a few steps away, the elevator door opened and a short, older man with a small amount of white hair over his ears and bald on top stepped through the opened door. He had a frown on his face. Meagan watched him out of the corner of her eye as he moved past her and quickly to the imaging desk.

"Where are my x-rays?" he grumbled loudly. "I haven't got all day."

"I'll check on them, Doctor," Catherine said as she picked up the phone and pressed a couple of buttons.

Air slipped slowly out of Meagan's pursed lips.

So much for a happy place to work.

She felt certain he would be the one, her boss and landlord rolled into one. The next three months were going to be the longest three months of her life.

"Oh, well. A job is a job," she whispered under her breath. Meagan loved what she did. She usually enjoyed her patients and the help she supplied in their recovery. She could give it one month, hopefully three months, and make enough money to wait on the next job. Meagan stepped into the elevator, turned her back to the wall and glanced at the old doctor one more time. As the elevator doors closed, she looked toward the ceiling and whispered, "As long as you help me, Lord, I can get through this. Don't let his grumpiness bring me down. My joy is not in him, but in You. I hate the thought of how unhappy his children must be. But that is what I signed up to do, so give me the strength to do it well." In her heart she knew, God didn't put you into something without giving you what you needed to get through it. Everything would work out. That she knew. She pressed the button for the first floor, then stepped back and leaned against the wall as it descended.

A Scripture passed through her mind, reminding her, she could do all things through Christ who strengthened her and a smile touched her lips. With an added vigor in her step, she walked to her car ready to face the next three months. She was armed with a smile and brave determination.

Making her way back to Oceanview Highway again, she turned right and followed it to Beach Boulevard. Turning left, she drove toward her new temporary home. The address was easy to find. The GPS was in line with Lauren's directions. She also had told Meagan the mansion wasn't far from the hospital and the girl was so right, less than five miles. That was always a blessing, living close to where she worked. The street on which the mansion sat ran parallel to the ocean with large homes on either side of the street. Before turning into the horseshoe drive, she paused momentarily.

Her gaze slowly covered the immense two-story structure. It was a stucco home with burnt orange scalloped-shaped clay tiles for the roof. The house had several windows, most rectangles and some rounded, all with arches above them. The home sat back off the road displaying a beautifully manicured front lawn. The semi-circle drive cut through a small scattering of palm trees as well as having extensions on each side of the house forming driveways leading to the back. A sidewalk ran from the front of the house, through the horseshoe drive, down to the street dividing the well-kept grass and hedged boxwoods.

The house itself was one big rectangular building, except for an addition that appeared to be added to the far right side, the south side. The addition extended farther out than the front of the house. Although the house was magnificent in size, it looked inviting. It had a peaceful, protected sense about it. That, she found strange after meeting…correction…after seeing the doctor at work. Turning into the semi-circle drive, she followed it to the front of the house.

Stopping near the front door, she put the car's gear in park, turned off the ignition, and slipped out of the Honda. She took a deep breath and released it quickly. "Here goes nothing." She marched up the steps to the front door.

Ringing the doorbell, she waited less than a minute before the door opened to a pleasant looking woman, possibly in her late fifties or early sixties, with short curling brown hair and wisps of gray throughout. "May I help you?"

"Hi. I'm Meagan Phillips. I'm the new x-ray tech who will be staying here." She introduced herself with a little bit of trepidation. Her misgivings were squashed within seconds.

"Meagan! Oh, how wonderful!" The lady threw the door wide open. "Come in. Come in. The doctor said you would be arriving today. I'm Helen Trent, the housekeeper. Call me Helen."

The first step inside took her breath away. She had never been in a home as lovely as or more beautiful than this. Meagan almost pinched herself to make sure she wasn't dreaming.

If Shelly could be here now, she would be jumping up and down with delight and hugging Helen. That thought brought a smile to Meagan's lips.

She blinked a couple of times to focus on the inside of the home again.

The first thing she saw was a long immense curved staircase leading up to the next floor. Pristine white edged the stairs and covered the spindles on the banister, while the wooden handle and steps were stained in the natural. Along the wall, below the staircase, hung a huge mirror with various pictures surrounding it.

Below those things sat a loveseat next to a table. Fresh cut flowers filled a clear vase on the entryway table emitting a sweet scent into the air.

Slightly to the right was an open space that revealed a view straight through the house, through the large glass windows across the back wall. The house set high as she looked out the window that exposed a pool and surrounding area. Beyond that the property edged downward toward a private beach with a long pier leading out to a boathouse. The ocean glistened a dark blue as white caps rolled up on the sand.

What a breath-taking view! How magnificent!

Helen ushered her in all the while babbling on about Meagan's visit and the good doctor's hard work at the hospital.

Meagan almost missed hearing Helen's words about the doctor waiting as Meagan continued to look around in such awe. When Helen's words sunk in, she snapped out of her daze. Suddenly, Helen had Meagan's undivided attention.

"I'm so excited about you coming. He's waiting in the study to meet you before going back to the hospital. The doctor said not only would you be working at the hospital, but you would be intermingling here with the girls. I think that is wonderful!" The woman practically clapped her hands as she spoke. Her enthusiasm was evident.

"They are wonderful girls. You'll love them. And the doctor, he works so hard he has very little time to devote to his girls. And there is never a woman around. Well me, and their aunt. But you can't count me…and well, I won't say anything about Mrs. Jennifer's sister. It's not my place. From what the doctor tells me, you will be so good for the girls. They need a woman's touch so much." Helen dragged the so out a little longer than normal. "Poor dears. Things have never been the same since their mother's passing."

Meagan's mind was still on the comment Helen had made about the doctor being at home. How could that be? Either he moved very fast, or that short grumpy old man wasn't him after all.

She would find out soon enough.

Moving to the left of the stairway, past the stairs to some double doors, Helen stopped. "Wait here," Helen said. "I'll be right back." Facing her, the woman squeezed Meagan's shoulders and gave her another big grin before opening one of the doors and disappearing behind it.

As soon as she closed the door, the front door swung open and two girls rushed inside heading for the stairs. Meagan turned and watched as they entered.

They both glanced Meagan's way but neither stopped their forward motion. The taller girl, slender in physique, had a sullen look on her face as she gave Meagan the once over. She then rolled her eyes upward and dashed up the stairs. The girl dismissed her from her thoughts right away...pretty much what Meagan had expected.

The other girl, however, bit her bottom lip as she slowed her steps. "Hello," she said softly.

"Hi."

That was all Meagan could say, because the taller girl hollered from the top of the stairs, "Come on, Rachelle!"

The young girl didn't say another word Instead; she lowered her eyes and flew up the stairs to join her sister.

Meagan smiled to herself. She knew it. She had figured they

wouldn't like her before she came, and it looked like they didn't want her to be there any more than she wanted to be there herself.

Helen returned, putting Meagan's focus back on the matters at hand.

Opening both doors wide, Helen said, "Come on in." She hurried Meagan along. "Dr. Ryan, this is Meagan Phillips."

Meagan stopped short.

The man's long slender hands rested gently on the clean shiny finish of the large dark oak desk. He rose, stepped around the desk, and walked toward her. He definitely wasn't the short, old man at the hospital. He stood over six feet tall, with soft brown hair, streaked with touches by the sun, combed neatly back. His skin was golden tan. The man either played a lot of golf or found any excuse to stay outdoors. Then she remembered this was an island. He probably indulged in a lot of swimming, sailing, and other outdoor activities. A flash of his back yard came to mind. Of course he did!

When his gaze rested on Meagan's face, she found herself unable to breathe.

He took her by surprise as he reached out and shook her hand, saying, "Welcome, Miss Phillips. Thank you for coming. Thank you for taking me up on my offer. I hope they explained everything to you in detail. I am speaking of my plans for you and my girls."

Nodding her head as she shook his hand, she made herself breathe. Meagan tried to speak but nothing came out of her mouth, so she kept on nodding. Her heart was pounding so hard she thought it would explode. Why? Was it fear?

A quizzical look crossed the doctor's face as he turned to Helen. "Does she speak?" The question was spoken almost in a whisper, but Meagan heard it.

She covered her mouth, feeling her face redden, and then started to laugh. "I'm sorry, sir. I didn't mean to be silent. You took me by surprise. You're not quite how I pictured you." Once the words were out of her mouth, she shut her lips tight and clamped her hands over them as a deep warmth swarmed over her face. She hadn't meant to say aloud what she was thinking.

The doctor let out a deep bellow. "Look at her blush, Helen. I do believe this is what the girls need." A smile spread across his face. "Dare I ask what you expected?"

"Ask. Ask away," Helen said. "I believe you are so right, sir. Just what the girls need," Helen added as she turned her gaze on her boss and then looked back at Meagan. "Ask her. I want to know the answer."

Meagan shook her head. "Again, I'm sorry," she said, holding her hands up in front of her as if to say stop. "I'm not getting started on the right foot here."

She shook her head again, but not saying anything this time. Instead she cleared her thoughts as well as organized them before speaking again.

"Let me start over. Dr. Richardson. It's nice to meet you." Her sentence didn't stop there…at least not in her head. She finished it with, I think. But Meagan didn't dare say that aloud. Instead, her mind wondered why she had reacted to him the way she had. He seemed like a nice enough man and probably a wonderful father and doctor.

Of course, she had to admit he was nothing like she had imagined when she had talked to Shelly a few days ago when the job was first offered.

The proof was in the pudding, her grandma used to say. In this case, the proof would be in the children. They would be the true test of how things would go at the house.

When the doctor took her hand again, squeezed it, and then said, "I look forward to your stay. I hope you will be able to help my girls," warmth shot up her arm, followed by tingles that went all the way to her heart. Meagan wasn't so sure anymore about where the proof was coming from. The good doctor could be the test.

She swallowed hard, trying to force down the strange emotions that raced through her. "I'll do my best, sir."

Chapter 4

After the welcome speech and the long list of things expected of her were stated, Dr. Richardson gave Meagan a set of keys. "Drive around to the south side of the house. Toward the back you'll see a private entrance that leads to your living quarters. You have your own garage."

She nodded as she accepted the keys. The clip held a small device as well as the keys. The device was a hard square of black plastic with a button in the middle. It must open the garage. She liked the thought of having such privacy and easy access. "Thank you very much."

"Would you like help getting your things inside? I could come assist you."

"I'll manage. Thanks again." Quickly, she thanked Helen as well and then dashed out to her car and drove around to the south side like the doctor had said.

This part of the house might not be an addition after all. Everything matched the rest of the structure so well. The stone looked identical and kept the same design of the house, rectangular with arched windows.

The original owner may have used this part of the home to house his help or even some distant relatives.

Meagan was looking forward to seeing the inside. An outside

door into her part of the house was visible. Hopefully the garage had a door that she could enter from. Talk about private as she came and went. That would be nice. She would know soon enough.

Pressing the button, the garage door rose. She slipped in with the car. It did have another door. Great. She pressed the button again and closed the large door. A light came on and stayed on…for how long she did not know. Meagan liked the security in that.

Closing her eyes, she leaned her head back against the headrest and took in a quiet breath. Silence was all around her. In that tranquil moment her mind remembered her reaction to the doctor.

There went the peace. Disturbed, she opened her eyes, turned the rearview mirror down some and looked at her own reflection. Pointing her finger at the mirror and speaking to her reflection she said, "With your new job and the added stress of helping the girls, you don't need any more complications. Get a grip on yourself."

Shaking her head she wondered what she had gotten herself into. She had no idea. All she knew was she had to get some distance between her and that handsome doctor…her boss…her new boss and landlord. How was she going to work for a man that made her nerves tingle from the tip of her fingers to the depth of her heart? No one had ever, in all her thirty-plus years, affected her that way.

"Enough!" she shouted as she flipped the mirror back in place. Enough of thinking about him and the way he made her react. She had to concentrate on why she was there. It was a job. A job to make money to make the rest of the needed repairs to her home. A job to do what she was well trained to do. A job like any other… well almost.

Taking in a quick deep breath and releasing it instantly, she climbed out of the car. "Home sweet home. Thank You, Lord." In no time she had her baggage out of the car. Meagan connected the two cases, hung the strap of her laptop on her shoulder, and then wheeled the luggage behind her as she headed for the steps to the door.

The key unlocked the door easily, and she pushed it open. Glancing around in the garage and at the garage door, she thought she didn't really need to lock this door. She'd be fine with the automatic garage door opener. Pulling the luggage up the two steps to enter behind her, she walked into her new lodgings.

First impressions were usually right.

If that was still the case, she was going to love living here. Sniffing the air, everything smelled so clean and fresh. Standing inside the door, she saw the kitchen to the left and the living room to the right.

The color tones of the rooms were soft. She liked that…pleasing to the eyes. The entryway was a small area. The wall she faced upon entering had a door that probably served as a coat closet. This small area doubled as the separation of the two rooms. Perfect.

A single rattan mirror hung on the wall to the right of the closet door. It hung over a small bamboo entryway table. The bouquet of dried flowers on the table looked so real, she was tempted to sniff the fragrance, but they weren't real. It consisted of daises, carnations, violets, and other flowers that Meagan did not recognize, but the arrangement was bright and cheerful.

A glance to the right opened up a nice sized living room with plush, overstuffed furniture. Looking back to the left, she stole a glimpse of the kitchen.

One good thing about having her meals with the girls, she wouldn't be doing much of her own cooking. That would be great since this was another way she and Shelly differed—not that Meagan couldn't cook. All good Southern girls knew how to cook.

She just never cared for it before.

Rolling the luggage into the living room, she parked the bags in the middle of the floor, pulled her cell out of her purse, and keyed in her mom's speed code number. In two rings she heard her mother say hello.

"Hey," Meagan said. "I'm here. Just walked in and had to say, Mom, you'd love it."

"Hey, sweetie. Glad you made it safe and sound. So I'd love it. What's so special about it, besides you're staying in a mansion?"

Meagan curled up on the big soft couch and settled in. "It's a mansion all right, but you'd never know it by the wing I'm in. It's different from the rest of the house. The main part of the house was decorated on a grand scale with high ceilings and such, but my place reminds me of some of the resort apartments we've rented down in Florida. You know what I mean, like the couch I'm sitting on. The print is of seashells and starfish. And the coloring in the fabric of the furniture and draperies are soft beige, brown, and a touch of burnt orange with swirls of light blue like waves of the ocean. And of course, there is an over-stuffed wing chair to match the sofa I'm sitting on."

"I can see it in my mind."

"But the big thing is I'm looking out a picture window. It looks out onto the backyard facing the pool, but you can look out past that and see the ocean. It's amazing!" Meagan could almost see her mother's smile come across the line. This was her mother's dream retirement place. Nothing like Meagan ever dreamed of or cared for, for that matter, but her mother loved beaches and everything that came with it. "The only thing I don't like about it is the floor. It's hardwood flooring with a high polished shine finish. How in the world do they expect me to keep it like that?"

"You poor dear. You'd better hope it's the newer type wood floors that keep that shine. Just pass a dust mop over it to collect the dust, and then use a damp mop of warm water and vinegar. That should keep the shine. You better hope it's not the old fashioned kind like your grandmother used to keep polished. That would be a lot of work."

She shivered. "We'll know soon enough. For the house's sake, they better hope it's the new kind."

They both laughed.

"Mom. I wasn't joking earlier though." Sighing, Meagan looked out the picture window again. She slipped her arm up on the back of the couch and rested her chin on her forearm. "It's beautiful, but it's more than just the vast ocean. You wouldn't believe everything. I'm sitting here looking out at the back yard. The grass, what little there is, is so green, so lush. All around the edges by the house and along the fence are flowerbeds with luscious bold colored flowers. I wish I could tell you the names, but you know me."

Her mom chuckled. "You don't know any of them."

"You're right. But wait till you hear about the rest of the back yard. A short distance over to the left side of the yard I can see an Olympic-sized swimming pool and a patio surrounding it. They even have big old planters filled with thick green ivies and palms. Farther beyond the pool to the left there is some sort of building structure and behind that appears to be a lighted tennis court."

"It's already dark there?"

"No. I mean I can see these huge poles with lights on them, and they are spaced out like in a big rectangle shape. So I'm guessing it's a tennis court. They must play a lot. But I'm just guessing. The fence is too high to see what's hidden behind it."

"It sounds wonderful dear. If it's tennis, I know you'll love playing."

She smiled. "I'm sure I will, if that's what it is and if it's allowed. But wait. I've saved the best for last. At least you'll think so. I can see where the back of the yard stops and the sand begins. It goes all the way to the ocean. Their back yard backs up to the beach. And it looks like it's their private beach. The fence on both sides of the house goes down to the beach area." She sighed. "And there's a pier that goes out into the ocean. At the end there seems to be like a boathouse to one side. I'm in paradise, Mom."

"It sounds like it. But you've never liked the beach before. What makes you like it this time?"

Meagan shrugged her shoulders. "I'm not sure. I think it's because I can see the beauty of it, yet I don't have to be on the sand getting it in my shoes. I get the joy of hearing the roar of the ocean without feeling the grit between my toes. It's the best way to view the ocean…at a distance, but yet close. I don't know. I just know it's so peaceful looking, Mom, yet so massive." Meagan paused for a second and then said, "Maybe I'm just getting old and my tastes are changing."

"Girl. Don't do that to your momma. If you're old, what does that make me? Ancient?"

They both laughed. Meagan felt her eyes starting to tear up, she was laughing so hard.

"Well, dear. I'm glad you like it already. Maybe before your three months are up, I can come out for a visit and get to enjoy some of that beach with you. Or better still, you do a re-sign and I come out in July or in August for your birthday."

She smiled. "That's a great idea. I know you would love this place. And my three months could turn into six, so who knows? Maybe that will work."

"We'll see. Have you met the doctor yet, or the girls?"

"I met the doctor all right, but we'll talk about that later. The housekeeper, Helen, you'd love her. And I've seen two of the girls so far, but we haven't spoken yet. Right now, before I get too comfortable, I need to get up and go unpack. I just wanted to let you know I'd made it safely. Tell Shelly I'll call her as soon as I get settled."

"Okay, dear."

"Tell Pops hi for me, and I love you both. And if you see Troy, tell him I called. Love him too." On that they said good-bye and Meagan pressed end to disconnect the line.

Glancing out through the window one more time, she said, "I can't wait to see my first sunset and my first sunrise." A smile spread across her face as a peace settled over her.

Chapter 5

It took about thirty minutes for Meagan to unpack her things. She had learned to bring the bare minimum when she flew. If she had had time to drive over in her own car, she would have included some of her personal belongings such as a couple of her own bath towels, her pillow and blanket, some things from her medicine cabinet, and a few things from her kitchen…a little bit of home on the road. And of course she would have brought her guitar and some of her CDs as well as her CD player. Not enough time this time.

After some clothes were hung up and others put in the dresser drawer, she picked her cell back up and punched in the speed dial code for her sister's house.

Before the first ring even finished, she heard, "It's about time!"

"I can't believe you answered so quickly."

In her ear, she heard the familiar laughter of her sister, Shelly. "I was trying to time you. Get it just right. I have to admit, I was off a little. I figured you would have been in your own place about thirty minutes to an hour ago. I even remembered to add a half hour for you stopping off at the hospital and checking it out. I know you do that every time. Then you get in your place and call." Shelly sighed. "So I missed it by half an hour. I'd say not bad. Now give me the scoop."

"Mom didn't call you?"

"Actually, she did. She called while I was in the laundry room and left me a message to call her back, but it was too close to the time I thought you'd be calling, so I figured Mom could wait. A little while anyway."

Meagan chuckled as she wished she could see her sister's face right now. In her mind, Shelly was grinning like a Cheshire cat, that cute little smug look on her face saying, "I was so close. Maybe next time I'll be right on the money."

Meagan had to tell Shelly. "Truth be known, sister dear, you were right. The thing is, this place is so beautiful, I had to take time to soak it all in. It's even better than you could imagine." Meagan went on to share some of the details with her sister as she had with her mom.

Afterward, Shelly sighed. "Oh, Meggie. This is going to be a job you'll never forget. I feel it in my bones."

Leaning back against the soft cushion and closing her eyes, Meagan said, "I do believe you're right, little sister."

"So have you met the rich old man yet?"

Laughter bubbled out of Meagan's mouth. She couldn't hold it back no matter how hard she tried. "Sorry. Didn't mean to laugh in your ear."

"He's that ugly, huh?" her sister asked in a deep voice.

"On the contrary." A smile touched Meagan's lips as she heard herself sigh.

A squeal crossed the line. "So, are you saying he's cute? Tell me. Tell me." The energy in her sister's voice raced across the line.

"Calm down, girl." Meagan heard a knock. The sound was muffled so she needed to go in search of where it was coming from. "Hold on a minute, Shel. I'll be right back. Someone is knocking...I just don't know from where. There's a door facing the backyard, but I can see through it. No one's there." And she didn't believe anyone could get into the garage connected to her wing of the house.

Standing, she listened again for another knock. It came and she followed the sound carrying her cell phone with her. "Hang on. It's got to be where this apartment connects to the house." The sound took her down the hall, past the bathroom and bedroom doors. At the end of the hall was another door. At an earlier glance, Meagan had assumed it was a hall closet, or a linen closet. Looking closer, she now saw the deadbolt on the door. No one deadbolts a closet door. That had to be the connecting door Lauren had mentioned.

"Who is it?" Meagan asked. She guessed it was probably Helen. But then again, it could be one of the girls coming to check her out.

"Miss Phillips. It's me. Dr. Richardson."

"Oh." That was the last person she would have expected. By now, she figured he had gone back to the hospital. She whispered to her sister, "Hold on another minute."

Quickly, she unlocked the deadbolt and turned the doorknob. When the door opened, she saw her new boss filling the frame of the door.

"Yes, sir. Can I help you?"

"I just wanted to make sure you found everything you needed. The kitchen and bathroom should be stocked with necessities. Also, I wanted to let you know we will be eating in about one hour if you would care to join us. You could meet the girls tonight…if you are up to it. Unless you are too tired and need to rest. It can wait until tomorrow. It is up to you."

Meagan swallowed hard. "Uh. Sure. Tonight, I mean, is fine." She practically tripped over every word.

The man's gaze slid down to the phone in Meagan's hand. "I am sorry. I did not mean to interrupt anything."

She shook her head no as she held the phone up and pointed at it.

"I mean, you didn't. It's just my sister. I was letting her know I was here safe and sound." Shrugging her shoulders she added, "You know family. They tend to worry."

He rubbed his chin and arched his brow as he listened to Meagan with what seemed to be amused curiosity and then nodded as if he understood.

"I will let you get back to your phone call." His gaze slipped to the phone in her hand and then returned to her face. "See you later." He turned and walked away.

Slowly, she shut the door and turned the lock. Blowing out a gush of air, she leaned her back against the door. Shaking the thoughts that were about to creep into her head out of her mind before they began, she looked down at the phone and told herself, "No. Don't go there." When she finally returned the phone to her ear, she heard her name being called over and over.

"Okay, Shelly. I'm back."

"Wow! Was that him? If he's half as good looking as he sounds...wow!"

Meagan felt her face redden as warmth spread across it. She didn't want to think wow...but couldn't help herself. Shelly's word fit perfectly. Although she had resisted thinking words such as wow, handsome, and awesome only moments ago, she couldn't help that her sister repeated them to her now. It was hard enough to control her thoughts. There was no way she could control Shelly's.

Instantly, Meagan started chanting in her mind, this is a job... this is a job...this is a job. To Shelly, she said, "Don't be silly. He's a married man...in more ways than one."

"Wake up, sister dear. He is a widow! Seven years a widow," Shelly reminded Meagan.

"Yeah. Well. My guess is he plans to stay that way. If he hasn't found a new wife in seven years, the odds are, he isn't looking. Besides, I'm pretty sure, since he owns the hospital, he's married to his work."

"Oh. That's too bad." Meagan heard the disappointment in Shelly's voice. "Well it still sounds like you're in heaven. And you're going to get to enjoy it for at least three months, if not six."

Meagan had to admit, Shelly's voice didn't sound nearly as disappointed as Meagan actually felt. She forced a smile to her lips as she realized her sister was right in her own little way. Meagan was there for a job and the pay.

In the scheme of things, she was given a beautiful place to pass the time and do what she was called to do. How blessed could a person be?

"It is gorgeous. I'll take some pictures soon and text them to you. But the big test is in an hour. I get to meet the girls. If we don't click, he could send me packing tonight. So say a little prayer for me. I know I will. But you know what the Word says, when two or more come together and ask…" She didn't need to finish her sentence. Shelly said the prayer aloud as Meagan was in agreement with her. They finished the prayer, said their good-byes, and she disconnected the line.

And then the strangest thing happened. A sudden desire to stay here in this beach town overwhelmed Meagan.

That shook her to the core. Not only did she want to stay, she also wanted to make a difference in all three girls' lives. She wanted to help them in any way God would allow. If she was being totally honest with herself, she wanted a chance to get to know Ryan Richardson better as well. Maybe there was a reason she felt something when she first met him.

What had come over her?

She had no idea, nor did she know how to make the feeling go away. Even more so, she didn't want it to go away. She looked forward to the next three…maybe six…months of her life.

Chapter 6

Meagan took a quick shower. She wanted to be fresh when she met the girls. Could she handle it? *Keep the desire strong, Lord. The one I felt less than one hour ago. I want to help the girls, Lord. Lead me.*

She prayed a quick silent prayer.

Three girls were about to size her up. Meeting strangers was not her most favorite thing in the world. In fact, she would put it right below having a root canal.

Sure she was a travel tech. This meant she had to meet new people all the time, but those were co-workers, people who chose to get into the medical field. Same as her. They had common interests. But this...this was so new, and she wasn't quite ready to face her fate although the desire to help them was strong.

Should she dress up for the first meeting? Or should she dress casual? Looking her best was a must for the first meeting. First impressions last. But still, she needed to be herself. Would it make any difference whatsoever how she dressed? Those girls probably knew what their dad was up to, so they probably wouldn't want anything to do with her anyway.

All of a sudden she remembered something she had learned in one of the Beth Moore Bible studies, or in Joyce Meyer's teaching, or maybe both. The tongue was your most powerful weapon. She could destroy her stay here before it truly began...if she wasn't careful.

A smile crossed her lips. It wasn't too late. She hadn't spoken any of those thoughts aloud. Instead, she said, "This will work. I will be a good influence. The girls will love me, and I will love them."

After she spoke those words aloud, she thought to herself, who in the world was she trying to fool. She sighed.

She wished she were more like Shelly. Her sister never met a stranger. Then she shook those words out of her mind. That was the devil lying to her.

It would work out. She and her sister were more alike than she gave them credit for. Besides, God brought Meagan there for a reason and He would be using her. He picked her to be brought there for the girls and He would supply whatever she needed for them.

In an instant some words Shelly had said the other day flashed through her mind. "Just be yourself. My kids love you. So will his." That helped Meagan's confidence even more.

She took another deep breath and then pulled out a bright yellow T-shirt she had bought in Alaska. Blue jeans and T-shirts. That was Meagan. She was not going to put on airs. This was her normal dress when she wasn't in her scrubs.

The only exception was Sunday morning church. When she went on Saturday night, or any other night for that matter, she wore blue jeans and a neat shirt, usually button down with a collar. Sometimes she dressed it up with a vest. And when winters were cold enough, she added a sweater. They were still in the spring now, plus she was indoors, so nothing extra was needed.

After dressing, she glanced in the mirror at her reflection. That proved how nervous she was. This mirror was a full-length mirror, and Meagan never looked at her total reflection.

The only mirror she used was in the bathroom, and then she only looked at her face long enough to slap on what little makeup she wore and to fix her hair. How else would she know if it looked okay? Her hair was so thick, she only wore it two ways…up in a ponytail or down loose around her shoulders, but she still wanted to be sure every hair was in place.

Tonight she pulled it back into a ponytail. Her bright shirt reflected on her clear complexion. The natural rose in her cheeks did more than any make-up could have done. Meagan touched her eyelashes with mascara and the lids with a soft brown eye shadow.

"Like it or not, here I come." She started for the hall door and then stepped toward the living room eyeing the back door and then the garage door. "Which way should I go? Should I use my back door and go around? Or should I walk through the house?" She didn't know how to get to the kitchen cutting through the house. She shrugged, sighed, and then turned to the hall door. She might as well get used to using it and learn her way around the mansion.

Slowly, she opened the door and dared to walk through. Meagan had no earthly idea where to go. She knew she was on the bottom floor, so she decided to head down the hall in the direction of the front of the house…she guessed. From there, she would wander around and follow the smell to the kitchen.

She hadn't gone far when a voice stopped her.

"Who are you?"

Meagan stopped in mid step and then turned slowly toward the voice. Through an opened doorway, she saw a huge room, almost twenty feet long but not quite as deep. The room was filled with workout equipment. Looking in the middle of the exercise room, she saw a young girl in shorts and a fitted athletic top lifting free weights over her head and then bringing them back down even with her shoulders. Her blonde hair was pulled up on the top of her head and wrapped around to form a knot. One big clip secured it. This had to be the youngest of the three, the twelve-year-old.

"Hi. I'm Meagan Phillips. I'm the new rad-tech at Jennifer Lane Memorial."

"Oh. You work at Daddy's hospital." She nodded as if that explained everything.

How many other hospital workers had done this? How many had worked at the hospital and lived with the family? Maybe there was more to it than even Lauren Woods knew. Lauren had talked like this was a first time try to have the temp live in the home and get to know the girls.

Maybe getting to know the girls was the only part of this that was new.

"I start tomorrow at the hospital. For tonight, I was trying to find my way to the kitchen. Your dad invited me to join y'all for dinner."

The girl bent forward till the free weights touched the floor and then released them. "Hold on a minute and I'll walk with you to dinner, but it's not in the kitchen."

Megan blushed as she remembered where she was. Of course it wasn't in the kitchen. Not in this big mansion. They probably dressed for dinner, too, and then ate around the elegant dining room table.

This was going to take some getting used to.

The young girl disappeared out of view from the doorway. Meagan wasn't sure where she had gone or what she was doing.

When the girl reappeared, the answer was obvious. She had washed up, brushed her hair, leaving it hanging down, and pulled a T-shirt on over her workout top.

"Daddy wouldn't like it if I came to the table in my workout clothes. First off, he'd notice I'm not a little girl anymore. That alone would be hard for him to handle. Second, he would think it was disrespectful. At least we don't have to dress up like he used to make us."

The twelve-year-old led the way down the hallway, around a corner, down another hall, then cut through a big room that appeared to be a family room or den, a very nice one, although no one was in it.

Next they went down another hallway, and then a left into the dining room.

By the time they had reached that room, a heavenly aroma wafted through the air. This would be the first job she had been on where she didn't have to eat her own cooking. What a blessing! Home cooking and she wouldn't have to lift a finger.

"Thanks for the directions. I'm not sure I could find it again, though."

The young girl tilted her head slightly and shrugged her shoulders. "No problem. You'll figure it out. You look to be pretty smart."

"Thanks." Meagan glanced around. The table was set, yet no one was in the room. Maybe they were too early.

"Don't worry. The rest will be here shortly. Daddy sits there." She pointed to the head of the table as she talked. "Jessica there, Rachelle here, and I sit on the other side next to Daddy."

That left four empty chairs, but only one had a place setting. It put her in the chair next to his youngest daughter. "Looks like I sit here, next to you."

"That's what it looks like to me, too." No sarcasm was in her voice. She spoke it as a fact.

"What's your name?" Meagan figured she might as well start getting to know her.

"TJ."

Meagan noticed that although the girl seemed friendly enough, she never smiled, plus she talked older than her years. That was sad for one so young. Mandy, her niece was only two years younger and she grinned all the time.

Smiling at the girl, she said, "I like that. My grandfather was named JD. It didn't stand for anything. In those days, a lot of men were given initials as their names. Two of his brothers were too. They were RT and LD."

"That's silly."

If Meagan wasn't mistaken, she could have sworn the girl almost smiled. TJ seemed to actually struggle to keep from smiling.

"No, really. And my grandfather, JD, when he went in the navy they added letters to his initials. They said it was mandatory. So he became J-a-y, D-e-e Phillips."

The girl laughed, which touched Meagan's heart. It pleased her so to see that the girl wanted to be happy. Apparently she had been sad for so long, she had just forgotten how to laugh easily.

"It sounds like someone is having fun in here. What is going on?"

TJ jumped up from her chair and rushed around the table to her daddy who had just entered the room. She wrapped her arms around his waist and hugged him tightly. The love beamed from the little girl's eyes.

Her dad seemed to enjoy the attention himself. Maybe it was hearing the laughter that gave him pleasure. Meagan hoped so.

"Dr. Richardson," Meagan said as she started to rise.

"Sit. Do not get up on my account." He indulged his daughter in a hug and then kissed the top of her head. "Good evening, Tamara. Where are Rachelle and Jessica?"

"I'm right behind you," a young teenager said.

He spun on his heel. "Hi, sweetheart. Now where is Jessica? Then we can eat."

"She's in her bedroom, Daddy. She said she's not hungry and doesn't feel like coming down." Rachelle passed him up and grabbed her chair, pulling it out to sit down.

"Tamara, run up and get your sister, please. I want you all to meet Miss Phillips tonight."

Meagan started to say, "Don't get her on my account," but instead kept her mouth closed.

Helen came sweeping into the room from another doorway. Her hands held a platter filled with a large roast already sliced. Potatoes and carrots garnished the edges all the way around.

"Perfect timing," she said as she laid the tray near Dr. Richardson's plate. "I'll be back with the peas and the drinks in a minute." In a flash, she disappeared behind the same swinging door she had entered.

By this time Dr. Richardson had settled in his chair at the head of the table.

Moments later TJ came rushing back in the room and fell into her seat.

"Where is your sister?"

TJ raised her eyebrows, glanced at Meagan, and then back to her father. "She's coming. I told her what you said. She'll be here."

The two girls passed their plates to their dad, and he put the food on their plates and passed them back. TJ held her hand out for Meagan's plate so she handed it to her. This was different…but so far so good. Meagan wasn't complaining.

She started to say not to put too much, but the oldest daughter came strutting into the room. Her hair was spiked with pink and green highlights. The skirt she wore was so short; Meagan couldn't believe her own eyes. She had seen the hair-do earlier with the top sticking up…but the colors the girl must have added later.

"Okay, Dad. I'm here. What's the big deal?" Her tone held her contempt for being summoned to join them after she had expressed her desire to stay away.

When Dr. Richardson looked up at the sound of his daughter's voice, he almost dropped the spoon he was using to put potatoes on Meagan's plate.

"What in the world?" he boomed.

Jessica walked over to the chair to the right of her father, pulled it out and plopped down in it. "I went shopping with Aunt Karrie today. She took me to her hairdresser and got me a new do. It's the style for teenagers, Dad. Don't be so up-tight."

Meagan watched in silence as the doctor put down the plate and spoon, took a deep breath, and then turned his total attention on Jessica.

"When we get through with dinner, you will go straight to your bathroom and shower that mess out of your hair. It better be a rinse and not a dye. Do you understand me? It better wash out or I will personally shave you bald."

Her eyes spread wide as she crossed her arms over her chest and pouted. "I told Aunt Karrie you wouldn't like it."

"I will speak to her later. But do I make myself clear?"

"Don't yell at Aunt Karrie about the color. I did that myself." Her voice was pleading.

"Where did you get the color?"

"I talked her into buying it for me."

He shook his head as if he understood everything. "Like I said, I will talk with her later. And you are not off the hook yet. We, too, will be talking about this…in private."

"Yes, sir," she said, almost as if she was saluting an officer in the military.

He closed his eyes—blue Meagan thought—as if he was collecting his control. When he opened them back up—yes, they were blue—he carried on as if nothing had occurred. The doctor finished putting food on Meagan's plate and then returned it to her via TJ.

Helen returned with a bowl of peas in one hand and a pitcher of iced tea in the other. She set the peas down on the table as she said with a surprised look on her face, "Glory be."

She said it so softly Meagan almost believed she had imagined Helen's remark. The widened eyes glancing at Jessica and then at Dr. Ryan told Meagan that it had been Helen's reaction to the new hair-do. Helen walked around the table filling the glasses one by one that had only ice moments before and then she disappeared behind the door again.

The doctor filled Jessica's plate and returned it before any conversation began. TJ and Rachelle were talking diagonally across the table about a tennis tournament that was coming up this weekend while Jessica kept her eyes trained on her plate.

Meagan took the opportunity to bow and give thanks silently for her job, a wonderful place to stay, and the meal. She took an extra second to ask God to bring this family together in peace. To Meagan they all seemed to lack joy.

As she was finishing her prayer, she noticed silence had returned to the room. She opened her eyes and found everyone's eyes trained on her.

She smiled a tight-lipped grin and said, "I was giving thanks for my meal. I hope that's all right." Even if it wasn't she would continue, she thought to herself.

"Of course. In fact, next time, we will bow our heads too and you can ask blessings over our food as well," he said.

She glanced around at each girl for only a brief second and then said, "I'd be delighted."

A frown swept across Jessica's face as she rolled her eyes.

TJ twitched her lips, almost into a smile. It wasn't as cheery as before, but two smiles in such a short space of time. That had to mean something.

Rachelle just looked at her father not responding in any form or fashion.

As everyone started eating, Dr. Richardson said, "Girls, I would like you to meet Meagan Phillips. She is our new x-ray tech at the hospital. I invited her to stay in the south wing of the house. She is going to be joining us for the evening meals. Breakfast also, if she would like. And girls, she will be here for you too, when she is not working. I realize you are all at a time in your life when you sometimes need a woman's—"

"Dad," Jessica screeched.

"Let me finish. I was going to say a woman's perspective. I believe you have questions that you need answers to, but you do not want to ask me. I understand how that would be difficult. And although Helen has been with us a long time, I thought you might want a younger woman's input. She has agreed to be here for you, when she is not at the hospital."

Meagan's mind and ears were taking in every word and trying to make sure she understood what he was expecting of her.

"I'm too old for a babysitter, Dad." Jessica's face showed her frustration at the thought of actually having a babysitter to answer to.

"Me too," the other girls said in unison.

"I don't baby-sit," Meagan said quickly.

Although that was what she had thought it would be in the beginning herself, watching them interact before dinner gave her a good idea that God planned her to be there and help these girls learn about Him.

Their dad might be able to buy them everything in the world, but you can't buy happiness, nor can you buy joy…or salvation for that matter. It's a gift freely given, but you have to know about it to ask for it.

Meagan realized quickly that these girls missed out on having a loving mother to show them about Jesus. It might not be what the good doctor planned, but God was in control.

"No. She is not here to baby-sit. And she will not be at your beck and call, either. You will see what I mean. Let's give it time."

A peace swept over her as the realization of all that had come about became clear in her head. Every eye was on her with blank expressions behind them.

Boldly she said, "I can be a friend."

TJ's blank look changed to a sweet smile…one Meagan returned instantly. TJ was looking for a reason to be happy. Seven years ago, she had been five.

The girl probably didn't even remember her mother well. TJ probably wanted to just be a happy kid, but her family didn't seem to be in the happy business. Meagan would work on that.

A chair scraped the floor as Jessica pushed hers back abruptly and rose. "Well, I don't need a friend, either. I've gotten by seven years without help from anyone, and I can get by for another seven plus years. Thanks…but no thanks." On those words she stormed out of the room.

The doctor had his elbows on the table and dropped his face into his hands. As he rubbed his forehead, he shook his head and then he looked up and said, "I am sorry, Miss Phillips. I should have known this would not work. I waited too long. Maybe six years ago it would have worked, but—" He cupped his hands together, and then he rested his chin on them interrupting his own words.

"I like her, Daddy," TJ said. "She can be my friend."

Meagan felt the warmth spread over her eyes as she fought back the tears that wanted to creep in at hearing TJ's statement. She blinked her eyelids quickly slapping the moisture away.

Rachelle offered Meagan a smile. She didn't commit herself, but she didn't say she didn't want Meagan around.

Dr. Ryan Richardson looked at his two younger girls and smiled. Meagan had to catch her breath and check the tears that still wanted to form. What a loving father he was. Why had they all drifted so far apart? She knew the mother's death had a lot to do with it, but that had been seven years ago. By now they should have moved on and started a new life without her. A smile touched his lips. "Let's not let this good food go to waste. Everyone, eat."

The roast was delicious, Meagan had to admit, but her appetite kept her from eating much. She did however, taste a little of everything.

The girls did as they were told and dug into their dinner. Meagan noticed Ryan Richardson's appetite wasn't as big as he had thought when he filled his plate earlier.

One day at a time, she told herself. God put her there for a reason and she would do her best to help bring the light they needed into their sad lives.

Chapter 7

After tossing and turning all night, Meagan was amazed she awoke on time. She did not want to face another run-in so soon with the whole family, so for breakfast she opted for a banana out of her own kitchen. Sure, Dr. Richardson had invited her to join them in the dining room this morning, but it probably wasn't part of the original plan. He had said if she would like—Maybe later, but not her first day of work.

Later, dressed in her scrubs, she started the Honda and pulled out of the garage. As she drove down the driveway and pulled out on the street, she noticed the quiet as the start of the morning rays filtered through the palm trees. Going down the road, her gaze was drawn to the water, to the glimpses she caught between each home. It was amazing. The calmness of the deep blue shade of water made it postcard picture perfect.

I wonder if it snows here in the winter? That thought flashed through her mind.

Probably not. The answer came just as quickly. This town was in the southern-most part of the coast of South Carolina. If it did, it probably wasn't much. Meagan had had enough snow in the last few years of her life in Maine, Massachusetts, and Alaska. She was ready to stay out of it for a while.

Turning right onto the street leading to the hospital, she laughed at herself. What did any of that have to do with her anyway? Winter was a long way off. It was the beginning of spring. She would probably be long gone before summer arrived…so what was it to her? Even if she got a three-month extension that would only have her working through the first part of September. She would be gone long before winter came to this little town.

Turning her thoughts around in her mind, she took in the businesses along the street.

On one side there were dress shops, sporting shops, clothing stores, dime stores, and souvenir shops, while on the other side she noted a post office, some cafes and eateries, as well as a few more souvenir shops.

Enough about that.

She needed to concentrate on her job, if she wanted to keep it at all, she thought as she crossed the bridge and neared the hospital.

Pulling into the parking lot, she parked the car and locked the door. In no time she was in the building and heading upstairs on the elevator to the imaging department.

"Good morning, Catherine," she said. "I'm all ready for orientation with whomever. Policy and procedures, here I come," she said with a lot of enthusiasm.

That got a chuckle out of the receptionist.

"Don't you come in all bright-eyed and bushy-tailed in the morning?" She lifted the corners of her mouth up into a smile. "I hope it's contagious. Another day like yesterday and I'm liable to call in sick for a week or two. And, by the way, you can call me Cat. Everyone else does."

Meagan smiled. "I learned a long time ago, this P and P orientation was a part I had to endure everywhere I went, so I might as well make the best of it."

They both laughed.

At least now, Meagan knew yesterday had been a bad day for Catherine. Cat, she corrected herself. She seemed to be in much better spirits this morning.

"There is fresh coffee behind me on the other side of that partition," Catherine said as she pointed toward a wall that didn't reach the ceiling. "Donuts and muffins are fresh too. Help yourself. You have time. Tom won't be here for about ten or fifteen minutes."

"I'll take you up on that coffee." Meagan slipped around the wall and found the pot of coffee.

Pouring a cup and adding cream and sugar, she stirred the concoction as she walked back around to the front desk and sat in the chair off to Catherine's side.

"Is it okay if I sit here…Cat?" The first time saying it was a little different, but Cat seemed to be a happier person anyway, and that was what Meagan liked. Happiness.

"Of course. So how was it at the mansion last night?" Catherine's eyes lit up as she changed the subject quickly on Meagan. For an instant Cat's energy and glow reminded Meagan of her sister. She would have confided in the whole experience of dinner with her sister, but not with this total stranger. At least not now, and she probably wouldn't later…but who was to say this early?

The question, however, being so unexpected, caused Meagan to almost choke on her first sip of coffee. Using a napkin, she dabbed at her mouth hoping to hide her shock. She wasn't about to start gossiping in the hospital or anywhere else for that matter. With composure in place, she said, "My living quarters are beautiful. I'm lucky to be able to stay there."

Catherine sighed a blissful sigh. "Yes, you are. Any single woman in this town would give her right arm to be staying at his place."

Meagan felt the warmth flood her cheeks. She needed to correct this path of questioning Cat had them on, before it became a widespread epidemic. "Catherine. I mean Cat. I'm not staying there because of the doctor. I'm there for the girls. And I'm staying in a separate wing away from the whole family."

Cat raised her brows and then dropped them as she pursed her lips and started shaking her head. She clucked with her tongue and said, "I know. Too bad, but one could always dream."

Biting her tongue, Meagan paused a moment before speaking. She wanted to ask but didn't want to send the wrong signal with her question. "Do you know his girls? Have you met them before?"

"I've seen them around. Never met them though."

"Oh," Meagan said. "I met them last night. I sensed sadness in them. I don't believe any of them have gotten over their mother's death yet."

Cat pulled a face. "I guess not. How can they, when their father is still grieving so?" she volunteered freely.

This gave Meagan something to ponder. She wasn't here to counsel the father, but if God gave her the opportunity and the right words, she would let Dr. Richardson know he needed to move on through his grief so his girls could grieve as well, and then they could all get on with their lives.

Cat changed directions again in the conversation and started giving Meagan the names and low down of each person that walked past the front desk, after they were out of ear shot, of course. Meagan found herself wishing the supervisor would come in so she could start orientation.

Tom had taken the full ten minutes Catherine had said in the beginning. She obviously observed people closely.

The morning was spent familiarizing herself with the layout of the hospital through Tom's direction. She learned where the x-ray rooms were located, the whereabouts of the films and other supplies, the QA room, and the computer where the patients were logged in and out so they could be charged accordingly. The x-ray equipment they used was familiar to Meagan.

She followed Tom through a couple of patients' processing, and by the end of the day, she handled the last three from start to finish.

"I don't think you'll need any more direction. You seem to already have a handle on everything…which makes my job easier." Tom seemed pleased.

Meagan was glad, because she never knew what to expect from one job to the next. Some places were so different from others. Rules varied with each, but this hospital seemed to run smoothly without a lot of behind the scene problems. For that, Meagan was relieved.

By the end of the day, Meagan had met most everyone in imaging and some of the doctors and nurses in emergency. As small as the place was, Meagan felt within a week she would know just about everyone. The hospital consisted of only three floors. Patients' rooms filled almost half of the bottom and second floor. The business office and admitting as well as emergency filled the rest of the first floor. The rest of the second floor housed the blood bank, imaging, treatment rooms, an exercise room, and a small cafeteria. The top floor, she was told, held the research department. Most of the research was for the treatment and cure of cancer, but some other diseases were studied there also.

Walking out to her car at the end of her first day, she concluded that she liked this hospital very much. Mostly, she liked the way it seemed to run. She hoped time wouldn't change her opinion.

On the short drive back to the Richardson's home, Meagan took time to offer up a prayer of thanksgiving and to ask for guidance with the girls. With the music turned off, after a long day of work, praying in the quiet stillness of her car was a very relaxing and peaceful way to end the day. What better way to spend the quiet moments than to talk to God?

"It was a good day, Lord. Thank You for sending me here. I hope I can make a difference in Jessica, Rachelle, and TJ's lives. The obvious thing they are missing is You, Lord, so give me the opportunity and the words to share You with them. They are still in pain over the loss of their mother. Please, Lord, help the pain to subside. Give them peace. In Jesus' name I pray."

Turning into the drive and heading toward the garage, she glanced at the car clock. If her schedule stayed the same, seven a.m. to three-thirty p.m., she was going to add a walk into the end of each day. Not the beach, of course, but she may walk down the street and up the main road past the little shops she passed going to work. By next week she should know if it would work. It all depended on the things she could arrange to do with the girls.

Opening the door and stepping into her place, she stopped. Surely, she had to be dreaming. "I know I left my robe on the chair this morning, along with a couple of magazines lying on the couch."

She peeked around the corner and looked into the kitchen. Her glass from last night and the one from this morning was washed and in the dish drainer.

"Pinch me. I must be dreaming." Even her various bottles of vitamins were placed neatly in a corner of the countertop. She always left them sitting haphazard on the counter where she put them down. It was a bad habit, one she wanted to break, but hadn't succeeded in yet.

Quickly, she slipped back around through the living room and then down the hall to the bedroom. Her bed was made. "I know I didn't do that."

Helen must have cleaned her place for her. She couldn't let her do that. Meagan worked for the doctor just like Helen. The woman had enough to do. She didn't need to take care of Meagan as well.

Glancing at her watch, she decided it wasn't too early to go in search of Helen and get things straight.

Still in her scrubs, she went through the door that joined her to the rest of the house. "Hopefully, I'll find my way," she whispered to herself as she walked. She passed the exercise room.

So far, so good. Maybe soon she too could use that room. She would have to remember to ask.

Meagan made a few turns, maybe a few too many, then backtracked a couple, and then turned a different direction. This time she ended up in the den...the big room she had passed through last night.

TJ was watching a tennis match on CNN Sports.

"Hi," Meagan said as she started to pass through and go find Helen as she originally planned. A twist in her spirit, made her stop. Maybe this was an opportunity being placed before her. *Use it,* she said to herself. "Is it okay if I come in?"

TJ turned her head around quickly causing her long blonde hair to fly out and then down about her shoulders. "Hi. How did your first day go?"

Meagan took that as a yes and went over to the chair opposite the couch TJ was sitting on. "It was good. I enjoyed meeting everyone and pretty much knew the equipment. They didn't have anything I haven't already used at one hospital or another."

"Great. Did you see Daddy?"

She thought for a moment. "You know, I don't believe I did. You would think in such a small hospital, I would have. But we never crossed paths."

The disappointment TJ felt showed on her face. Why? What difference would it make if Meagan saw Dr. Richardson during the day or not? Meagan didn't know. "I'm sure I'll see him one of these days. I know I didn't see everyone today, because yesterday I saw a doctor I thought was your dad, who wasn't of course, and I didn't see him today either. So I'm sure in time I will see your dad at work."

TJ shrugged her shoulders. "Do you play tennis?" she asked as she pointed toward the TV. "I was watching the news on the Zurich Open, the WTA Tour. Serena Williams, USA, and Angelique Kerber, Germany and so many others. They're awesome."

"You must love it. I noticed you have a tennis court in your back yard. And yes, I do play. Not great, but okay. Maybe we could play sometime."

A smile lit the young girl's face. Her beauty shone through. "I'd like that. Did you hear me say last night about my tournament coming up?"

"You and Rachelle were talking about it. Yes, I did hear. When is it? And what is it? School, YMCA, or some kind of local thing?"

TJ sat up on the couch giving Meagan her full attention.

Meagan saw how much this meant to the young girl. Someone was taking an interest in her love of a sport.

The young girl explained the school had been playing matches among the students and the semi-finals would play Thursday night. "I'm one of the twelve trying to make it to the semi-finals. Eight of us will be in the semi-finals. There will be four matches going on at the same time starting at four in the afternoon. The winners of those four will move up and play each other Thursday night at the semi-finals. Of course, we will have a short break between the afternoon matches and the ones Thursday night. The two winners of the semi-final matches Thursday night will go on to play the match for the finals Friday night. I plan to go all the way. Whoever wins Friday night's match will go to the state playoffs. And I want to be that person."

"Oh, TJ, that sounds wonderful! You sound very motivated. I didn't know you played so well." Meagan scraped her bottom lip with her top teeth, finding the courage to continue. "Maybe our playing together wasn't such a great idea after all."

TJ slouched back down on the couch again. A frown slid down her face.

Meagan realized she had said the wrong thing. "Wait a minute. I didn't mean I wouldn't play or that I didn't want to play. I meant I wouldn't be much of a challenge to you. I play, but—"

"That's okay. You don't have to." TJ shrugged her off, the defeated sound still in her tone of voice.

"No, sweetie. You misunderstood me. I'd be honored to play you, but I'm not much of a challenge. I play for fun and exercise. I'm really not that good. I chase the ball more than I return it."

A smile wiped the frown away as she jumped up from the couch and rushed over in front of Meagan. Dropping down to her knees, she said, "Oh, don't you worry. I'll go easy on you. I'm just excited that someone here will play with me. Rachelle used to, but now she just takes me where I need to go. She's more into her music. Thank you so much."

Meagan squeezed TJ's hands and stood up, pulling the young girl to her feet with her. Hugging her, she said, "I'll be happy to play any evening and on Saturdays or Sundays after church."

"Great. And will you come after work Thursday and watch me play? I want Daddy to, but I doubt he'll make it. He never has time. Usually Helen or Rachelle comes."

"I'd be delighted."

TJ hugged Meagan this time and said, "Thanks. I'm so excited. I better go do my homework so I can get a workout done before dinner." She started to run off, but turned back. "Bye. And thanks again. See you later."

"Hey. Can I use the exercise room, too?"

"Sure. Whenever you want. I try to get in there about four forty-five or at least by five p.m. That way I have time for a good hour workout. Then I take a few minutes to get cleaned up before dinner. Maybe you'll join me sometime. Two working out together makes the hour fly by." She smiled one more time and then took off.

Meagan couldn't help but offer up a quick prayer of thanksgiving. And she added, "Lord, it is so nice seeing that little girl smile more easily. Please use me to help her."

It will work out…all in God's time, she heard in her heart.

Looking around trying to reorient herself, she decided she better try again to find Helen. Now she had more things to talk to the woman about. Meagan felt a deep smile creep over her face.

One thing for sure, she had the time.

Chapter 8

By the time Meagan made her way to the kitchen and found Helen bouncing around preparing dinner, she wondered if she would ever learn her way around this house. The fragrance of an Italian kitchen had wafted down the hall and led her to it. Roasted garlic, tangy tomatoes, parmesan cheese…all rolled together to make Meagan's mouth water.

"Something smells wonderful," Meagan said.

"Lasagna is baking in the oven, and I have some green beans with butter and bacon simmering on the stove."

"I know now, if I'm going to eat what you cook every night, I definitely have to start exercising and playing tennis with TJ. If not, I'll get fat in no time." She laughed as she spoke.

Helen dropped the pan she was rinsing in the sink and spun around on her heels. "Glory me, child. Are you saying Tamara and you are going to play tennis together?"

Meagan walked over to the coffee pot. "Do you mind?" she asked, and then answered, "Yes, we are."

"Of course not. Help yourself. It should still be fresh enough. That's wonderful that you are playing tennis with her. I know she's excited to have someone show an interest in the sport she loves. If I could I would, but my hip never lets me enjoy many sports.

Besides, I'm a little too old to run around in one of those skimpy skirts." She laughed as she slipped the pan in the dishwasher.

"Glad to do it. I love tennis." Pouring a cup of coffee and adding the cream and sugar, she said, "First I want to say thanks for picking up in my apartment, but please don't do it again."

"Oh, dear. You like your privacy. I'm sorry. I wasn't meddling."

Meagan slipped into a chair at the little table in the center of the kitchen. "You misunderstand, Helen. I have nothing to hide. That's not the problem. I don't want you doing work you don't have to be doing. I can pick up after myself. Wash my dishes. You know what I mean. You have enough to do without picking up after me too. This house is huge."

Helen dried her hands and poured herself a cup of coffee. Then she went and joined Meagan at the table. "Child, I really don't mind. It didn't take more than fifteen minutes to pick up in your place. I just want your stay to be pleasant here. I feel it," she placed her hands over her heart, "here. I know God sent you to these kids…and I want to help them in any way I can. I'm just trying to give you more time to spend with them. Besides, I've lived here since before Ms. Jennifer's death. I have a routine and I promise it doesn't keep me busy enough."

A smile touched Meagan's lips as she heard what the woman said. Great! She was a believer too. Meagan couldn't stop her mind from wondering why she hadn't been trying to share God with them, but Meagan didn't have to ask. It was like the woman was reading her mind.

"Let me tell you just a little bit, so maybe you can understand why the family is the way they are. Ms. Jennifer was a wonderful woman and a good Christian. She took her girls to church every Wednesday and Sunday. She shared the Bible with them in other ways too. Jessica had just accepted the Lord as her Savior right before her momma's passing. That lung cancer hit Ms. Jennifer and took her in three month's time. Dr. Ryan didn't go to church before, so he sure didn't want any part of Ms. Jennifer's God when He took her from the doctor. I tried to help him see God had a reason for taking her. God knows why but we may not know until we reach heaven." She shook her head slowly.

"Dr. Ryan wouldn't listen to anything I had to say. I even tried to help the girls. Jessica blamed herself. Rachelle didn't know whom to blame, so she tried to be a momma to little Tamara. I think that was a way for her to fill her minutes of the day so she wouldn't have to think."

Helen stopped long enough to take a swallow of her coffee and Meagan drank hers too. She didn't want to stop Helen from telling her the background she needed to know to help her do the right thing when it came to the children.

Setting her cup on the table, Helen continued. "And little Tamara didn't know what happened to her momma or her happy home. Her momma and happiness disappeared at the same time. This place used to be filled with laughter, but since Ms. Jennifer's passing, no one really laughs anymore. I try to keep joy in the house. I prayed and prayed for seven years for something to happen to help bring them out of their grief. When I saw you, I knew you were the answer to my prayers."

Meagan felt herself blush. "I don't know about being the answer, but I do know God sent me here. So He does plan on using me in some small way. So while I'm here, let's see what we can do to help those girls."

Lifting her cup in the air like a toast, Helen said, "Here, here." Then she drank the last swallows of her coffee.

"The good news is, as you probably already gathered, I believe TJ and I have already connected."

A chuckle slipped from the woman's lips. "Has her daddy heard you call her TJ yet?"

"No. But I noticed he called her Tamara last night. And that's what you've called her in our little talk today."

Smiling, she shook her head. "Don't you worry. You do what the Lord leads you to do. You seem pretty comfortable calling her TJ, so follow your heart."

Meagan reached across the small table and laid her hand on Helen's. "Thank you for sharing."

Glancing at her watch, she said, "Well, I'm going to find something to work out in. I'm meeting TJ in the exercise room soon. Now we have two things to connect us so far. And by the way, Thursday I'm going over to the school to watch her in the semi-final play offs. Do you want to come with me?"

"Gladly. Thanks for asking."

"I'll slip back here and change, and then we'll go from here." Meagan finished off her coffee, rinsed her cup out in the sink and set it down. As she started to exit the kitchen, she turned back as she smelled the cheese and tomato sauce baking and said, "Can't wait till supper. I'm going to go burn off some calories before I take all those in tonight."

"Supper is served at six-thirty. See you then."

Meagan gave a slight wave of the hand as she slipped out the swinging door into the dining room. "I'm going to concentrate and get it right on the first try this time," she said softly to herself as she started finding her way back to her side of the house.

Easy enough. She did just as she said she would. In her apartment, she looked in her dresser drawer trying to find something that would work as an exercise outfit. She didn't think she had brought any, but wasn't sure. Her first instincts were correct, but she did however, bring a swimsuit. She could wear that under a pair of shorts...or just wear the shorts and a T-shirt. Tomorrow after work or during her lunch break, she would go buy an outfit or two. Cat could tell her where, because she for sure didn't see a Wal-Mart or anything that resembled it coming onto the island.

Meagan was the first one in the weight room, so she started with some stretching exercises. When she had done toe touches and some side twists and was about to do lunges, TJ walked in.

"You're here. Glad you made it." TJ tipped her head in Meagan's direction and then started doing some of her own stretching exercises.

"I'll need this workout for sure today. Helen made lasagna for supper."

TJ twisted and stretched as she said, "She makes the best. And she adds cheese to her garlic bread."

"My mouth is watering already." Looking around the room, Meagan wasn't sure whether to start free weights tonight or to just use some of the machines. Since she hadn't worked out in the last few weeks, she decided she would take it easy the first few times. She started on one of the machines.

After checking the weight, she moved the pin up and lightened it some, and then sat on the seat and pulled down the cold steel bar with the intent of doing two sets of eight with two variations. By her fifth or sixth evening working out, she would move up to sets of twelve.

First, she pulled the bar down behind her head to shoulder level and then slowly raised the bar back up extending her arms. After the two sets, she would do two sets pulling the bar down chest level and returning it back up slowly. This should help loosen up her shoulders, getting her ready for tennis tomorrow evening. Whatever exercise she did tonight, she would keep it at two sets and by next week or the week after, she would move up to three sets of everything.

"I can turn on some music if you would like. I usually do my workout in quiet, so I can concentrate, but I don't mind music if you want it," TJ said.

"Quiet works fine by me. It gives my mind time to rest. If you decide to talk, feel free," Meagan said.

"I probably won't. I'm used to quiet."

It started out that way. TJ used the machines tonight, just like Meagan, but with heavier weights. Meagan enjoyed the butterfly, the leg roll, the calf extensions, and leg raises before she headed to the treadmill. TJ ended her workout on the stepper. And that was when the conversation began…but Meagan didn't start it. This brought a comfort to her, knowing that TJ broke her own routine. The girl decided talking was a little more important than concentration.

TJ talked about the competition. She even said how much she wanted to one day be a professional tennis player. "Vania King was seventeen, I believe, when she started making money playing the sport. If I work hard and stay at it, by the time I'm in high school maybe I can be the youngest professional tennis player…if my dad will let me."

"You never know. But make sure you keep your studies up too. It's important to be well rounded. You know…brain and brawn." Meagan touched her temples with her pointer fingers when she said brain, and when she said brawn she made a muscle with both arms.

They laughed.

They talked some more as they finished their walk and stepper; making plans for the next day's match, their match for fun. As time passed, they barely noticed it. The talk came so naturally. Meagan was very pleased as they went their separate ways to go get ready for dinner. In fact, at the present, Meagan's social calendar was filling up nicely. She had plans for Wednesday and Thursday already. If Thursday went well for TJ, Friday would be booked also. A sense of satisfaction filled her as she realized she was making headway with TJ. And to think she hadn't even been there a week yet. The Lord moved quickly.

Meagan showered. When pulling out a clean pair of jeans and her favorite red T-shirt, the Boston Red Socks, she paused, wondering, "Should I make a little effort in my appearance...my dress?" She looked at her reflection in the mirror above the dresser holding the red shirt up under her chin as she asked.

Just as quickly, she twisted her tightly pressed lips as she realized what she had said...and why she had said it. Meagan felt foolish. "You're too old to be playing games, girl. And besides, you're not here to impress the father. You're here to help the girls. Wear the T-shirt."

Living alone, she was used to having her own little conversations. Sometimes she would pick up the phone and talk these things out with Shelly, but she didn't dare let Shelly know how she was thinking about her new boss. Meagan thought better than that. She would never hear the end of it, and Shelly would be pushing her every day to flirt with the doctor. Meagan was not a flirt! Never had been. Never would be.

Besides, she was in no position here to be a flirt. She was asked here for a reason, and Meagan's love life had nothing to do with it.

Quickly, she slipped on her jeans and red T-shirt, and then stepped into a pair of tennis shoes. After she tied the laces, she tied her hair up in a ponytail. No make-up. No fuss. Meagan was going to be plain old Meagan. Take it or leave it.

A few minutes before six-thirty, she slipped into her seat in the dining room. TJ came bouncing in behind her.

"That was a good workout. Are you going to be sore tomorrow? Because I don't want any excuses when I beat you. I'm looking forward to it." She smiled.

Meagan snapped her fingers. "Rats. You figured me out already. When I lose tomorrow, I was going to use that old excuse…you made me exercise too hard. You took advantage of me, because you knew my muscles were going to be sore after our workout."

Both of them doubled over laughing hard. Meagan felt her eyes start to tear up from the laughter. Each time they caught each other's gaze, they'd laugh again.

Before it stopped, she heard, "There is too much fun going on in this room. Stop all that laughing."

Meagan immediately stopped and her gaze flew to the door where the voice had come from. There filling the doorway was the good doctor, wearing a most serious look on his face that matched that stern tone that was in his voice. No one moved. No one breathed.

Chapter 9

"That was a joke, people. Let me in on what was so funny." Dr. Richardson entered the room and walked past his chair to Tamara. Leaning down, he kissed the top of her head. "I love hearing you laugh, sweetheart. That is something you have not done a lot of lately."

"Oh, Daddy. I laugh all the time. But Meagan is so funny. She's already making up excuses as to why I'm going to beat her tomorrow when we play tennis."

He ruffled the top of her head and then sat down. "Do not feel bad, Miss Phillips. Tamara beats everyone she plays. She is one little tennis pro, my little girl." He said this as his gaze full of pride rested on TJ. She appeared to love every minute of it.

This was good for her, Meagan thought. She wondered how often TJ got to hear her daddy praise her. Maybe this was the perfect opportunity to talk about her tournament with him. "I'm sure she does. That's why she's playing in the semi-finals of the tennis tournament at her school Thursday. Are you going to be able to go watch her play?"

TJ had been watching Meagan as she spoke, but as soon as the question was out of Meagan's mouth, her little eyes averted to her daddy with great anticipation. "Can you, Daddy? Can you come? I'd love for you to see me play."

"I will try, sweetheart. You know how hard it is for me to get away from the hospital early."

Her smile slowly disappeared. "I understand, Daddy. No problem."

Meagan's heart broke for the young girl. Couldn't her father see how much his presence would mean to her?

"You know what, TJ? You'll win the first round. If he doesn't make it for that, maybe he'll make it for the second round…the one that will put you in the finals for Friday night when you win." Meagan saw a light flicker in the girl's eyes, but as fast as it sparked, it disappeared again.

Dr. Richardson's eyes shot daggers at Meagan before he looked back at his daughter and said, "I will do my best…like I said before."

About that time, Helen pushed the swinging door open and entered the room carrying a long casserole dish filled with piping hot lasagna. Meagan saw the steam rising. "Garlic bread is on the table in that basket. And the green beans will be out on my next round."

Rachelle and Jessica strolled into the dining room together and slipped into their seats. "It smells good, Ms. H," Jessica said.

Tonight she looked like a normal teenager, well normal in Meagan's thoughts of teenagers. Although today out in the world spiked hair was the new fad…again, tonight there was no added spray paint in Jessica's hair, nor was it sticking up.

"Hello, girls. Nice of you to join us." Both knew, by the look on their faces, their dad was letting them know they were late coming to the table.

"Daddy," Jessica said as she sat down, "I was on the phone with Aunt Karrie. She wants us all to come to a party at her house Friday night. It's a special dinner to raise money for something or other. I don't remember. Do you remember, Rachelle?"

Before her sister could answer, TJ said, "I can't. I hope to be playing in the finals Friday night."

Dr. Ryan sighed before he spoke. "Your aunt is always hosting a party for one reason or another. I doubt we will be there."

"You never go to her parties, but Daddy, this one we're all invited to. It's not just all-old people. This is the first grown up party she's invited us to. And besides, she has a friend, who has a nephew that she wants to introduce me to. She said he was *so* cute and I would like him." Jessica pouted as she spoke.

"The answer is still no."

"I'll be at TJ's match. So I'll gladly get her home safe and hang around till you get back…if you three want to go, Dr. Richardson," Meagan offered sweetly.

He cut his eyes at her but didn't say a word. That was the second time tonight. He turned his attention immediately on Jessica and said, "Pass your plate down." The tone said, "End of conversation." Everyone at the table got the message, including Meagan. So no one brought the party up again. In fact, the whole room went silent.

The only thing said after that was when the doctor asked Meagan to say the blessing before they began to eat. The only sound heard was Helen's shoes squishing as she walked in the room with the beans and went around the table pouring the iced tea. She poured each glass carefully and then left the remainder of the glass pitcher sitting in the middle of the table.

By the time she walked out, the doctor had dipped up everyone's main dish and the beans were passed around. Each ate in silence. Meagan hated it as she chewed her food tasting the wonderful flavor. All she could think was, what a perfectly horrible way to ruin a marvelous meal! She glanced around the table. *Had any of them even noticed the strained silence? Or was this the way they normally sat at the dinner table and ate?* Last night could have been for her benefit.

Everyone seemed to be too comfortable, sitting, eating in silence.

When everyone was just about finished, Helen swished her way back in, removing some of the dishes and asked, "Who wants banana pudding? I made it fresh today."

"Oh, I do."

"I do."

"I do." All three girls responded practically together in agreement.

"Meagan, do you want some pudding?"

She smiled at Helen and said, "I'd love some, but I have no more room. I'm about to bust. Your lasagna was wonderful."

"Glad you liked it."

"She is the best cook around. We are lucky Jennifer found her… how long has it been? Ten years?" the doctor guessed. The smiles that had been on the girls' faces when banana pudding was mentioned disappeared at the sound of their mother's name.

"She was pregnant with Tamara, so almost thirteen years ago," Helen said.

"I stand corrected." He bowed his head slightly. "And I can honestly say, without a doubt, she has never fed us anything that did not taste good. She has a way in the kitchen."

"Thank you, sir. It's my pleasure. Let me get everyone's dessert. How about you, sir? Are you eating any tonight?"

"I think I will pass for now. Maybe later. I would like to have a word with Miss Phillips before she heads back to her part of the house." Turning his head in her direction he said, "Would you join me in my study?"

Meagan knew she had no choice. She would have loved to say, "Maybe another time." Or "No, not tonight." But she didn't. Instead she nodded her head and said, "No problem."

A gentle squeeze touched her right knee. TJ was trying to give Meagan her support. How sweet.

Well, she wasn't going to worry about it. He was her boss, that was true, but she hadn't done anything wrong. And in the end, the Lord was in charge. He would keep her protected. He had her there for a reason. The doctor wouldn't run her off that easily, even if he wanted to.

God would change his thinking, and the good doctor wouldn't even know what made him change his mind.

Quickly, in her mind she prayed for God to help her not overstep her boundaries or say anything she shouldn't say.

Chapter 10

Meagan let him leave the table before her. She didn't want to seem overly anxious. But now, standing outside his study, the place she had met him for the first time yesterday, she found her knees a little wobbly. She wasn't afraid of him, but she had no idea what he wanted to talk to her about. Meagan was always a little organized... at least in her actions. Not so much in things around her in her daily living, but always in her work world and her actions toward others. This meeting fell under work. She wished she knew what it was about so she could be prepared in her thoughts.

"My strength comes from you, Lord. Lead me in what to say or keep me quiet. Help me to obey You, Lord." She prayed this softly before knocking and entering his study.

Doctor Richardson rose from behind his desk. "Please. Have a seat." He motioned to a stuffed green leather chair that sat off to the side. Next to it was a dark oak end table matching his desk, with a lamp perched on top.

This was probably where he sat in comfort to read some of the books he had on the many shelves on all four of the walls. At a ninety degree angle from the table was a matching couch and a coffee table that sat in front of the two pieces.

The doctor walked over and lowered himself on the couch near the end with the chair. "Thank you for coming. We need to get a few things straight."

"No problem, sir."

"First, I want you to know, I already see a difference in Tamara. I do not know how you connected so quickly with her, but—"

"She was desperately seeking someone to hear her," she said interrupting him. "I just happened to come along at just the right moment." The truth be told, it was God's timing. He was never too late or too early…always right on time, but the doctor wasn't ready to hear that.

"Yes. That is great."

She started to smile and thank him for noticing, but her smile froze half way as he continued with his words.

"But I will not tolerate you telling me what I should or should not do with my girls."

Her blood started to warm as the word "but" formed on her lips, but then she heard in her heart…*stay quiet.* So she remained silent as he continued.

"I love my girls. I have tried to give them everything they wanted and needed all their lives. I thought between Helen, Karrie, and myself they would not miss their mother so much. I see now they need a woman role model for them in their lives. *That* is why I hired you." He rose from the couch and looked down at Meagan before he started pacing around the room.

Meagan followed him with her eyes, except when he crossed behind her, not knowing where this would end.

"I have done all I know to do. Their mother was a wonderful woman. And I know there will never be anyone to take her place. I have neither looked for another wife, nor do I want one." He paused again in his walking and his ranting, and then came back over to the couch.

Sitting back down, his voice a bit calmer, he said, "I want you to do whatever you can to help my girls feel…I cannot say *loved* because you do not know them…feel mothered. Tell them things a mother shares with her girls. Things that will help them be better women as they grow older."

He dragged his fingers through his hair, as he still seemed to be searching for the words he was trying to say to her.

"Be there for them…but do not, I repeat, do not tell me how to be there for them."

Meagan wanted to tell him a thing or two about being a dad not a father. How his girls may have everything money can buy, but they didn't have him. They needed him…not his money.

She had to bite her tongue hard, almost in half, to remain silent. Meagan was certain it would be a bloody mess she bit so hard.

Through direction and answered prayer, she slowly opened her mouth and much to her amazement, gentle words came out. Thank God for answered prayer. "Dr. Ryan. I assure you, it's easy to love your girls. I may not know them yet, and yes, I've connected with TJ without a problem…but I guarantee I already feel love for all three of them and I will do my best to give them all the special love and attention, words and guidance, I feel led to do. I will do the job you hired me to do."

He raised his brows and asked, "And you will not try to pull me into your duties with them?"

"No, sir. I will not try to encourage you in any way." *But that's your loss…and your daughters,* she thought but didn't say.

"And one more thing before you leave. Why do you call Tamara, TJ?" he asked.

Meagan thought for a moment. Closed her eyes and saw the little girl come to mind. TJ. Tamara. "Well, sir, that was how she introduced herself to me, so that is what I know her as."

"Well, her name is Tamara. Tamara Jane, not TJ. Try to remember that."

She rose and as she was heading out she said, "That is a pretty name. I wonder why she prefers TJ?" Shaking her head, she continued in her departure.

He called out to her as she was walking out the door, "Tamara. That's her name."

Meagan smiled as she closed the door behind her. "But TJ is who she is at the moment. Time will tell."

Chapter 11

Meagan's second day of work turned out differently than she had expected. It was the same when it came to Cat talking about everyone who passed near imaging and Tom running a few minutes behind but always the eager beaver when he arrived. No. That was still the same. Even emergencies were the same with twisted ankles and a little boy with a broken arm. Someone always had broken bones to be x-rayed.

The difference today was God used her with a walk-in.

Cat had gone to lunch. Yesterday, the front desk was closed from twelve to one while she was gone. This was normal according to Cat.

Today Meagan slipped by the gift shop in hopes of finding that they carried workout clothes. They did and she picked up a couple of leotards and spandex shorts along with tops to wear with each for a comfortable workout. Glad this hospital had its own little gym or it wouldn't have had this type of merchandise.

With that taken care of and finding she was not hungry, she returned to imaging by twelve-fifteen.

While she was sitting at Cat's desk, a woman came up to her. Meagan was about to tell her they were closed until one, but when she looked up and saw the look on the woman's face, she couldn't turn her away. Her face was pale white and lacked any emotion whatsoever. She looked to be in shock. It also appeared the woman had cried all the tears she could and didn't have anything left. Meagan's heart broke for her.

"Hi. May I help you?" Meagan asked.

The woman swallowed hard and then said, "I need to get my lungs x-rayed."

Sometimes doctors sent patients in for a follow-up, or even had them come in to be x-rayed checking on a suspicion or lack of anything to explain a pain. "And who referred you?" she asked so she could find the information sent over by the doctor's office on the patient.

"No," she said as she shook her head. "I need to be x-rayed. I need to make sure I don't have lung cancer."

Meagan knew what she was supposed to do, but at the moment protocol didn't seem to be required. She watched the woman's face as water filled her eyes, about to spill over. The moment before they toppled, she blinked and squeezed the water away.

"Miss…what did you say your name was?" The woman hadn't, but Meagan found that a polite way to get answers.

"Lisa. Lisa McCullah."

"Ms. McCullah, follow me." Meagan brought her around to one of the smaller offices in the back so they could talk privately. She showed Lisa to a chair and then Meagan pulled another chair out from behind the desk and sat near her.

"What makes you think you have lung cancer?" Meagan asked.

"I'm forty years old, and I have smoked since I was nineteen. My mother, who never smoked a day in her life, just died three days ago from lung cancer." The water was back in her eyes. "It should have been me…not her. Or if she got it without smoking, surely I have it. I need to be checked."

Tears started falling like a bad leaky faucet. Drip. Drip. Drip. They fell one right after the other down Lisa's face. Meagan reached over and laid her hands gently on top of Lisa's and let her cry. When she finally stopped, Meagan gave the woman a couple of tissues.

Lisa wiped her face and stood to her feet. "I'm sorry. I know I sound foolish. I should have consulted my own physician first."

"No," Meagan said as she rose. "You don't sound foolish at all. You sound like someone who is in pain. You are grieving the loss of your mother." Meagan's heart reached out to this woman. The pain, the suffering felt when someone's mother died, Meagan could only imagine. "You loved her very much, didn't you?"

"Yes," she said as she sniffed.

Meagan pulled another tissue out of the container and handed it to her. "I bet she loved you too."

The woman nodded.

"What you need to do now is focus on the good memories and the good times you shared. Don't think about the last few months. It won't hurt to get checked, but go through the proper channels so your insurance will pay for it. Most of all, don't feel the need to be the one who is sick. Thank God you are alive. Do you have children?"

"Yes. I have two, a boy and a girl. Both are teenagers."

"That's great. See? You get to share more of your mom with your kids. And throw away those nasty cigarettes. No need to aggravate your lungs. Go home and love on your kids." Meagan hoped she was doing the right thing. In her heart, it was the right thing to say and do.

Lisa looked up at Meagan. Small tears trickled down Lisa's cheeks again as she said, "Thank you." Her hand went out as if to shake hands, but Meagan gave the woman a hug instead.

"It will be okay. Do you believe in Jesus as your Savior? And did your Mom? Was she saved?"

"Yes."

"Then remember to be absent of the body is to be present with the Lord. Your mom is in good hands," she whispered.

Lisa reached out, this time hugging Meagan. "Thanks so much. You just don't know how much this means to me. I was so afraid, but for some reason I don't feel the fear anymore. Thank you again." She walked out of the room, not smiling, but not crying. She seemed to be at peace.

Nothing could go wrong. That was enough to brighten up the rest of the day…or so she thought. Then all of a sudden she heard a bellow from the other side of the short wall, the one that separated the front desk and the coffee area. Glancing at her watch, she saw the front desk was still closed for another fifteen minutes, but the loud man hadn't settled down any. Meagan decided to go see if she could be of any help.

The moment she rounded the corner, she saw the doctor she had seen on the day of her arrival. *Mr. Pleasant,* she thought. *Yeah, right.* Too late to turn away. He saw her.

"May I help you?"

"I'm Doctor Peters, and I'm waiting on my films. They should have been brought to me by now, but they haven't. I've called up here several times and you don't answer your phone. So I'm here now to get them. So give them to me," he said, stiff-lipped.

She had no idea what x-rays he was referring to, or where they might be at the moment unless she took them herself. "Dr. Peters. What is the patient's name? Why don't you have a seat and I'll see what I can find."

"Don't you know where they are? You should have already brought them to me. Where did you stick them?"

She looked at Cat's desk, where he was pointing. Meagan learned early the tech usually ran them to the doctor, but here Cat sometimes took them...when there were several patients to x-ray. And sometimes even when she was busy checking people in for x-rays, the doctor's nurse would stop by and pick them up. And so far...until now at least, everyone had been pleasant.

"Find my films!" he boomed.

At that moment, Dr. Richardson walked up. "Is there a problem here, Dennis? I can hear you yelling down the hall. We don't need that. This is a hospital," he reminded the doctor.

The top of Dr. Peter's baldhead turned red, as he apparently was embarrassed that the big man caught him.

"Yes, there is a problem. This woman can't keep track of her films on her own desk. She acted like she didn't even know who I was or where my x-rays were. I believe her supervisor needs to have a talk with her."

Oh great, Meagan thought. Just when she was having such a wonderful day, this obnoxious man had to spoil things.

"First off, Dennis, obviously you don't know who this woman is. The main thing is she is not the one responsible for keeping up with the films. If I'm not mistaken, Cat is at lunch. This office is closed for another ten minutes. You need to get with the schedule around here. And furthermore, you have no business talking to this young woman or any other woman or man for that matter, the way you were just speaking. Do I make myself clear?"

Dr. Peters grunted as if he couldn't believe his own ears.

"I believe you owe her an apology. And the next time you come to get x-rays, or deal with anyone else in this hospital, show a little respect. You want it…then give it out first." Dr. Richardson shook his head and walked away.

With his mouth hanging open, the other doctor watched his boss storm away. Dr. Peters seemed to be shocked. Probably because he was the one reprimanded, not Meagan.

Of course, Meagan too, was left a little dumbfounded. She stood there staring at Dr. Peters, not knowing whether to search for his x-rays or walk away. Out of the corner of her eye, she noticed Cat standing perfectly still a few feet from the desk. She apparently caught the ending at least.

All of a sudden everyone moved at the same time. Dr. Peters turned and stormed off as Cat rushed over to the station while Meagan dropped down into the chair.

"You go, girl," Cat said.

Meagan's eyes widened as she threw her hands up in the air and said, "What in the world just happened here?"

"Mr. Obnoxious-pain-in-the-rear just got knocked down a peg or two and by the boss no less. It's about time!"

Patients started coming up to the desk so the two of them had no more time for discussion of the incident that had just taken place. That worked for Meagan, because she wanted to forget it. She wanted to reach back to what happened before and recapture the peace and presence of the Lord.

The rest of the day was uneventful. By the time she got home, she was ready to unwind with a good game of tennis with TJ. The air seemed to have a slight chill in it, so she slipped on a pair of warm-ups and a T-shirt, and then her tennis shoes.

Cutting through the house, on the first try, Meagan found Helen in the kitchen. "Good afternoon."

"Hi, there. I'm cleaning chicken for supper. Hope you like it.

Help yourself to some coffee. How was your day? Are you getting used to the routine yet?"

"Love it cooked just about any way." Her mouth started to salivate at the thought of baked chicken with that teriyaki and garlic flavor she loved so much. That was how she cooked it, anyway. She had no idea how Helen prepared it, but felt sure she would love it.

To distract her thoughts, she asked, "Do you have some orange juice or apple juice? I feel the need for a zap of vitamins," she laughed as she said it. "I'm about to play tennis with TJ. Need all the strength I can get. She'll win by her youth and energy alone."

Helen laughed. "She'll win because she's great." As Helen continued to pull the fat and extra skin from some of the pieces of chicken and rinse them well, she said, "In the fridge. Help yourself.

Meagan opened the refrigerator and pulled out a pitcher of orange juice.

"By the way, I am amazed at how quickly Tamara has taken to you. In the beginning, after her mom's death, her sister, Rachelle, protected her from others. She always played games with her and kept her mind occupied so the loss wouldn't be so obvious to the young girl. But now that Tamara is a little stronger, and a preteen, more active in school functions, Rachelle has focused on her music. Now Tamara runs around like a tough little cookie so no one can bother her. She hasn't wanted to be with anyone except her little friend, Mary. Other than Mary, Tamara has kept to herself."

Meagan knew what she was saying. It had to be the Lord who brought Meagan here for just that purpose. He would open the door to each girl's heart at the right time and Meagan prayed for the strength and wisdom to step in.

"But since the first night you came, she latched on to you." Shaking her head as if trying to figure it out, she said, "Another thing is, since you've come she's been smiling again. She hasn't been smiling much lately, but night before last, you turned a smile up on her face and it doesn't seem to be going away. I'm so proud."

Meagan had poured some juice and sat at the table listening to Helen. "I'm glad to hear you say that. The first thing I noticed with the whole family was that no one seemed happy. You were the only joyful spot in the entire group."

"I can remember the days when happiness filled this home. I've tried different things over the past seven years to bring it back, but to no avail. But when you got here, it was like a little ray of sunshine, or a little ray of hope infringed on this household. I'm so glad."

After another sip of her juice Meagan said, "I know God sent me here to help these girls. I'll do my best to reach out to all three of them."

Rinsing the last piece, Helen washed her hands, and then reached in the cupboard. Pulling out a casserole dish, she said, "You've got your work cut out for you. And with God on your side, I'm sure you won't miss."

Meagan laughed. "Since I never had any kids of my own, I'm not sure how to approach them, but I'm praying about it. He'll open the door. One at a time I'm hoping, and I plan to be bold and walk through." Standing up, she swallowed the last sip of her orange juice and stepped over to the sink to rinse out her glass. Meagan was glad for Helen's input.

By now, Helen had worked herself and the dish with the chicken down the counter, seasoning the meat. "If I can help in any way, let me know," she said.

"Don't forget the games are tomorrow. I'd like for us to go together, if that's okay with you. I'd planned to pick you up after work. It should be okay if I go in my scrubs…right?"

"You'll be fine. I'll be ready."

As Meagan headed out the door, she waved bye with the toss of her hand. A joy filled her heart as she agreed whole-heartedly with Helen: with God on her side, she couldn't miss.

Chapter 12

Meagan sat in the family room as she waited for TJ to join her. Her wait wasn't more than five or ten minutes. It gave Meagan a little time to think about her life and the road she was on. She knew her own planning and conspiring didn't choose the path she was on. No. She was there because God led her there, and He had a purpose for her. Meagan prayed that she would follow His plan and not her own. She knew that it was easy to get into the flesh, thinking, *What about me?* Right now she was surrounded by beauty, a beauty she had never before felt, but she knew it was only temporary. In her mind she whispered, *Help me stay focused.*

"Great. You're ready," TJ said as she dashed into the room.

Meagan stood up. "I hope you have a racket for me. Otherwise, you've won by default. *By de-fault I didn't bring my racket,*" she said adding a flair of a Cajun accent.

TJ laughed at Meagan's corny joke. "No such excuse. I have a racket for you. In fact, you get to choose between a couple. Maybe you'll find one grip better than the other...depending on your taste."

Of course, she thought. *They have everything.* Tightness started to grow in the pit of her stomach. She was about to play tennis with a young girl who could probably shut her out, but that didn't matter. They were here for a reason far more important than the game they were about to play. Focus!

"Don't look so gloomy. We're going to have fun...remember?" TJ said as she led Meagan out to the back yard and around toward the tennis court.

Meagan's eyebrows flickered as she realized her fear was written all over her face. A forced chuckle fell from her lips. "Yeah. Sorry. I'm starting to question my own sanity here."

When they stepped onto the court, she glanced around taking in the beauty of the ocean. "How great this must be, playing tennis with such a beautiful backdrop." The smell of the saltwater teased Meagan's senses as the rush of the waves sounded in the air. Powerfully magnificent, there were no other words that would come close to describing it.

TJ stopped in mid-stride as she was stepping into a little equipment room off the front of the court. This was part of the structure that hid the tennis court from Meagan's view through her picture window. "I hate to say it, but I've lived here all my life and never thought about it before.

Meagan nodded as she remembered TJ was just a kid. Most people don't appreciate things like beautiful views until they get a little older in life.

By the time the racket was found and they started playing tennis in the heat of the game, the view was lost on Meagan too.

After four intense games, Meagan was pleased at the fact she won the third one. "Enough. Enough. I give. I'll take my little victory and relish it. Three losses are more than I can bear for our first time." Exhausted, she waved her arms frantically over her head as she said, "Truth be told, I can't go any more today, TJ. I probably didn't help you much, but I'm ready for a drink...then a shower."

TJ, still full of energy, jumped the net and ran up on Meagan. "No. This was great. I loved it. Thanks for playing." Her enthusiasm was abundant. She reached for Meagan's racket. "Start up toward the house. I'll put these away and catch up with you." She lifted the rackets up over her head and took off toward the building.

"You'll get no argument from me," Meagan said even though TJ couldn't hear her. Meagan ambled away one slow step at a time. The energy young people have. It was amazing. TJ caught up with Meagan before she reached the back door.

"Let's get some Gatorade. It will replenish our electrolytes. We'll get our drinks and crash in the den."

"Oh, no. I'm too sweaty. Let's go sit at the kitchen table or outside on the patio."

The young girl laughed. "Go," she said pointing inside the house. "Sit. I'll get the drinks."

Meagan didn't argue any more. She went and plopped down on the love seat in the family room. Leaning back against the cushion, she thought about the bonding between her and TJ. Meagan was glad, but she knew she needed to do more. She needed to get close enough for the girl to open up to her, let her bare her little broken heart, help her to grieve the loss of her mother, so she could move on. Also she needed to find a good Bible-based church near here for the girls to attend and become a part of. She would try to find one Saturday, and she would invite TJ to join her Sunday.

Friday was there before she knew it. TJ had won both of her matches Thursday, which placed her in the finals. It had been a long day at work. Meagan thought it would never end, but it did...all of it. Her work, the race home for Helen, the food picked up on the way and then wolfed down, and then the final match all ended. In two cars, they returned to the Richardson's for a little celebrating.

"I was amazed, watching TJ play. She isn't just good...she's great!" Meagan said as she pulled down glasses. Pressing one glass at a time against the ice dispenser on the door of the freezer, she began to fill them as Helen grabbed a couple of liters of soft drinks. "Six glasses, right?" Meagan asked making sure she was filling the correct number of glasses.

"Let's see. You, me, Tamara, her friend Mary, Rachelle, and Stan. Yeah. Six." Helen then filled each glass with soda. "That little bit of a girl started playing when she was only four years old. It's one of the things her mom was teaching her before she passed away."

That explains TJ's passion for the sport, Meagan thought. *It is her way of staying close to her mom.* Meagan wondered if the doctor realized that. "I knew she played a tough game when I played her, but now I see she was holding back on me…giving me a break. She let me win my one and only game. I'm so grateful, but now I have to get better." This was definitely the way to get close to the young girl, and Meagan had made up her mind to give it her all for all three of the girls.

As Helen filled the glasses, Meagan set them on a tray. When the job was completed, Meagan snatched up the tray and headed toward the swinging door.

"Let me get that tray," Helen said.

"Please," she said as if to say, *Don't be silly,* stretching out the "e" in please. "I got it. Just hold the door open so I don't spill any."

They joined the others in the den. The four young people were gathered around sitting on the couch and chairs talking about the games from last night and the final tonight. TJ was the center of attention and seemed to love it. After Helen took her drink, Meagan stepped in front of each of the young people and waited as they took a glass.

When it was down to one, she grabbed it, set the tray aside, and raised her glass in salute. "To TJ. She's the best."

"Here, here," Helen said.

"Go Tamara!" cried Stan and Rachelle in unison.

"TJ, you did it!" shouted Mary.

Different ones made quick comments of praise as they raised their drink to their lips.

"I'm glad you beat Katie," Stan said.

Helen had said Stan was a friend of Rachelle's. Seeing how close he sat next to her on the couch, Meagan wondered how good a friend he truly was to the middle sister.

She also wondered if Dr. Richardson knew anything about Rachelle's friend. The girl was sixteen, old enough to date, but as little as the doctor was around, she wondered if he even noticed. Stan made himself right at home, as if he had been there a number of times before. Meagan shook the thoughts out of her mind. She was building a scenario without all the facts.

"Me too," Rachelle said. "Katie was bragging around school this morning about how she would take you down tonight with her eyes closed. I tried to tell her not to underestimate my little sister. She only laughed and said you were just a kid." She winked at her little sister. "You made me proud."

Mary grabbed her little friend's ponytail and tugged, and then the two of them giggled.

Laughter and conversation were flowing freely when Dr. Richardson walked into the room. "Are we celebrating a victory here or something?"

TJ squealed, slammed her glass down on the coffee table as she jumped to her feet and ran to her daddy. "I won! I won!"

He opened his arms wide, and she threw herself into them. "I knew you would, sweetheart. I never doubted it for a minute," he said as he spun her around. When they stopped, he slowly lowered her to the ground.

A glow beamed from TJ's face. The girl lived and breathed for her daddy's attention and approval. She hugged him tightly, clinging to him. "Thank you. I wish you could have come."

"I wanted to, baby. I am sorry."

She shrugged. "I know. It's okay. Come on, Mary. Are you finished with your coke?" As the girl nodded, TJ said, "Good. Let's go play some X-box in the game room."

Dr. Richardson looked at his watch and one of his brows raised. "This is a school night, Tamara. I probably should run Mary home."

"Oh, Daddy. You're so funny," she laughed as she spoke. "It's Friday night!" she said as they headed out the door.

Stan rose from the couch and said, "I was going to drop Mary off on my way home, Dr. Richardson."

Rachelle jumped up, her long blonde hair flying freely behind her, and grabbed Stan by the arm. "Let's order pizza. And while we wait on it, I'll beat you in a game of pool." Her hair flew out as she spun around and tugged Stan to his feet.

Meagan watched the doctor's eyes, as he seemed to observe his daughter growing up right before them.

"That's okay, isn't it, Dad? Besides, Tamara didn't eat with us before the match and we only grabbed a burger on the run back up to the school for Meagan, Helen, and myself. I'm sure Tamara's starving because I'm hungry again."

TJ must have heard them because she stuck her head back in the door and said, "Pizza. Great idea!"

As the doctor stood there saying nothing, Rachelle led Stan around her dad. As they were passing him, in a softer voice she said to her father as she touched his elbow gently, "Dad, you should have been there tonight. You would have been very proud of Tamara. She reminded me of Momma—her intensity of the game, her concentration on the ball. It was amazing. Just like how Momma used to play. Every one of Tamara's opponents was older than she was...Thursday and Friday, but she put them down. Beat them easily." Rachelle let her hand drop from her dad and pulled Stan on out of the room with her. "See you later."

With all four of the kids gone, the room grew very quiet. Meagan couldn't take her eyes off the doctor. *What had he been thinking as his girls passed him by?*

Helen didn't seem to wonder, or at least she didn't wait to find out. "I better go order the pizza," she said as she grabbed the tray and the empty glasses and then shuffled out of the room. "They think of the ideas, but don't seem to follow through. If I left it to them they would be waiting all night for the pizza."

Before Meagan looked away, the doctor caught her gaze. His face went cold immediately. "I know! I should have been there. I missed last night, but I truly meant to be there tonight."

"I'm sure TJ understands," Meagan said but thought differently. The poor girl was used to her daddy not being there for her.

"No, really. The truth is we got so close tonight on one of the tests we were running. I lost all track of time. I knew we were about to have a big breakthrough any minute, and we almost made it tonight."

"You don't need to explain anything to me, sir. Tell TJ if you don't think she understood. Have a good night, sir."

She started to slip out of the room, trying to avoid a confrontation. For she knew if he asked her opinion, she'd give it. Sometimes, Meagan didn't know when to keep her mouth shut, but she was going to try tonight.

"Miss Phillips," he said, and the tone wasn't saying goodnight. It said, *turn back around. We are not finished here.*

She took in a deep breath and released it slowly. Shucks. Not fast enough on her escape. She tried. She would have to work harder on that in the future. As she slowly eased back around, she said, "Sir?"

"I am glad you went tonight…you and Helen both. I am sure it meant a lot to Tamara."

She nodded. "No problem, sir. I wanted to be there. Glad I made it, too. Your little girl plays one heck of a tennis match. She wants to be a professional tennis player when she gets older…did you know that?"

"Yes. Well, no. I did not know it. I do know she plays well, though." He dropped his shoulders as he added, "I know I should take more time for all my girls…do things with them. I know it, here," he said as he pointed to his head.

"And I want it here." He dragged his hand down to his heart. Then all of a sudden he threw his shoulders back, stood tall, and said, "Never mind. I know. That is all. You do not have to tell me anything." His voice grew gruff, almost angry, as he spoke.

"I didn't say anything, sir. What you do or don't do with your kids is your business, not mine. I remember what you told me Wednesday night." She wanted to smile, but didn't dare. Meagan had basically voiced her opinion without saying a word. The main thing was she could tell he got the message loud and clear.

Dr. Richardson looked down at her. Raising his hand and pointing his finger, he opened his mouth as if he were about to say something, but then he closed it again without uttering a word. He raised his hand higher and raked his fingers through his sun-streaked hair. Then he shook his head slightly, his gaze never leaving Meagan's face. Silent seconds passed.

Suddenly he drew in a deep breath, dropped his hand to his side as his fingers formed a fist, turned on his heel, and stormed out of the room.

Lifting her hands into the air, Meagan said to a completely empty room, "What did I do?"

Chapter 13

Meagan left the den not knowing which way to turn. Should she go join the girls in the game room? Maybe she should go find Helen. Meagan could tell her what just happened and see what she thought it was all about, what he meant by storming out without a word, but she didn't really want to understand Ryan…the doctor. He could be so confusing. It was best to leave well enough alone.

The doctor had to take more time with his girls if he wanted a deeper relationship with them. There was no other way, and he knew that.

So what was he afraid of? Losing them? Like he lost his wife? At the rate he was going, he may lose them anyway.

She shook her head. Probably not. His girls loved him a lot, if TJ and Rachelle were anything to go by. Although she hadn't gotten to know Jessica at all, Meagan felt down deep the teenager loved her father too. One thing Meagan knew for sure was he was not as close to his girls as he could be. If only he would make an effort, but he wasn't even trying to reach out to them. And that was a shame. After God, family was the most important thing in a person's life.

For a second or two, she flirted again with the idea of joining the kids and playing pool with Rachelle and Stan, not X-box with the younger ones.

Meagan had never been too good at holding the long narrow stick braced on her fingers, then sliding it just right, hitting the little white ball making it smack into one of the others. Her balance was never very good, but she liked the challenge of the game.

Her mom and dad played a lot of pool. Both of them were very good at it. In fact, Pops had a few trophies where he had won or come in second in a few pool tournaments.

Sighing, she shook her head. "No. I think I'll go give Shelly a call before it gets too late." Glancing at her watch she saw it was a little after nine on the East Coast. "It's barely after eight at home. Shelly should be running around cleaning up the kitchen," she whispered and then thought, *Unless they went out for dinner.* It was Friday night. At Shelly's house that meant "family night."

Meagan liked the idea of calling Shelly. Her sister could usually see things clearly for her, or at least attempt to make sense out of things that Meagan couldn't. Besides, Meagan had gone five days… well, almost, since last talking to Shelly, and things could have happened around home. Shelly was her lifeline to home. She needed to get the scoop and Shelly would have it…if there was any to be had.

Back in her part of the house, she took her phone off the charger and keyed her sister's number. As she was about to hang up, she heard, "It's about time. I haven't heard from you since you got there."

Good ole Shelly. She would never change. A force of energy in herself. Always in fast motion. "Hey, Shel. Missed you too. How are the kids? I definitely miss them." Meagan plopped down on the love seat and hoisted her feet up on the coffee table.

"They're great. Of course, they miss you too. Every day they ask if I've heard from you. And Kirk wants to call you. I tell him you're at work. You'll call when you're free."

Meagan's heart dropped. She loved Kirk and Mandy and

wouldn't hurt them for the world. "I'm sorry, Shel. Give both of them a hug and kiss from me. You wouldn't believe how fast things are happening here. You remember TJ, the twelve-year-old?"

As Shelly acknowledged the remembrance, Meagan told her everything. She told her about the tennis the two of them had played, about the young girl's passion for the game, about TJ's wins and Meagan's losses, and about TJ's tournament.

She also mentioned the lack of TJ's dad being there for her. She even told Shelly how quickly she and TJ had bonded. In their conversation Meagan also told her about Rachelle. "Nothing has happened there…yet, but since the tournament started, I've been able to talk a little to her. Jessica, the oldest, that's another story. With her, it's more of a lack of Jessica being around. How can you connect with someone who isn't even here?"

"Sounds like you're making great progress, sis. And you thought it would be like babysitting. It sounds to me like you've already connected and that you really care about these girls."

Meagan leaned her head back on the sofa and sighed. "It's weird. I do. I can't explain it, but I know it's God. He's going to use me in a big way with these girls. Pray for them…and me."

The next one she told Shelly about was Helen. Shelly had to love Helen as quickly as Meagan had.

"She sounds like a treat. I know I'd like her," Shelly said.

Meagan yawned in Shelly's ear. "Sorry," she said in the middle of her yawn as she glanced at her watch. It was now after eleven Eastern time. "It's past my bedtime. I can't believe we've talked this long."

"You should hear yourself. I can tell you are where you should be. God definitely sent you there. Even though I didn't hear much about that handsome boss of yours, it did sound like you and TJ have connected. Rachelle doesn't seem that far away. You'll find something there to connect you with her. Kirk is calling me. I gotta run too, so go to bed."

"Love ya, Shel. Tell Mom hi for me and catch her up on the things going on for me."

"No problem. Will tell her the juicy tid-bits first thing in the morning."

"Y'all pray for me, that I say and do the right thing," Meagan said.

"You know we will. Night, sis. We love you."

"Kiss everyone for me," Meagan said and then punched the button to disconnect the line.

A shower, a good book, and bed for me now, she thought. And as soon as her shower was complete, she found Dee Henderson's latest novel and crawled into bed. The only thing bad about taking one of her books to bed, Meagan found herself fighting sleep to stay awake to finish one more chapter, then another, and another.

The next morning, Meagan woke to a knock on her door. She had stayed up till three reading. She knew that would happen, but she had completed about half or maybe a little more than half of the novel.

Rubbing her eyes, yawning, and stretching, she climbed out of bed and padded down the hall. Meagan opened the door a crack and peered around it. She saw the back of TJ as she was walking away.

"You gave up too soon, TJ. Come back. I'm awake," she said, her voice sounding a little crackly.

Spinning around, already dressed in jeans and a sweatshirt, the young girl rushed back over to the door and stepped inside. "I hope I didn't wake you."

"You did, but that's okay. It's time to get up anyway." She raised her wrist to check the time as she closed the door behind TJ. No watch. It was on the dresser. "By the way, what time is it?" Meagan asked.

"Nine-fifteen. I just thought we could talk a little this morning. And if you wanted, I could show you around the island a little. You can't have seen much since you arrived. You've been too busy working and keeping me company."

"Follow me," Meagan said. She led TJ to the kitchen. "Have you eaten?"

"Oh, yes. On Saturdays we always have doughnuts, so we can eat whatever time we get up. Nobody gets up at the same time."

Glancing down at her watch again, she added, "In fact, right about now Rachelle is getting up, well, really in about fifteen minutes or so. Jessica on the other hand, you won't see her until noon…no matter how late or early she comes in."

Meagan was busy making a pot of coffee while TJ talked. When the water started dripping, she said, "I'm going to scramble some eggs. Would you like some?" She asked anyway, because the young girl had a voracious appetite.

"Sure. You got any orange juice?"

"Yes, I do. Your daddy supplied my kitchen well."

She laughed. "Daddy didn't do that. It was Ms. H. She takes care of everything."

"Oh." Meagan didn't want to go there, so she pulled down the plates and got out the eggs. She kept herself busy so she wouldn't have to get into that conversation…talking about the doctor.

"Speaking of Daddy. Did he say anything to you last night?" Apparently TJ didn't want to leave him out of their conversation.

Meagan cracked the egg a little harder than she intended, shattering parts of the shell.

Good thing she was scrambling them. The yolk busted as the white and yellow slid through her fingers oozing down into the bowl below. At least no shell fragments fell into the bowl.

"Ah…nothing important…Why do you ask?" She turned to face TJ for a moment as her mind tried to remember what exactly Dr. Richardson had said to her last night.

She remembered how he made her feel. She remembered he almost said something but then he turned and left her standing there…as if it was her fault his relationship with his daughters was the way that it was.

She cracked two more eggs in the bowl. While beating the eggs, her thoughts continued. Like she was the reason he didn't have a close relationship with them. Meagan hadn't even been around them a full week yet. Maybe her being there and her quick connection pointed it out to him. She cast those thoughts out of her mind as her eyes rested on TJ.

The young girl shrugged her shoulders. "I don't know. It was just weird. Daddy got up early, as usual, but instead of rushing off to the hospital like he's done as long as I can remember, he hung around in the dining room and talked to me while I ate."

"That's good, honey. He probably wanted to get the entire scoop on the final match. He missed seeing you win your victory. Your dad probably figured you could give him a play-by-play account of the game." Meagan turned back to scrambling the eggs in the melted pat of butter as they cooked. "Do you want toast?"

"One slice."

"Me too. Would you put two in while I'm finishing up here? The eggs only take a minute to cook."

The girl jumped up and got busy. She seemed to know where everything was stored. It was apparent to Meagan that TJ had been in this part of the house before. Meagan felt a jolt in her chest. Shaking her head, she frowned. *What difference did it make?* So what if TJ had been in here sharing breakfast with some other woman who lived in their home before her.

Who was she? She found herself wondering, and then she wanted to scream. She sounded jealous…besides which, she had no business wondering anything. She squeezed her eyes closed trying to squash the question right out of her mind. It was none of her business. She worked for the man. An employee. *That* was who she was. So what was it to her who had stayed in this wing of the house before? It was none of her business; that's what it was.

Minutes later, while they sat at the table enjoying the meal, TJ shared the conversation she had had earlier with her dad. Afterwards, she said between bites, "It was nice. Usually, he's so busy we only see him at dinner and for a short time before we go to bed at night."

That saddened Meagan's heart. The girls needed more of his time. She hoped she found a way to convey that to the doctor before her time came to an end. She would. No room for doubt in her mind. Meagan was there for a reason, and she knew it was to help those girls grieve their mother's death and to move on with life. Part of that would have to come from their dad moving forward too. She would make him see it as time went on.

Apparently something had gotten through to him last night for him to stay and have breakfast with his girls. That was a start she had to admit.

"Maybe he's trying to change that, sweetheart. He's trying to spend more time with you. In fact, you should probably be over there right now talking to him instead of being here with me."

TJ took another bite, chewed it up, and swallowed. "No. We did have a great thirty minutes, but when I said I wanted to check on you and show you around town, he thought that was a wonderful idea. He even said he should have thought of that. He should have offered to take you around town."

Meagan felt her cheeks burn. "Nonsense. Nowhere I've ever worked traveling has the boss shown me around town."

Swallowing her juice, TJ set her glass down. "But Meagan, you're more than a worker for my dad. You're a friend for all of us."

"No, sweetie. I'm your dad's employee."

A shocked look spread over the young girl's face. "But you said you wanted to be our friend."

Meagan laid her fork on her plate and reached across the table. Laying her hand gently on TJ's hand, she said, "I am your friend. And I want to be Rachelle and Jessica's too."

TJ dropped her gaze from Meagan's face to the table.

"Sweetie, don't be sad. I really am your friend. You opened up your heart so quickly to me and I couldn't resist."

She looked up and smiled at Meagan. "I know. I felt the same way. You made me feel so special so quickly. You treated me almost like I think a mom would treat her daughter."

Warmth spread through Meagan's insides. That was a very sweet thing for TJ to say, but she wasn't sure how to respond. TJ didn't seem to expect a response. Instead the young girl went on to explain.

"No. The reason I looked so sad was because you want to be friends with Rachelle and Jessica too. You can forget Jessica. Last night, I heard her when she got in. Rachelle had just come up the stairs. She stayed up playing her guitar after Stan left. Anyway, they stopped outside my door. Rachelle was telling her of the fun we all had tonight and she mentioned you in it. Jessica got so uptight and loud. She warned Rachelle to look out. She said you were like all the other women who came around here. You wanted Daddy and his money. She said you didn't really care about us. We were just extra baggage you had to deal with."

"Oh, sweetie. I'm so sorry she feels that way. I hope you know it's not true."

"I'm full. That was good." TJ sat back, rubbed her stomach. "Don't you worry about me. I like my new friendship and I'm going to make the most of it while you are here, for however long that is. I hope that's okay with you."

Meagan felt a grin spread across her face from ear to ear. Of course that was all right by her. She saw progress already with the youngest. TJ was hungry for a friend...not a friend...more of an adult to take an interest in her, giving her direction. That was what Meagan believed and she knew that was why God had sent her to an area of the country that was the last place Meagan would have chosen for herself.

"That is more than okay by me, sweetie. Thank you. Now, you go in the living room and turn on some music or TV to keep you occupied while I clean up in here and then go get myself dressed. We have a day on the town planned."

TJ stood and as she was walking out of the kitchen she said, "Besides if you were after my daddy and his money, I'd hope you'd get both. Then you would stay here forever. I'd have a lifetime friendship...with someone treating me like a friend and like a daughter."

The girl didn't wait for a response. Good thing because Meagan felt her mouth drop open.

Meagan, get Dr. Richardson, as TJ so youthfully put it was a little more than she had been thinking herself. All she could do was gape after the young girl. A strange thought swept through the back of her mind. *That might not be so bad.*

Meagan wasn't sure which shocked her more…TJ's words…or her own thoughts.

Chapter 14

Meagan slipped on her normal attire—blue jeans and a T-shirt—but covered it with a navy-blue jersey she had gotten while in Maine. Before leaving her apartment, TJ tossed a cap to her and said, "This will keep the sun from burning the top of your head. This may be spring and the breezes are nice, but the sun is shining and it could burn your scalp."

Slapping the cap on top of her head, Meagan thought she she should probably pull her hair back in a ponytail, but decided against it because she wanted to feel her hair flying in the breeze. The baseball hat would keep her hair out of her eyes, so that would work perfectly.

It was a typical April day on the island according to TJ. The temperature reached the high fifties and the slight breeze in the air stirred Meagan's hair as they stepped out the back door of the mansion.

"I still don't see why you don't want to take my car. I can drive us around the island. That way, I'll see more."

"There are only two correct ways to see the island. One is on roller blades. The other is on bikes. Do you blade?"

Instantly, a picture flashed in Meagan's mind reminding her of a day a few years back. A chuckle slipped through her lips. "You could say I do…but not very well. I mean, I know how, but the last time I did it was about three years ago with my niece, Mandy. We went up and down my street and around the neighborhood for about an hour. It was fun. And I only fell once. But the next day, I hurt like the dickens."

A smirk slipped across the young girl's face as a low giggle gurgled up from her throat. "That settles it. Bikes for us. Come on." She led Meagan around the pool and to the left of the building they had gone around the back of to play tennis Wednesday evening.

When TJ opened the door, Meagan saw it was the garage. The place was so big. She had never seen one this large except in the movies. It could accommodate about six cars, but there were only two parked in it—a black Lexus and a silver Mercedes convertible. The Mercedes sat all by itself in the middle of the garage. Meagan had never been good at makes, models, or years of cars, but she could tell this one was several years old, five or better. The Lexus appeared to be rather new. In her gut, she guessed the silver car was the mother's.

How sad for those kids and for the doctor, if that were the case. For them to have to see it every time they came out to ride a bike or get in the car to go with their father somewhere…the memory…the constant reminder. She sighed.

Maybe he had good reasons for keeping it. Maybe, he was going to give it to Jessica. Meagan guessed it could be a wise financial decision to give it to his daughter instead of selling it outright and buying her a new one, but Meagan doubted it. The man apparently had enough money to buy what he pleased. It was probably here for sentimental reasons. And if he kept this, what else did he keep, reminding him and the girls every day of the mother who was no longer around? How could anyone move on with life?

TJ walked straight to the bikes, as if not even noticing the car's existence, making her way to the backside of the garage. There stood five bicycles of various colors, four girl bikes and one bike for a guy. Each had a helmet strapped on the handle bar.

"Which one do you want to ride?"

"Blue's my favorite color, so how about that one?"

TJ raised her brows then lowered them. "That was my mom's favorite color also. In fact, that's her bike. Daddy keeps it in good shape. Keeps the chain greased and the tires aired."

A knot formed and twisted in Meagan's stomach. "I can ride another one. No problem."

"Please ride Mom's bike. It needs to be used…or given away."

Smart girl. Meagan knew which got her vote: *Get rid of it!* But she didn't voice it. Her premonition had been right. She wanted to ask if the car was her mom's also but didn't dare. She prayed soon TJ would bring up her mom in a conversation so Meagan could help her open up and grieve her loss. Releasing a pent up breath of air, she felt sure TJ would talk about it at the right time and God would give Meagan the right words. She would wait.

Quietly, Meagan stuffed the baseball cap in her back pocket and then slipped on the helmet while TJ pulled something out of her jacket pocket. The girl then stuck it in the leather pouch behind the seat of her bike, and then she flipped the flap over it and buckled it closed. Slipping on her helmet, she grabbed the handlebars and then knocked the kickstand up with her left foot. Next she rolled the bright red bike, turning it around in the garage heading toward the large closed door. As she neared the door, she pressed a button.

Meagan grabbed the handlebars of the blue bike and followed TJ out of the garage through one of the big doors that had opened.

They mounted their bikes and peddled down the driveway. As

they rounded the house, Meagan saw Dr. Richardson stepping out of the front door. She wondered if he was headed to the hospital. He wasn't dressed for it.

TJ waved as they passed him. He watched them pass as he waved back.

"Maybe we should stay home so you can be with your dad. He didn't look like he was going to be working today," Meagan said as they peddled their bikes down the driveway, side by side.

"He's not. He took the whole day off. He'll be here when we get back." TJ reached out and tapped Meagan on the arm, getting her undivided attention. They both stopped in their progression down the massive driveway and looked at one another. "I have to tell you this. You're not going to believe it, but he almost came with us biking. But then he decided I might enjoy it more with just you. Kind of a girl thing, he said." TJ laughed as she was telling Meagan. "I thought it was cool that he even thought about it."

Meagan's stomach twisted and then did a flip-flop as she wheeled her bike to the road. What was that all about? It was a good thing he didn't go with them, right? She questioned herself: had she wanted him to be a part of the outing today?

No. Of course not!

His not coming was for the best. He was her boss, not a man for her to take notice of. Dr. Richardson, no matter how good looking, was way out of her league. Her thoughts were interrupted when TJ started talking again.

"We're going to make our way to the bike path along the coast. I'll show you places that are really busy in the summer time but right now are pretty much closed down. The island is a tourist town in the summer, but a quiet little place the rest of the year. We'll stop along the way at various places I think you might enjoy. While we're out, we'll grab lunch. Follow me."

Meagan smiled. As tiny as that girl was, she was always ready to eat. At least she had been so far this week…every time Meagan could remember.

They both mounted their bikes and rolled down the street. TJ took the lead and Meagan followed. In no time, they were wheeling on the bike path that ran along the coastline with the ocean in its grand scale out to their left. The path couldn't have been more than forty to fifty yards from the water's edge and running parallel with the water, but it was built about six to eight feet higher than the shore. In various places they had steps that led down to the sand.

As much as Meagan had always claimed to hate the beach, she found herself entranced by it today. Why? She didn't know. Maybe it was because she was fully clothed with very little chance of the gritty sand working its way next to her skin to irritate it and her.

Waves rolled in and then flowed back out again. Sailboats floated out in the water as the wind moved them along. Not many were out there, but there were a few, and the scene was beautiful… almost like a painting. Moored along a couple of piers they cycled past were schooners in their slips, masts tall but bare, and no movement onboard.

"Not much action going on right now," TJ called out over her shoulder, "but stay through the summer and the waters will be packed full of boats out a ways from shore. And over there," she pointed a little ahead of them but still to the left on the beach area, "is where you rent kayaks and jet skis. Even sailboats if you want. But if you don't want to get out in the ocean, you can go down to the channel. There you can rent canoes and paddle boats and even fishing boats to have fun in the channel."

Water sports had never been a great love of Meagan's. The truth be told, other than swimming, she had not really had the opportunities to try many of them out…except fishing. She had tried that and didn't like the worms or the hooks or the sun burning up her skin…but the things TJ mentioned, all but the fishing, sounded like they had possibilities.

The wind blew across her face as she kept pace with TJ. As much as everything sounded intriguing to Meagan, she doubted she would be around long enough to find out about the active summers.

But what if I am?

They cycled down the bike path along the coast for a good thirty minutes or more before TJ pulled over and parked her bike at a stand set for bike parking. Meagan parked next to her.

Looking around Meagan asked, "Y'all just leave your bikes and go off? No one bothers them?"

"Why would they? Besides, I thought we'd walk down to the lighthouse. It's the one the town got its name for."

Meagan smiled. She couldn't remember ever leaving bikes parked out in the open without locking them down with a chain and lock. Otherwise, you'd come back to nothing. Even with the lock and chain, sometimes you'd still come back to nothing but a cut chain. It was sad to realize that about her hometown but even more reason to enjoy where she was at the moment.

It also dawned on Meagan that she couldn't recall Helen or anyone else for that matter, locking the front or back door when they left for the tennis matches. There had been no locks on the garage or the equipment room around back. She liked the feeling of trust everyone seemed to have on this island. She strapped her helmet on the handlebar and replaced the baseball cap on her head.

Another good thing she found here. Come to think of it, Meagan couldn't think of a single negative thing about her stay here on

Lighthouse Isle, except maybe that one doctor she had seen her first day and had the displeasure of meeting later, Dr. Dennis Peters.

Meagan followed TJ down the stone path to the lighthouse. It reminded her of a barbershop pole, red and white stripes curving upward as they circled around the pole.

"Does it light up at night?"

"Yes, but it's run by electricity now." TJ went on to tell her the town tale of the lighthouse keeper filling his containers with oil and walking up the steps all the way to the top so the light would burn all night, warning the ships that land was close as well as some rocks.

"I notice the rocks all around but before we got here there were a lot of sandy shores without the rocks."

"This is about the only place that has a rocky shoreline on the whole island. The place is a tourist attraction now. People can climb to the top and walk outside and around it. The rails are high, so it's safe," TJ said.

"I like it from here. I'd have to really think on it before I'd commit to going to the top." Wrinkling her nose, she said softly, "I have a little fear of heights."

"We can't go up now anyway. It's closed to the public. We're just going around the outside."

TJ led Meagan around the bottom of the lighthouse. She even had them stepping on some of the larger rocks. As she started to go farther out, Meagan said, "I think this is far enough. Some of those rocks seem to be pretty high off the ground."

"Three, maybe four feet tops."

"This is enough. Let's go back around the other side."

TJ shrugged and smiled as she started them back away from the water to the other side of the lighthouse.

Meagan tasted the salt on her lips as the wind off the water brushed across her face.

Back at the bikes, she saw TJ pull something out of her satchel attached behind the seat of her bike but paid little mind to it. Her thoughts had been on the good things of the island. Instinctively her mind slipped onto thoughts of Dr. Richardson. He was a good boss…a kind man to work for…and for all intents and purposes, a good landlord. But his mind had been preoccupied since day one. If only he would take the time to smell the roses so to speak…or in this case, smell the saltwater. If he could learn to enjoy his girls and his life, he would be so much happier…more at peace with life. And then she thought, *Today was a good start for the man.*

As TJ led Meagan down some steps that led to the sand, she asked, "So what are we about to do?"

"I thought you might want to do a little shell shopping. Well not shopping. More like collecting. We look for them on the beach. I brought this in case you did."

In her hand she dangled something. It looked like a cloth bag with holes all over it. That was what she had pulled out of the pocket of her bike.

"You drop the shells you find in this. The sand falls through the holes and you don't bring much of the beach home with you. It has a draw string on top to close the bag so none fall out on the way home."

"Sounds great! I haven't done this since I was a kid. I remembered enjoying the shells once we got them home and cleaned off all the sand, but mostly we bought them from a gift shop and played with them in the sand."

"This is a good area." TJ pointed toward an empty pier that led out into the water, but motioned toward the sand just this side of it.

"You may find sand dollars, angel wings, or some whelks in all sizes. That's our state shell. Those you'll find in abundance out in the waters, but the animals are still in them and you'd have to suit up to go out in the cold waters this time of the year."

"I'll pass on that part of it, but looking around in the sanded area will work for me." She shocked herself saying that. Since when was rooting around in sand fun to her? Somehow this place, or this little girl, was causing some weird changes in Meagan's likes and dislikes.

They started out toward the water's edge by crossing through the soft sand, and then started walking on the firm damp sand... strolling slowly alongside the shoreline.

"TJ, I've got to say, you have given me reasons to like the beach. Never, before today, in all my years, have I ever cared much for the beach. In fact when the job offer came, I hesitated. In fact, I almost turned it down." And part of her had thought it was a glorified babysitting job. But she didn't need to share that with TJ. They had come too far.

Her eyes widened as if shocked. "That's un-American. No, that's inhuman. Everybody loves the beach." The young girl started jumping ahead and playing dare with the waves as they would roll up and back out again. Each time she grew closer and closer to getting soaked, but in the nick of time, she would leap away from the water.

Meagan laughed with TJ as the girl played. She even found herself caught up in the action of the timing and she would scream to TJ, "Look out!" as a wave would rush in and almost catch her. "You're going to get your shoes and pant legs wet. And even though the air is not cold, I'm sure the water is. You might make yourself sick if you get wet."

The young girl laughed in response and ran out toward the water's edge again and then as it started to roll back in, she waited until the last possible second before dashing back toward Meagan, laughing the whole time. "Try it. See if your reflexes are fast enough."

Meagan found herself tempted but restrained herself. Never could she recall enjoying a walk on the beach before. All of a sudden she saw a couple of shells and ran to them. "TJ!" she shouted. "Look what I found!" She ran over and scooped up a couple of cone-shaped shells. They looked like a baby shell compared to some of those she had seen in the gift shops.

All of a sudden, she screamed and dropped the shells to the ground. "The shell started moving in my hand!"

Laughter peeled from TJ as she ran up on Meagan. "You found a couple of baby whelks. The little critters are still inside."

Meagan felt her eyes widen in disbelief. "You've got to be kidding!" She squatted down and watched the two shells she had dropped. Slowly some spiny-looking fingers or legs eased their way out of the darkness of the shell. Inch by inch, one of the shells made its way toward the water.

Suddenly, a wave rushed up and with their attention distracted they were almost overwhelmed. TJ yelled, "Look out!"

Meagan turned in time to see the wave. She jumped up and tried to run the other way but didn't move fast enough. The water covered her left foot before rolling back out again. As the water rushed back out, she looked down behind her and both shells were gone. *Good,* she thought. She didn't want to take the animals' homes.

Her eyes searched the sand some more. She found more shells. This time it looked like sand dollars. She had seen that kind before…in a store for sale…not on the beach. No animals lived in them. She squatted down and picked them up, grabbing as many as she could get a hold of.

TJ snatched Meagan's hand and tugged her to her feet. "Come on," she said. "There's more."

They walked for at least a mile, if not more, watching down by their feet and around. Both managed to find more shells. Some of the sand dollars were darker than others and some were almost pristine white.

"Don't pick up any whelks if the animals are still living in them," Meagan pleaded.

TJ laughed.

"I mean it."

They found a few varieties of shells. Meagan didn't know the names of them, but figured she'd find out from TJ or look them up on the Internet. This was fun. "In the past," she said to TJ, "I've seen some of these shells before, but they were in a souvenir shop waiting to be purchased. It's much more fun to collect them this way."

After filling the bag about one third of the way, they turned and started back toward where they had parked the bikes. The next few minutes were spent in compatible silence; no joking around, no playing in and out of the water. Meagan enjoyed the sound of the water as it rushed on shore, and then eased back out again.

TJ settled down and appeared to be in deep thought about something. Suddenly she said, "I don't know about you, but I'm hungry. Let's get something to eat." She dashed ahead toward Papa Joe's where the scent of cooked food floated down to the shoreline, calling hungry stomachs to come eat. "Papa Joe's stays open all year round. Lucky for us. Most everyone else closes down until summer."

"I think I've worked up an appetite," Meagan admitted as the aroma touched her senses and a hunger pang twitched her stomach. Riding bikes and walking beaches must give people strong appetites…all that exercise…all that energy expended. She couldn't remember ever being so hungry before. Taking long strides, she caught up with TJ.

"I've enjoyed this morning with you, Meagan. Is this what it's like…I mean a mother and daughter relationship?"

Caught off guard, Meagan wasn't sure how to respond. Finally, after a quick silent prayer lifted up to God asking for guidance, she said, "Yes. It could be. I remember some times with my mom over the years where we played and hung out together. In fact, we still do…at times. But it's not always playing. Sometimes mothers give advice to their daughters on how to wear their hair, or make-up, or they check their homework." She thought for another second or two and then added, "Mothers also correct their young or punish them when needed. That's how they teach them right from wrong. Things like that…but more. It's hard to put it all in words."

Stopping in her tracks, TJ grabbed Meagan's hand and squeezed it. "Thanks. It's been great. I know Daddy loves me, and so does Ms. H. Even Jessica and Rachelle love me. They are there for me when I need them. But today was different. With you, I felt different…like maybe I could talk to you about anything."

"Oh, sweetie. You can. I'm here for you."

TJ lifted Meagan's hand and caressed the back of it against her cheek. "I do know. In fact, I was hoping I could talk to you about Mom. Maybe not today, but soon. I don't know. Maybe even today. Who knows?" The young girl shrugged her shoulders as a smile spread across her face. She squeezed Meagan's hands, and then TJ turned her face up toward the sun and seemed to soak it in. "It's a beautiful day!"

Swallowing a hard knot that had caught in her throat, Meagan said, "Whenever you want, I'm here for you." They locked eyes as a special friendship passed between them.

"Let's go. I'm hungry."

They walked the last few steps in silence. Meagan didn't want to push, but she knew they were getting close to TJ releasing her emotions that over the past seven years had built inside her. Meagan prayed God would give her the right words for TJ...at the right time. Although Dr. Richardson and Helen had given the girls everything, there was still one thing they didn't have...the knowledge of Christ and a relationship with Him. That was the reason she believed God sent her there...to be a channel to get the message to the girls.

All in God's time, she told herself. *All in God's time.*

Chapter 15

"First things first," TJ said as she led them to a table out back. This way they could hear the seagulls cry and the roar of the Atlantic Ocean, yet at the same time not get sand in their food. "We'll sit out here and eat. Then maybe when we finish, we can walk a little more on the beach, or go sit out on one of the piers so we can talk. I'm feeling, I don't know, almost relieved and at the same time excited." Her words flowed quickly, rushing out of her mouth. "Does that make sense?" The young girl pulled a face at her question then continued in the direction of the table she had picked for them.

Following behind carrying the tray holding her ham and cheese po'boy with fries, and a Diet Coke to drink, Meagan said, "I'm glad to be here for you, sweetie." This was probably something she should have talked about a long time ago with someone, but better late than never. *Who knows,* Meagan thought. *Maybe the young thing hadn't been ready to talk to anyone before now. Every person grieves in his own way and in his own time.*

Lunch was eaten in silence although the air was filled with the sound of the roaring ocean and the steady chatter from around the other tables. The lunch crowd was in full force. Being between seasons didn't seem to affect the business. The food must be really good.

Meagan saw anticipation twinkle in TJ's eyes as she savored every bite of her burger. That sparkle wasn't for the food for a change. Meagan could tell that TJ was looking beyond the moment…yearning for a chance to reminisce with someone or just remember times with her mom in her own mind.

When they finished, Meagan reached in her pocket to pull out some cash, but TJ insisted on paying. "This is Daddy paying. He gave me the money and said, 'Take her to lunch and anywhere else she wants to go.'" TJ laughed as she mimicked her dad's voice by deepening her own. With a half smile, she added, "And I do as I'm told. If you want to catch a show at the cinema or go check out the shops, we can do that too. I have more cash." She raised her brows and smiled a silly grin as she held up the money. Then in a more serious tone she said, "He wanted you to enjoy your visit around the island. But if you don't mind, we'll talk first. Who knows how we'll feel afterwards…if that's okay with you."

"Great by me."

The silence was only for a moment as they headed to the pier out back of Papa Joe's. At the end, they sat and let their feet dangle over the edge. Meagan waited for TJ to open the conversation on her mom. She didn't want to influence her one way or the other. At the moment, Meagan wasn't sure what TJ wanted to talk about in regard to her mom. Maybe she wanted to talk, or maybe she wanted to ask questions. Meagan waited and was startled by the first words out of TJ's mouth.

"Why?" TJ looked straight up into Meagan's eyes. "Why did my mother have to die? Why couldn't she have lived long enough to raise me? I was only five." Squinting, her eyes moistened along the edges of her eyelids. "Sometimes it's hard to remember her."

As Meagan thought how to answer that, TJ continued. "In the

beginning, after she first died, I could crawl into Mom's bed and lay my face down on her pillow and cry. Her scent was there and pictures of her floated through my mind. After a week or maybe two, the scent was washed away. Then I found another haven. I would go into her walk-in closet, take her robe off the hook, and lay down on the floor. Her scent would be all around me. Still the pictures were clear."

Meagan realized she needed to stay silent and let the girl talk for as long as the words would flow.

"This went on for months. When Ms. H couldn't find me, she knew where to look if she needed me. I think I was almost nine before Dad packed all of her things away. Sure, the smell of mom had been gone for a while by then, but the clothes were still a part of her." Shrugging her shoulders she added, "Who knows? Maybe Ms. H sprayed Mom's perfume in the closet occasionally, to keep me close to Mom or to keep her memory strong in my mind. I don't know. But I do know that was how I got through the first few years. And playing tennis, of course. Don't get me wrong. I didn't play with anyone. Just that machine Mom had out back that spit out the balls. I watched her so much and she had played with me some, to where I started playing with that. I pretended it was Mom playing with me. Against the machine, I had to get good or I wore myself out chasing the balls I missed that rolled off the court."

Meagan watched, as a memory seemed to flash through TJ's mind. A smile crossed her lips. Maybe keeping things around was meant to help the kids after all. Meagan wondered if maybe she had judged Dr. Richardson too quickly.

Sighing, TJ, said, "That's about the time Rachelle started doing more things with me. She never liked tennis, but she played it with me, knowing I liked playing it with Mom. Then she introduced me to the guitar and the piano. That's her thing. I've told you that before. She's talented in music and can sing like an angel." Then focusing her eyes on Meagan, TJ asked again, "So why did God take her so early?"

Drawing in a slow full breath, Meagan said a little prayer silently in her head. *Lord, lead me. Give me the right words.*

Tightening her lips, she released her accumulated air and said, "That's one question only God can answer. And I'm sorry to say, you won't get that answer until you face God on judgment day." Lifting TJ's hands and squeezing them gently, she added, "And by then, you won't be wondering. You'll probably be too excited knowing you're going to get to see your mom."

This was probably a time to introduce salvation to her, if she didn't already know the message. In her heart she heard God tell her to be gentle. "I'm guessing your mom was saved. Do you know about salvation? What that means? How you get saved?"

TJ nodded. "Ms. H takes us to church sometimes, or should I say, she used to, until Daddy put his foot down. I heard him tell her not to be filling our heads with such nonsense. If God was real, He wouldn't have taken Jennifer, that's my mom, from him and us. Ms. H argued, but Daddy always wins."

Meagan told TJ a little bit about Jesus, His birth, His life on earth, His death, and His resurrection. "To see your mom again in heaven, you need salvation for yourself. Your own personal relationship with Jesus. I'm going to make sure you know more about that before I leave. But remember, God has a plan for you. He loves you and your family. He didn't take your mom to hurt you… maybe it was to save her from the pain she would have had to go through here on earth with the cancer she had."

A tear fell from TJ's eye and then another. "I never thought about that." Before another second passed, more tears flowed.

Meagan pulled her close and wrapped her arms around the young girl. "You cry, sweetie. It's good to mourn the loss of someone you love. Crying is part of it. Remembering is part of it, too. You need to talk out your feelings. Grieve your loss of your mom."

Her tears soaked Meagan's shirt.

"If you don't, you'll never get to move on. The main thing to remember is your mom loved you, your sisters, and your daddy very much. She wouldn't have left here for the world if she could have stayed."

"How do you know that?"

"Because she's your mom, and moms want to be in every part of their children's lives." Wiping the wetness off the young girl's cheek, Meagan said, "And you can still let that happen by keeping her in your heart but letting go of the pain. It's okay to remember. You'll remember moments with her. You'll talk about your memories. You'll cry. But one day, you'll realize the crying stopped and the smiles replaced the tears. That is when you know you are healed."

Pulling TJ back in her arms, she hugged her close. More tears came and even some hard sobs, but eventually the tears slackened and TJ pulled in a couple of deep breaths before sitting back up.

"Thank you," she whispered.

"Sweetie, I'm always here for you. Share your memories with me any time. You might even try sharing some with your sisters, or Ms. Helen, or even your dad. As you start to share the memories aloud, the sooner the grief will flow out of you and the healing will begin." She winked. "Come on. Let's head home. I'll take you on in a match. Who knows? Maybe this time I'll win."

The young girl laughed, bringing a sparkle back into her eyes. "You're on." As they both rose and started to leave, TJ said, "Don't tell Daddy we had this talk. Let me talk to him about it."

"No problem, sweetie. What's said in confidence stays in confidence."

TJ hugged her and then turned. Grabbing Meagan's hand TJ headed them back up the beach toward their bikes.

Chapter 16

After being beaten badly in tennis, Meagan showered her loss away under a hard stream of hot water. When dressed in her usual attire, Meagan joined Helen in the kitchen to help prepare dinner. Her contribution to the meal was preparing the salad. "You are spoiling me rotten. When I get home, I doubt if I'll remember how to cook."

"It's a pleasure having you here. I mean it from the bottom of my heart. I can already see a difference in Tamara. You are a God-send." All the while talking, Helen kept busy preparing the meal.

While Meagan was washing tomatoes, rinsing lettuce, shredding lettuce, and chopping green onions, black olives, and carrots, she told Helen about the excursion. She told her about the many shells they found and the different types. In detail, she talked about the biking they did, as well as the playing on the ocean shoreline without getting wet…well almost. As wet as her foot got, it didn't take long to dry out. And as it dried, on the ride home, the sand fell away from her shoe. For that she was very grateful.

"I didn't know you could have so much fun at a beach," Meagan admitted. "We had a great time. TJ also opened up to me today about her mom and how much she misses her."

"I'm glad you and TJ are bonding. The young thing needs to talk to someone. She never really talked to me much, but I tried to keep the memory alive as long as I could, till I thought she was old enough to handle the loss better." Shaking her head, Helen said, "I just didn't know what to do. I thought her dad would help her through her loss. And I thought he would help the other girls, but he couldn't even help himself. By the time I figured that out and tried to get the girls help through the church, Dr. Ryan came unglued and wouldn't let that happen."

She must have seen Meagan's eyes widen in fear for the man's eternity because Helen went on to say, "Oh don't get me wrong. Years ago, the doctor loved the Lord as much as you do today. He got angry with God and hasn't gotten over it. I'm sure you've heard of that before. Some people turn against God in their grief, but usually they come out of it. I'm afraid the doctor never did."

Wringing her hands as she talked, she added, "And when you came, I knew you were sent here by Him. You are a breath of fresh air that's come into this house and I know it needs airing out. You're just the woman to do it."

Smiling, Meagan said, "Don't go giving me any of the credit. If I'm used by God, that will be His doing. I'm just a vessel. But I am starting to love the girls. I hope He does allow me to help them…all of them if possible. Speaking of God, where is the nearest Bible-based church around here…preferably full gospel, but if not, that's okay."

Clapping her hands in excitement, Helen said, "Just a couple of blocks over. Bethany, House of God. You can't miss it. Go two blocks down and three over, away from the beach. It's the big building that takes up over half of that block. It's the one the family used to go to."

As Helen finished the last minute touches on dinner, Meagan set the table. They continued chatting each time Meagan reentered the kitchen. Helen was such a loving woman. Meagan sensed Helen thought of the girls as family, even though there was no blood relation.

As usual, TJ was the first to arrive to the dinner table. By the time she walked in, plates and silverware were already positioned, and Meagan was just finishing putting ice in the glasses.

"I'll place them around," TJ said as she stepped over to the sideboard where Meagan was putting down the last glass.

"Great. If you'll do that, I'll take the ice bucket back in the kitchen and I'll bring the pitcher of iced-tea back with me." Meagan turned as Helen walked in carrying a platter of pork chops.

"Those smell scrump-de-a-licious," TJ said. "My mouth is watering. Did you make my favorite potatoes?"

"You know it, honey. New Orleans style smothered potatoes."

Meagan stopped in the doorway as she was coming back into the dining room and looked at them as her brows rose in question. "Where did you get that recipe?" She couldn't recall a New Orleans style smothered potato.

"My mom picked it up when she was staying with her cousin down in New Orleans."

"It's sliced potatoes, simmered in a little oil and water, covered with onions and chopped red bell peppers, sprinkled with Tony Chachere's seasoning. You cook them slow over a medium to low burner, turning them occasionally. Her cousin, Charlotte, keeps us in supply. This little girl here," she said as she placed both of her hands on TJ's shoulders, "would go crazy if she didn't have her favorite potatoes at least once a month."

"Sounds good. I just never heard of smothered potatoes being called New Orleans style. My mom cooks them too, but she doesn't always add the red bell peppers and sometimes she uses Season All and red pepper instead of Tony's."

"It sounds like we are recipe swapping in here. Are you picking up any new ones, Helen? You know I will always be your taste-tester. I don't mind."

Meagan turned to find the doctor dressed casually, in a pair of dark brown slacks and a tan pullover sweater. It looked light, yet warm enough for the cool temperatures they were still having in the evening…and she had to admit, he looked very handsome.

His hair looked soft and shiny, as if blown gently by a breeze and every strand fell into perfect place. Her fingers tingled at the thought of running them through the softness.

So intent on his presence, she failed to notice Rachelle and Jessica enter the room. Not only had they already come in, but they were already seated at the table.

"That's not a bad idea. I'll have to get a couple from you, Meagan. Remind me. You all sit. I'm going to go get those potatoes and the green beans. I'll be right back."

Meagan started pouring the tea as she walked around the table, one place at a time.

"So girls, how was your outing today?" the doctor asked.

Feeling warmth spread to her cheeks, Meagan let TJ answer.

"Oh Daddy, we had so much fun. This woman has never hunted for shells before in her life. Can you imagine that? We collected so many. And I taught her how to chase waves without getting wet." TJ laughed as Meagan couldn't help but smile as she remembered the fun they had and the small soaking that came with it.

Rachelle's eyes were upon them, watching their every exchange. Jessica ignored the talk, of course. She had no interest at all in how their day went and made it obvious.

"Your island is beautiful. I must admit. I never liked beaches before, but TJ showed me a side of your beach that I couldn't resist." Laughter bubbled from both of them as they eyed one another.

Helen re-entered the room and placed two steaming bowls on the table. The doctor started filling the plates with the pork chops as they were passed to him. The bowls of potatoes and beans were passed around and each added their desired amount to their own plate. Meagan liked that better.

"I'll have the rolls out in one second. They are already buttered," Helen said as she whooshed back out of the room.

TJ started to speak but was interrupted by Jessica. "I had a great time today, too, Daddy. I'm glad you stayed home. It was fun in your library, looking through the family albums with you. The memories of the good times we've had over the past few years. I hope we do it again sometime soon."

Her father looked at his oldest daughter and smiled. "I enjoyed it too, baby. And Rachelle, I want to thank you for making your old man happy, playing all those pieces for me this afternoon. You are gifted, young lady. And I am very proud."

Her cheeks blushed as she quickly looked down. The long soft strands of blonde hair fell as a veil covering most of her face as she quietly said, "Thank you, Daddy."

The conversation softened to a dim mumble as everyone started filling their mouths with food. Helen had slipped in with the rolls and vanished again behind closed doors. After about ten minutes, she came back in and poured some more tea. "Everything taste all right, young ladies?"

With a full mouth, TJ said, "Wonderful, Ms. H. Love it all."

Rachelle and Jessica nodded in agreement with their sister.

"I can see why they call these New Orleans style smothered potatoes. They have a kick. 'A little spice is nice, a lot is even nicer.' That's what my momma always said. She's originally from New Orleans," Meagan said, "so I guess most things she cooked were New Orleans style. I probably grew up with it so I never recognized it as being so different, until I started traveling of course. Then I learned what different was."

"Your job takes you all over the world?" the doctor asked.

"So far, I've stayed in the States. I'm starting to check out some of the businesses that send their workers to other countries...but there aren't as many job openings traveling that distance. It's probably because the pay is so much higher or different. I don't know," she said shrugging her shoulders. "I'm thinking about it though."

"I am glad you took this one. I can see a difference in Tamara already." He nodded his head at his youngest daughter, as she looked at him in question. "Do not get me wrong, young lady. You have always been a little fire-cracker," he said still looking at his daughter. Then he turned his attention back to Meagan. "She has always been outgoing, but she seems...I don't know." He shrugged as he spoke. "Happier? Bubblier? If that is a word. Do you girls see what I am talking about in your little sister?"

Jessica grunted.

A smile spread on Rachelle's face as she said, "Yes, Daddy. I saw it within a couple days of Miss Meagan's arrival."

"Call me Meagan, please. TJ does. You two may also. In fact, I wish you would."

A jeer twisted on Jessica's face as Rachelle said, "Meagan," and then smiled.

"Dessert, anyone?" Helen asked as she came in with a tray of chocolate cake already sliced and on saucers.

"Me. Me. Me." TJ sang out clearly. "I'll take some," Rachelle replied at the same time.

The doctor and Meagan both said thank you in unison, letting Helen know they would eat some. Jessica frowned. Either she didn't like hearing them speak together or she didn't want any of the cake. Meagan wasn't sure which it was.

"One thing for sure, when I get back home I'm going to have to buy all new clothes or shed some pounds. I haven't been here long and I'm seeing a pattern of over-eating. Usually, wherever I go, I have to cook for myself, so I don't eat much. It's no fun cooking for one. But Helen, everything you make is wonderful. I haven't tasted anything I don't like yet."

The older woman beamed as she strutted around the table placing a saucer to the left of each of them.

"Dig in," she said as she carried the tray, platter, and the two bowls, almost empty, back into the kitchen. The whole family had a healthy appetite.

As dinner was coming to an end, Meagan wanted to make her invitation known to everyone at the table. With the pleasant mood and everyone's belly satisfied, she blurted out, "I'm going to Bethany in the morning. TJ is going to go with me. And I wanted all of you to know if any of you would like to join us, you're more than welcome. I found out the service starts at ten-thirty, so I'll leave about ten minutes after."

"It's right around the corner. You don't have to leave so early," Jessica said in a dry tone.

"Did you want to go? I'll leave a little later if it would help you, if you want to come with us."

Jessica shook her head, almost agitated. "No. I don't think so."

She then frowned and looked down at her cake that was half eaten.

"I might go with you two," Rachelle said. "We'll see."

Meagan glanced at the doctor. For the first time tonight, he was quiet. That wasn't a good sign, but she couldn't worry about it. At least he wasn't forbidding them from going like he had done to Helen however long ago that was. He was silent and his eyes were trained on the plate in front of him. It wasn't so much so that he was interested in the cake, Meagan thought, he just didn't seem to want to share his thoughts at the moment so he remained still.

The last of the dessert was eaten in silence, but Meagan didn't let that worry her. TJ was happy and starting to heal from within. She had the freedom to grieve the loss of her mother. This was what all of them needed to do.

Rachelle appeared to be interested in going to church with TJ and Meagan. Jessica, now that was another situation all together. She would pray on that and God would open a door. Right now Meagan had to focus on TJ and Rachelle.

As everyone started leaving the table, Meagan rose and started clearing the last of the dishes.

"Leave that for Helen. I want to talk to you in my study." On those words, the doctor turned and left.

For remaining silent for the last five to ten minutes, his few words spoken now spoke in great volumes.

The girls had already slipped out of the dining room so none of them heard the command. So be it. She would join him, but first she would finish taking these dishes to the kitchen. He could wait one minute…and hopefully she would muster up the courage to face whatever his problem was tonight. He had seemed so happy only minutes before. What a pity.

Unfortunately it took less than a minute to carry the saucers into the kitchen. Not much time to build up courage.

As she placed them on the counter, Helen said, "I'll get that. Don't you worry. That's my job and I enjoy doing it."

"Well, I don't mind helping. Besides, I got a royal command to see the master. I'm not in any rush to get into his study."

Helen's brows rose. "He seemed happy every time I walked in the room. And I know TJ is. And truth be told, Rachelle and Jessica had a good time with their daddy today. He did too. I know. I watched them every time I passed. There was a difference in the atmosphere here today. It was almost like years ago. Almost. Not quite, but almost."

Meagan drew in a deep breath. "Well let me go face his wrath and get it over with."

The little lady shook her head and her curls bounced. "Don't you worry, child. Everything will be fine."

Before entering the study, she knocked on the door.

"Come in."

She heard his deep voice bellow from the other side. Although the sound sent a jolt of lightning through her veins, she did as he said. Was that a case of fear? Or what? Meekly she said, "You wanted to see me, sir?"

"Sit, please."

Again, she did as she was told.

"Miss Phillips. Meagan. I do not want you taking my girls to church with you. I don't want their heads being filled with all the hopes and promises offered only to be snatched away. Do I make myself clear?"

Meagan felt a knot tighten in her stomach. When she had first walked in the room, deep down she was ready to fight tooth and nail at whatever his problem was. But his words came as a shock to her. Sure, she knew he had forbidden Helen. But that was five or six, maybe even seven years ago…shortly after his wife's death. Surely he couldn't still be angry with God.

He's a grown man who knows the truth. Besides, supposedly, that was why he hired her…to help his girls grow as young women. And in Meagan's mind, a major part of their growth would be their spiritual growth.

Again, a part of her was prepared to stand up and fight. Yell if she must. But another part in her felt pity for the man. How could he still hurt so badly? Meagan had never lost a loved one so she had nothing to compare with it. *The man must have loved deeply to still be in such pain. To be loved like that,* she thought, and then sighed.

Yelling wouldn't help, so she said, "Dr. Richardson. I'm glad you spent the day with your girls today. They all three enjoyed it immensely. You wanted to get closer to them, and you've taken the first step. I hope behind all this anger you are feeling right now, you do see the difference you've made in your daughters' lives today."

She didn't know if she stunned him into silence or if he was forming words in his brain for another attack, but he didn't say a word during the moment of pause she allowed…so she continued. "Well I also had a great day with TJ. I promised her I would not mention what we talked about. She wants to be the one to tell you. But we had a break-through today that I know helped TJ."

His gaze locked on her face but said nothing.

"You hired me to help your girls grow as young women, but none of them can until they can get past their grief. None of them, or you for that matter, has grieved for the loss of Jennifer Richardson. They need that. You need that. Obviously, you are still angry with God, but let me leave you with this thought. Yes, He took your wife at a young age. But she had cancer. She was suffering. If He had not taken her when He had, maybe her pain would have been more than she could bear. God does not allow us more than we can bear."

The doctor's eyes bore into hers, but he never said a word. She saw the muscles in his jaw jerking. Obviously, he was biting his tongue. For that she was thankful, but it didn't stop her.

"You're probably thinking, *But He let me and our children suffer.*" She nodded her head. "Yes. He did. And to think how much it hurt you and the girls…her pain would have been so much more. Would you have wanted her to suffer more than you have?"

The muscles in his face dropped as his eyes opened wide. His mind was churning. Obviously, he had never thought of it that way before. Good. Maybe she had made headway.

Thank You, Lord, she thought, *for the words You gave me.*

She thought she had made two steps forward, till he spoke his next words.

"The girls may go tomorrow, but do not encourage them to attend church with you every Sunday. Do not encourage them to worship with you. I am their father. I am trying to protect them. I am your boss and I am telling you not to go there. Do not entice my girls to church. Their spiritual life is none of your business. Do I make myself clear?"

Quietly, she rose to her feet. In her thoughts, she spoke to God. *He is my boss. I am to obey him, Lord. So help me. If I'm to say anything, give me the words. If not, keep my mouth shut and help me out the door.*

Nothing. She stood for several seconds in silence…listening hard for a remark to give the doctor. She still heard nothing.

Okay, I'll keep quiet. Finally, she turned and walked out the door.

As she closed it, she leaned back against it. "Give me the

strength, Lord, to stand strong for You…for them…for him. Their spiritual life is my responsibility as one of Your children. So is his. And that was a desperate cry for help if I ever heard one."

Chapter 17

The next morning TJ and Rachelle were both dressed and ready when Meagan went to check on them. By the looks on their faces, TJ was excited to go while Rachelle appeared a little nervous…as if she wasn't sure this was her next step.

"Jessica didn't want to go?" Meagan asked whoever would answer.

TJ's eyes darted to the top of the stairs while Rachelle said, "She's still asleep."

"No problem. Let's go," she said to the two.

From the outside the church didn't seem very big, but on the inside it was large enough to hold at least five hundred people if not more. When they arrived there were still several pews available for seating. The three made their way to the middle of the church and sat down. As people came in and sat near them or passed them, most greeted with a "hello," or "welcome to our service." People were pleasant and friendly. A man who led the music, played the keyboard as several singers stood across the front of the stage. Behind him were a couple of guys playing guitar. The sound was inviting for worshiping. The songs, although familiar to Meagan, TJ and Rachelle didn't seem to know. Rachelle picked them up quickly though, and when she did, Meagan heard that angelic voice TJ had mentioned yesterday. She hadn't exaggerated one little bit.

The music and singing led the worship nicely into the message. Meagan herself was so caught up in the worship; she no longer watched the girls or anyone around her. After about thirty to forty minutes of worship, the pastor came forward to speak.

Brother Terry Williams was anointed. Meagan felt the words coming from his heart and from God's Word. The man was so deep into what the Lord laid on his heart that the words flowed out naturally. Although the whole service lasted about an hour and a half, the time passed quickly.

Heading out to the car, they shook several hands and met a good many people, not that Meagan could recall one name. Once they got in the car and the doors were closed, the first words out of Rachelle's mouth were, "I'm so glad I came. I forgot how refreshed I felt coming to church. My heart responded quicker than I did."

Meagan's spirit leapt.

"I don't remember anybody. But I was young. I don't even remember coming here. I did see some of my schoolmates though. Did you?" TJ asked her sister.

"Yeah. I saw a few. I remember some people from years ago, also. A lot of them came to visit us at first." She got real quiet and then added, "I mean right after Momma died. They would have kept coming. They had even offered to pick us up for church, but Daddy basically ran them off. Don't get me wrong. He didn't do it verbally, but he let them know in his own way not to keep coming. So eventually, they quit. Ms. H tried to as well, but he stopped her cold."

Looking at first one and then the other, Meagan said, "I hope y'all enjoyed it. Your dad won't let me encourage y'all to come with me, but I will tell you that I plan to continue going and I hope you will both join me every Sunday morning. But it will have to be your decision. I, personally, think it will help you two…Jessica too, if we could get her to come with us." Meagan turned the key and started the car.

"Don't hold your breath."

TJ laughed. "Sorry. But Rachelle's right. Jessica is not going to come with us. I'm glad you're going and I will keep going with you. I want to learn more about Jesus."

"Count me in too."

Thank you, Lord, Meagan offered up silently, wanting to cry out with joy but held back. This was a step in the right direction. In minutes they were turning into the drive. Meagan found herself wondering if the doctor would be there, ready to scold or stop his daughters' desire to go. They would know soon enough. She didn't need to go looking for trouble.

They entered through Meagan's garage. Stepping in the apartment Rachelle said, "I'm sure Ms. H has lunch ready for us. After I change, I'll see you in the dining room."

"Me too," TJ said as they went on their way to their side of the house.

As usual, lunch was superb. The doctor was nowhere around. Jessica joined them, but once she saw her dad wasn't there, she grabbed her plate and took it up to her room.

"TJ tells me you play piano and guitar. Would you play for me? I actually play guitar myself, but when I fly, I don't get to bring it with me."

Rachelle's eyes lit up as she glanced at her sister, and then returned her stare to Meagan. "I would love to play. Maybe we could even find some things we could play together."

"Great. You guys play and I'll sing."

"That's okay, Tamara. We play. You listen." And then they both laughed.

"What's so funny? Let me in on the joke," Meagan said.

"I don't sing. I don't have rhythm and I never hit the right notes. I try, but it just doesn't come naturally. That's probably why I enjoy listening to Rachelle so much. She is gifted."

The older sister blushed as she pointed to TJ. "Stop it," she said.

"Really, Meagan. I don't know if you were listening to her in the service, but her voice is like an angel singing…or at least how I would think an angel would sound."

"I heard you say that before and I agree…an angel."

The three finished their lunch together and the girls helped Meagan carry the dishes into the kitchen. Helen jumped up from the table where she was sipping her after dinner coffee. "Meagan, you've got to stop this. It's my job. I'll get the dishes."

"Ah, Ms. H. It doesn't hurt for us to bring them to you. You've spoiled us all of our lives," said TJ. "We never do anything here. You do it all."

Helen gave TJ a hug and said, "Sweet child. It is so good to see you so full of life. So tell me, how did you three enjoy church this morning?"

Rachelle responded by saying, "We did. And we're going back next week. Why didn't you go? Don't you usually go to church?"

"Yes, dear. I do. I'll go next week with you three." She looked over the girls' heads and caught Meagan's gaze.

Meagan could guess what the woman was thinking: *He can't blame her, but praise be the girls are going to church.* That was a start.

"If you're not too busy, why don't you join us in the—" Meagan cut herself off, because she had no idea where they would be playing music.

"In the music room."

"Of course. Silly me. In the music room. We're going to listen to Rachelle play," Meagan finished saying.

Helen squealed with delight. "That's wonderful. I would love to listen. As soon as I finish up in here, I'll join you."

"I can help—"

This time Helen cut Meagan off. "No, you will not help me. Get on with yourself. All of you. I'll be there shortly."

As Rachelle was passing Ms. H, she leaned over and said, "Meagan is going to play with me on guitar."

A surprised expression crossed the woman's face. "That's wonderful, dear. I get a double blessing. I'll be there shortly."

In the music room, there was a piano, a couple of guitars, and a stereo. Speakers sat in various places all around the room. A couple of couches were placed at different angles across the room as well as large pillows that were tossed here and there. Meagan and TJ stood around the piano while Rachelle played and sang.

After a couple of songs, TJ and Meagan found them a place to sit so they could enjoy the music in comfort. Meagan sat on a couch while TJ found a spot on the floor with one of those big pillows, and then they sat back and continued to listen to Rachelle entertain them with another song by Sarah McLachlan.

Time passed and at some point Helen slipped in and sat in one of the chairs. After several songs by other artists, Rachelle stopped and said, "It's time I get to listen. Do you play the piano?"

Meagan knew Rachelle was talking to her. Standing and stretching she said, "Chopsticks is about it." They all laughed. "After listening to you, I don't think we need my rendition of the banging on the piano. How about the guitar? I see you have two.

We can play them together."

They each grabbed one and went and sat on the same sofa a little distance apart, yet facing each other. After several minutes, they agreed on a song and once the two of them got started, the music and singing went on for over an hour. Helen even joined in on the singing. Occasionally, TJ belted out a note or two. Meagan understood the laughter earlier, but it was all in fun and it didn't matter if they could carry a note or not.

While the four of them were having a good time, no one noticed as the doctor entered the room. He sat on the piano bench, trying not to break up the fun they were having. His face was hidden from view by a portion of the grand piano.

It was good to see his girls laugh again. Sure, sometimes they laughed a little at a joke or something on television, but they were experiencing life and finding something good in it. That blessed him.

Maybe it wasn't so bad letting them go to church with Meagan. He would have to think on it some more.

She had already worked her charms on Tamara and now Rachelle was joining them. This was good. Jessica was going to be the hardest to crack. Of course she was the oldest and had been closest to Jennifer. In a way, since she was on the verge of becoming an adult, she probably missed her mom the most.

He sighed as he watched, and a smile touched his lips.

Then he heard TJ say, "You guys do one of Daddy's favorites. Do an Elvis song."

Meagan shot a look at Rachelle. Her face looked lost, but when Rachelle strummed the first stroke against the strings, she blurted out, "You ain't nothing but a hound dog...."

The rest joined in, even little off-key Tamara joined them and no one seemed to mind. He saw Meagan doing her best to strum the right chords at the right time…and Helen was giving it her all.

This was wonderful. Yes, bringing someone in to work with the girls was the right thing to do. *She has been a plus so far…well most of the time,* he thought.

When the song ended, he couldn't help himself as he broke out in loud applause. "Very good, girls. You did well. Elvis would be proud!"

All faces turned toward him. His daughters laughed as Tamara jumped up and ran over to hug him, wrapping her arms around his shoulders.

Helen bowed her head saying, "Thank you, sir. I'm all shook up…a uh huh."

Everyone laughed.

Even Meagan. At first, the look on her face showed shock…or was it fear? He didn't know, but he had seen it before. Was she afraid of him? At least the look disappeared as fast as it came. That was good. Now everyone was enjoying the moment.

"Where's Jessica?" Ryan asked as he rose from the bench and moved to the inner part of the room holding his daughter's hand all the while. "Didn't she want to come down and play music with all of you?"

"Oh, Daddy," Rachelle whispered.

Tamara rolled her eyes saying, "You know she wouldn't come do this with us." Leaning forward slightly, she dropped her daddy's hand and raised her hands drawing quotes in the air as she said, "She's a big *teenager*…almost an adult. This is beneath her. Hanging out with her little sisters."

Helen jumped to her feet and said, "Sir, would you like a bite to eat? I can go reheat—"

Shaking his head as he interrupted Helen, he said, "Don't bother. Sit back down. I grabbed a bite earlier. I'm fine. Everyone relax. Sing another song." As he spoke he sat down near the group ready to enjoy more entertainment.

Tamara sat on the floor by his feet and rested her back against the sofa, hugging her knees to her chest. He loved his girls. Sighing, a warm glow spread through him as he sat back and enjoyed the contentment of being a family. Jennifer would have loved a time like this. In fact, if she were still alive, he felt sure they would have had many moments like this.

Shaking those thoughts from his head, he decided not to slip into the past at this moment. He wanted to enjoy this present time with the girls. That was one of the main reasons for hiring someone…to get closer to his girls…to bring them out of the shell they all seemed to have locked themselves into.

Maybe I caused that. That thought flashed through his mind, but then he shook his head. He immediately decided not to go there either.

Reaching out, he rubbed the top of Tamara's head messing her hair slightly. She looked up and laughed. The music and singing went on for a good while. Ryan even joined in on some of the songs.

By the time evening rolled around, Ryan said, "I hate to bring this to an end, but there is school tomorrow. Baths need to be taken. Maybe a light supper needs to be eaten," he added glancing at Helen. "Keep it very simple, Helen. Don't go to any trouble. Leftovers or sandwiches. It doesn't matter."

"I'll help," Meagan said as she put the guitar back where she had found it. "My fingers need a break. I haven't played that long in a very long time, but I had fun."

Everyone was on their feet moving around.

"I wish we could keep singing. I'm loving it!" Tamara said.

"I'm with Meagan." Rachelle slipped her guitar back onto the stand. "It was more than I'm used to, too, but I have to admit it was fun."

Everyone was leaving the room at the same time. Ryan reached out and touched Meagan's arm. "Hold a moment, please."

She looked up at him with wonder in her eyes. "Sir?"

"Do you have a minute? I'd like for us to talk."

"Sure."

Now that everyone had left the room, he was not even sure what made him stop her. And he had no idea what he was going to talk about. Why had he done such a foolish thing? But as he was thinking how foolish it was, he said in all sincerity, "I want to thank you for what you are doing with my girls. This was a wonderful way to come home and find them. And thank you for letting me be a part of it as well."

She smiled up at him.

He noticed how angelic she looked. Her face had a glow about it…so clean and wholesome looking. Her soft brown hair fell loosely about her shoulders. Who was this woman? She was at least ten years his junior. Why was he looking at her in this way? Women have been coming on to him for the last five or six years of his life, but none had caught his attention. She was not even trying. Why was he noticing her? Her brown eyes were warm and inviting. What was happening to him? Did it please him that much to see his girls happy? Sure. That was it. He was so overcome with joy at seeing his girls step slowly out of that shell they had wrapped themselves in that he was filled with an optimism that he had not had in a long time.

"It was fun, sir. The girls enjoyed it. Helen and I had a great time, too." She shrugged as she added, "So it was great for all of us."

"Yes. It was. Thanks."

He gave a slight nod of his head and she turned and left. The best thing he could do was leave it alone. He brought her here to help his girls, not himself. At least now his money was working in his family's behalf. Without meaning to, his gaze watched as Meagan walked away and a smile touched his lips.

Chapter 18

"Shel, you wouldn't believe it if I told you. Two months have passed and things just get better and better around here every day," Meagan said as she stood looking out at the ocean. Time had passed so quickly. The first of June and only one month left of her stay. Would he renew the contract? Would she get to stay longer? She found herself slipping into a daily comfort of being around this family. The younger girls made her feel as though she belonged. And the changes in them have been phenomenal.

"What's all that noise I hear?" Shelly asked.

"That's the waves. I'm standing on the Richardson's pier enjoying a close-up view of the ocean."

"Now I've heard everything. Things are changing rapidly over there. You are on purpose standing on a pier, and I'm guessing you had to cross *sand* to get to it?" her sister asked.

Meagan laughed. "Isn't it great? I'm changing some too. As God is using me to help Dr. Richardson's girls, they are changing me. I've come to love the ocean. Love the sand. Love it all!"

"I wish I were there with you. Have you told Mom?"

"About loving the beach? Yes. She said if they renew my contract for another three months, she's going to come out and visit for a week." She heard her sister giggle. "What's so funny? Mom always tries to come visit when I go to a new area. And you know how much she loves the beach. This time we'll get to enjoy it together. That will be a first. The two of you always enjoyed it in the past. Are you jealous?" she spoke teasingly at her sister while she laughed.

"No, sister dear. I'm glad to hear the joy in your voice. But I hear something else. You haven't said it, but I think you are falling for Dr. Richardson as well as his kids. I've never heard you so happy in all of our years."

"Don't be silly," Meagan snapped. "He's my boss. He's the girls' father. You always read more into things than is really there."

Shelly laughed and said, "If you say so, sis. When will you know if he is extending your stay? Like you said, you've been there two months now."

"Time has passed. It seems like only yesterday the girls started going with me to church…and remember that day I told you about when we all…all but Jessica, played and sang music for hours? That was seven weeks ago and now my relationship with TJ and Rachelle has grown so much. It's going to be hard to leave them when my time is up here." Meagan felt the tears sting her eyes as they started to form. She blinked them away before they could fall.

"You're starting to get mushy on me, sis. I just don't know what's come over you." Then Shelly's laughter spilled over the phone pouring into Meagan's mind and heart.

"Enough! To change the subject and keep your mind from where it is trying to go, TJ's USATA Junior's State Championship match is tonight. We're all going to Charleston to watch. Even Jessica will be with us. I think it will be great, and I know TJ will probably win."

"If not, she'll have next year or the year after. She's only twelve don't forget. Relax and enjoy it with her. Don't let her feel your stress."

"Got you!" Meagan released a relaxing breath and said, "You know me so well. Thanks. I need you to keep me straight. I was tensing over it, thinking she had to win because it means so much to her, but you're right. She has more years left to get to the top. TJ is just starting to explore her purpose in life. She even talked to me about accepting Jesus as her Savior. She has come so far in such a short time. I'm glad you convinced me to take this job."

"Meagan. Where are you?"

"Shel, I hear Rachelle calling me. I better go. It's been great talking to you. Keep me in your prayers."

As they said their good-byes, TJ and Rachelle came walking across the beach toward the pier. "We've been looking for you," TJ said.

"We're about to leave for the match. Dad wants to get an early start. He said we may do a little sightseeing on the way," Rachelle said as they walked toward her.

TJ shook her head. "I don't know what's gotten into Daddy, but he sure does love doing things with us now. Used to be he spent all his waking hours at the hospital, but now he's home every weekend. I love it."

"Me too," Rachelle said sweetly. "Come on."

They had stopped at the edge of the pier and Meagan walked toward them listening to the joy in their voices. *Thank you, Lord,* she whispered in her spirit.

When they walked in the back door and stepped into the den, they heard a high-pitched female voice saying, "Oh. I want to go with you all, of course."

TJ and Rachelle looked at each other, and TJ said, "Aunt

Karrie." Both scurried through the den toward the front door where the doctor was speaking with his sister-in-law.

The girls hugged their aunt as Jessica came bouncing down the stairs. "Aunt Karrie," she cried out. "Great! Are you coming too? Maybe this won't be so boring after all."

"Jessica," her father scolded.

She slowed her steps and wiped the smile off her face. "Yes, Daddy. It's going to be fun. Tamara will win the whole shooting match, I mean tennis match." The sarcasm dripped from her voice.

Meagan stopped short of entering the area. She didn't want to impose on a family gathering. She and their Aunt Karrie had met only once a few weeks in to her first month working there, and it hadn't been pleasant.

"You are going with us. Aren't you, Aunt Karrie?" Jessica thrived on her aunt's attention.

"I don't want to push my way in," she said to her niece as her gaze fell on the doctor. Meagan watched her work her feminine wiles on him. "I would love to ride with the family."

"I don't think there is room," Ryan said plainly.

"Yes, there is Daddy. Helen and Meagan can follow us in Meagan's car. Can't you, Meagan?" Jessica asked as she looked through the opened space to the den and caught Meagan's gaze in her own. The smile on Jessica's face didn't touch her eyes.

But that was okay with Meagan. She was glad to see the family bonding. "No problem. We'll follow in my car. You don't mind riding with me, do you, Helen?"

"No problem by me."

A smug look crossed Karrie's face, as she seemed to bask in her victory.

TJ slipped over to Meagan's side and hugged her. In a soft voice she said, "I want you and Helen with me…so if it's okay, I'll ride with you."

"No, sweetie. You ride with your dad and your aunt. Don't worry. We'll all be there together." Meagan's eyes rested on the doctor as she spoke to TJ, hugging her in return. The doctor didn't look too pleased. She hadn't seen that look in his eyes for some time. She sighed within thinking he should know her well enough by now. He should know she wouldn't try to keep TJ from being close to her family. That was part of her job, helping TJ relate with her family…allowing the love to permeate throughout the group of them. One day Meagan would no longer be there to encourage TJ or Rachelle, so they needed to bond with each other and their dad now, and Meagan knew this. Of course she would encourage it.

The drive to town, although in two separate cars, worked well. Helen and Meagan were able to talk freely. Helen started the trip out grumbling about Karrie, but Meagan helped her see that it was important that they all connect. "Karrie is a piece of Jennifer. The girls need that."

Helen grunted. "Yeah. Well maybe." She shook her whole body. "You are right, of course. That woman gives me the chills. You just don't know Karrie like I do. She is nothing like her sister. Besides, she's been after the doctor since Ms. Jennifer passed away. It's shameful the way she throws herself at him. He's never shown an interest though, thank God."

Meagan smiled a crooked smile. Afterward, she wasn't sure if she was grinning from listening to Helen come to her senses or from knowing the doctor had never been interested in Karrie or her ways.

They pulled into the parking lot behind Dr. Richardson and parked the car next to his. The university was large but he knew exactly where to go. Meagan saw the large lights, although off at the moment, looming around the tennis courts. When they climbed out of the car, the doctor and TJ walked over to them.

"This is where the matches will be played. Since we're a little early, we are all going to walk around the university. This will give TJ time to unwind. We'll eat afterwards, so she can keep down her food." He laughed as he hugged his daughter.

Helen walked around the car and met with them as Rachelle stood waiting with Jessica and Karrie. Soon the group gathered together. TJ held on to Meagan's hand and her father's as well, so the three seemed to be together. Meagan felt Karrie's eyes burning a hole through her. Part of her felt as if she could she should pull away from the young girl, but the other part of her was glad to be connected.

The stroll around the campus was enjoyable. This campus was much bigger than the one Meagan went to years ago. She started her career by studying at Northwestern in Natchitoches, Louisiana, and then finished in Shreveport. The last year of her studies was spent working in the hospital. She was hooked for life…helping the sick.

As a toddler, she had a brain tumor and for the doctors and medical people to help her, she had to have a CT scan. The big machine scared grown people, much less a little girl of four. But for some reason, Meagan had felt peace then. Now she uses her experience as a toddler to help others through CT scans and x-rays of various kinds.

Not only did she help the physical need, she tried to be used in their spiritual need as well. And glancing at the family members, she knew this was her purpose here in South Carolina.

Joy flooded her heart as she watched the difference in the family.

The closeness the girls seemed to feel with their father...so different from that first night at the dinner table. *Thank you, Lord.*

An hour later on the stadium seats, the six of them sat in a cluster. Rachelle and Karrie sat on either side of the doctor and Jessica snuggled close to her aunt, while Helen and Meagan sat on the seats near the doctor's feet. Meagan was content with that. She was able to keep her mind on the game and TJ's every move. Freely, she and Helen cheered the girl along clapping and yelling out at the right times.

By the time the last game started, Rachelle had moved down to sit next to Meagan. "Isn't she great? I knew she would do well."

"It was your encouragement all these years that's kept her motivated. I know that from different things she has said over these last couple of months," Meagan confided in the little teenager.

A wide smile spread across Rachelle's face. "Thank you." Then she screamed, "Go TJ!"

Meagan could just imagine the look on Dr. Richardson's face as he heard his middle daughter call Tamara that name. She sensed him cringe and couldn't help but grin from ear-to-ear as she envisioned it.

With the crowd's quiet moments then quick outbursts of applause over and over again until the last whack of the racket and whoosh of the ball, no one knew who the winner would be. TJ had made it all the way to the very finals and the two opponents were so evenly matched that it came down to the very last game to determine the victor. Although the opponent won in the end, TJ was a winner too. The stadium went wild for both players as TJ ran up to the net to shake the hand of her opponent. The smiles on both girls' faces were wide spread, their breathing heavy. Meagan could tell TJ took her loss in stride and was happy with the outcome.

A short time later, they were all seated at a large round table in a restaurant that the doctor had chosen. Meagan found herself seated directly across from Dr. Richardson as the aunt managed to maneuver herself to be seated next to him. As Meagan glanced around the table and watched the smiles and heard the chatter, contentment wrapped around her like her favorite blanket. This was worth every moment of the last two months of her life. She was reaping the reward right now.

All enjoyed the meal and the time together was pleasurable. TJ walked them through almost every stroke of her game. Everyone helped her to rejoice in the accomplishment she had reached in her young career as a tennis player.

"And the great thing," her daddy said to her, "is you have the rest of your life to get even better and work your way to the top." Glancing around the table at each of the faces, he added, "And I know we will all be there for you, sweetheart."

"Here, here!" "Go Tamara!" "You know it, TJ!" Different voices called out simultaneously.

Meagan took pleasure in hearing the joy in the family's voices. Helen patted Meagan's hand that rested on top of the table.

She turned and smiled at the wonderful woman. "Isn't it great seeing them like this?" Meagan whispered.

"You don't know how great it is."

The drive home was uneventful. Meagan stayed close on the tail of the doctor's car. When they all entered the home and settled in the den, Ryan said, "How about ice cream for everyone?" His gaze eased around the room resting for a second on each and everyone, but settled quietly on Meagan. His eyes stayed on hers a moment or two longer than the rest.

Karrie blurted out, "Ryan. You've already done more than you should with the hired help. Let them fix the ice cream for the five of us. We can go out on the terrace and enjoy the sounds of the Atlantic as we sit together and praise our girl, Tamara."

Meagan's heart froze. Her joy drained from within as her gaze dropped to the floor. Of course. That was all she was to this family, she reminded herself. The hired help. How could she have forgotten? Because they all made her feel like a part of the family... just like Helen. But quickly she remembered Helen had always kept herself apart at the dinner table. She never ate with the family. How had Meagan allowed herself to feel like more than the hired help?

Embarrassed for even thinking she was more to them than just a nanny, Meagan cried out, "That's a wonderful idea. Come on, Helen. We'll get the ice cream." And then she dashed out of the room making her way to the kitchen before she made a fool of herself. Humiliation loomed over her head, but at least now she remembered where her place was with this family.

Chapter 19

When Meagan opened her eyes Sunday morning, the memory of the night before washed over her. She had made such a fool of herself, thinking she had become more to the family than a woman there to help the girls grieve the loss of their mother. The doctor had made it plain over and over in the beginning. Why had she allowed herself to feel so much for them and to feel she was more to them than what she was?

How could she face the girls this morning? Looking up to the ceiling she said, "By Your strength, Lord. Help me not to make a fool of myself again. I'm here to share You with them, Lord, and no more. Thank You."

She took in a deep breath, tossed back the covers and climbed out of bed.

To her surprise when she met the girls in the den, Dr. Richardson and Jessica were there also. At first a tremor of delight swept through her, then her memory kicked in and she pushed thoughts of everyone going to church with her, out of her mind. Who was she kidding?

"Good morning, Meagan," the doctor said to her.

She lifted her eyes and linked with his gaze. "Morning." She didn't dare trust herself to say more.

As Helen slipped into the room with the rest of them, Ryan said,

"We are all going with you this morning."

Then his lips turned up into a smile as he corrected himself. "Actually, you are riding with all of us. I am driving. I don't believe your car will hold us all."

TJ rushed over to Meagan's side and grabbed her free hand, the one without her Bible, and tugged her toward the door. "Daddy pulled his car around front. Come on."

Then in a lower tone, she whispered, "You should have heard Daddy light into Aunt Karrie last night. I was so proud. It wasn't any fun once you left us…so needless to say as soon as the ice cream was eaten Daddy rushed Aunt Karrie out the front door and sent her on her way."

Meagan felt the smile that had settled on her lips, but she found herself biting her bottom lip to keep from asking questions…all kinds of questions that she knew she shouldn't ask. Instead, she decided to go with the flow of the family and see where it took her. The main thing was everyone…including Jessica and Ryan…was heading to church. What a step in the right direction!

When they returned home, Jessica opened the front door rushing inside. She hadn't wanted to go, and it had been obvious the whole time. She disappeared behind the front door as everyone else followed her inside.

The smell of a pot roast cooking attacked Meagan's senses when she entered. "I'll help you set the table," she offered as she turned toward the kitchen.

"Let's all go help. We'll get to eat faster this way. And Helen, join us at the table, would you?" Turning toward the stairwell, Dr. Richardson called out to his daughter. "And that includes you, Jessica. Come back down and join us."

In less than half an hour, they were all seated around the table.

Everyone had their food and drink, but before they began Ryan said, "Meagan, would you ask the blessing?"

About halfway through the meal, Meagan found her courage and decided to trust in the Lord and just be herself as Shelly had suggested from the beginning. Now was the time to share openly her thoughts and feelings with the girls. "TJ, I was so proud to see you walk the aisle this morning. I've been praying for you daily, and I knew the Lord was tugging at your heart."

Her grin stayed in place as the young girl blurted out, "Me too. I'm so proud, so glad, and so shocked. I didn't know I was going to walk down that aisle this morning. I hadn't planned it…that's for sure."

"That's the way it happens," Helen said.

"Your heart and your spirit were following God's call on your life." Meagan reached out and squeezed TJ's hand.

Jessica rolled her eyes heavenward but didn't say anything.

In a quiet voice, Rachelle said, "I've been talking to God lately, myself. I think He's tugging on me, too."

When Meagan looked to Rachelle, she saw the light reflect on the moisture in the girl's eyes. The Lord was working on this family for sure. She nodded in Rachelle's direction. "That's wonderful. If I can help you or answer any questions, sweetie, you know you need only ask. I'm here for you."

Jessica tossed down her fork. "May I be excused, please?" As she spoke, she didn't wait for permission. She rose and left the room.

"What's the matter with her?" Ryan asked.

Rachelle touched her daddy's hand and said, "Don't you remember, Daddy? She had just accepted the Lord into her life when Momma died. So she's probably scared. That's all."

He turned his hand up and squeezed his daughter's fingers. "You're right. I want you all to know how sorry I am that I haven't been here for you these past few years. I know Meagan was sent to us, to shake us all up…so to speak…and get our lives back on track." He glanced at Helen and added, "I know you tried. But I was headstrong and wouldn't listen. But both of you have my attention now. You two have worked wonders on the girls and I'm so thankful."

"It wasn't me, Doc," Mrs. H said. "If anyone, it was Meagan."

"Don't give me the credit. We all know it was God working in your lives. I'm glad He allowed me to be a part of it." Meagan toyed with the last little bit of roast on her plate.

"Hey!" TJ blurted out. "Let's don't get down here. Meagan sounds like she's about to leave us. Let's enjoy the month we have left."

Dr. Ryan laughed a deep laugh as he looked at his youngest daughter. "Such a wise woman at such a young age." Turning his face toward Meagan, he added, "And I have it on good authority that your three months is about to turn into six…if you'll accept it."

TJ and Rachelle started clapping and together they both shouted, "Stay, Meagan! Please stay!"

Joy surged from within. Looking at Helen, then the girls, and last but not least, at the doctor, she smiled and said, "I accept."

This would give her more time to connect with Jessica.

Only by Your grace, could this happen, she thought, *and I'm willing and ready.*

The pleasure on the different faces spoke volumes to Meagan. She couldn't wait to share it with her family…tell them the good news…all of it.

Chapter 20

The month flew by. It was the middle of June already and her mother was going to be coming up next week for a stay. Shelly tried to find a way to come also, but Kirk wasn't ready for his mom to slip off that far away, even if it was to be with Auntie Meggie. She laughed as she recalled her sister telling the story of how wide Kirk's eyes had become when he heard Shelly telling Brandon what she wanted to do. Her husband was ready to let her go when Kirk yelled out, "Don't leave me, Momma!"

"Brandon and I both wanted to laugh it was so funny, but because Kirk was so serious all we could do was promise him that Momma wasn't going anywhere. That was the only way to calm him down."

Kirk was a pleasure for Meagan, and she wouldn't be a part of hurting the little guy for anything in the world. "Y'all did the right thing. Maybe before the summer is out, we can all go to Florida. Enjoy the beach. My six months will be up by the end of September. Maybe the weather will still be warm enough. You just never know."

"Wow! That would be great." That perked Shelly up because she loved the sand and the water. "You shock me. And to think it is your idea."

"Shocks me too!" They both laughed endlessly over that alone.

The conversation had ended with Shelly saying how excited their mom was getting with the expectations of spending a lot of time by the water.

By now, Meagan had fallen into a routine at the hospital. She bonded with all the employees at Jennifer Lane Memorial, but her life at the Richardson's home was more important than the job at the hospital. She limited her friends to just the girls, so they could spend as much time as possible together.

Rachelle and TJ convinced her to hit the beach with them when she got home today. Part of Meagan was dreading that. As much as she had enjoyed it so far, it hadn't included putting on a bathing suit and getting out on the sand…barefoot and everything. Luckily it had been a warm day.

A commitment was a commitment. She wouldn't back out now.

Pulling into the drive and around to her garage, she made it home. Once inside, it didn't take long to slip on the one-piece TJ had talked her into buying…Hot pink with black curved lines. Not bad looking, but a little too much skin showed as far as Meagan was concerned.

She pulled on the hot pink cotton knit cover-up that matched the swimsuit and slipped her feet into a pair of black flip-flops.

Looking at her reflection in the mirror, Meagan said. "You don't look bad, girl. This beach life seems to agree with you." Then she laughed as she walked through the connecting door and headed toward the den.

Before entering, she heard voices that caused her to stop short.

"I'm telling you, darling. I'll talk your father into letting you go. It's a graduation gift for you. How can he turn it down?"

"Aunt Karrie, he'll say I'm still only seventeen and no daughter of his is going off alone to Europe," Jessica said.

Meagan didn't want to hear this conversation, but she didn't feel like going all the way back to her place and walking around the back way. She'd had a long day and was actually looking forward to relaxing on the beach.

She was about to clear her throat so they would know she was there when Karrie said something that caused Meagan to freeze.

"Darling. I'm working on your father...trying to make him realize he needs to marry. You girls need a mother, and what better mother than a blood relative? I know your daddy doesn't love me like that. But hey," she chuckled as she spoke, "I don't love him either. So it would be a perfect marriage. Then I could let you do all those things we've talked about."

"Aunt Karrie, thank you."

Meagan couldn't see what was going on, but she felt sure Jessica was hugging her aunt by now. That woman was going to ruin Jessica. Karrie for a mother was the last thing any of those girls needed. Tremors shook her body. She wanted to turn and run back to her apartment but didn't dare. Instead, she did as she originally planned. Clearing her throat she stepped through the doorway and kept walking. "Morning, ladies," she said, but didn't slow down to talk.

Making her way into the kitchen, she poured herself a glass of water and then added ice to it. Gulping it down, she refilled the glass. This time she sipped on the water, trying to think if she should say anything. It was really none of her business...but oh she wanted to say something...at least to the doctor...warn him what his sister-in-law was up to. She shook her head. Again, it was none of her business. Placing the glass in the sink, she slowly released the breath of air she had been holding.

The kitchen door swung open, and Helen walked in. "Rachelle

and Tamara are looking for you. They are out back on the deck putting towels and a blanket in the beach basket. I put some snacks in a sack and some drinks in the little ice chest. Have fun." She opened the refrigerator door and was pulling out a head of lettuce. Closing the door, she looked back at Meagan. "Are you okay?"

Meagan realized she hadn't moved since Helen walked into the kitchen. Her mind was still frozen in time, thinking of that conversation she had overheard, but this snapped her out of it. "I'm fine. I'll go catch up with them."

Leaving the kitchen, she made a pit stop by the bathroom near the back door. Luckily, she hadn't run into Karrie or Jessica this go around as she made a fast exit. Right now was not the time to have to face them. She was sure the feelings inside would reflect on her face, letting them know that she had heard their conversation.

"Go have fun!" she said to herself.

Just as Helen had said, the girls were in the back. They were ready to go. "It's about time," TJ said. "I was about to call out the cavalry for you. I figured you had chickened out."

"No. I'm going to the beach. It's hot out here, but are y'all sure the water is warm enough?"

"Probably not, but it's time to try," TJ said as her sister punched her in the arm. They both laughed.

"Oh me. I have this strange feeling I've been suckered into something a little too soon." Her gaze slipped out to the horizon. The waves rolled gently onto shore. It was a beautiful picture. Yes. This would be nice and relaxing.

"Do we want to bring a volleyball or something to hit around on the beach?" TJ asked Rachelle.

"Not today. I'd like to just lie out and read. It was a rough week for me with finals and everything. Now that school is out, I'd like to rest a bit. What about you, Meagan?"

"I'm for the resting. So I'm with you, Rachelle."

TJ snatched up the beach basket and started walking away. "Okay by me…this time. But next time we're going to be active. Play ball, shoot the curls, swim, something active. Got it? Good!"

Everyone laughed.

The day at the beach wasn't bad. Since Meagan didn't get in the water, sand didn't stick to her.

Now TJ and Rachelle were a different story. Those girls swam like fish. It was fun watching them dive into the waves and then swim farther out. Then they would float on their back and let the waves bring them to shore.

At times, Meagan got a little nervous. They seemed to get pretty far out before drifting back in, but once they were back and she expressed her concerns, they told her they did it all the time.

At the dinner table while everyone was eating, the doctor said, "It looks like some of you played in the sun today."

Meagan felt the tightness on her face and a little burning on her shoulders, but when she had looked at her reflection after showering, she hadn't noticed anything. She was starting to feel it now, though.

"Some of us did play, Daddy. But some of us just laid around." TJ's eyes rolled over to Meagan while she was speaking. "Somebody didn't want to get wet…or something. How can you go to the beach and not swim?"

Meagan opened her mouth, ready to defend herself, when Rachelle jumped in.

"She rested. She read. But Meagan said that was what she was going to do to begin with. So was I, till you challenged me with who could dive into the wave and swim the farthest out." With a smug look on her face, Rachelle turned to her daddy and said, "And I won."

He laughed. "Sounds like you all had fun. That's great. What about you, Jessica? What did you do today?"

Her blue eyes darted toward Meagan then looked back at her dad. "Nothing, Daddy. Just slept late and hung around the house."

"Why didn't you go to the beach with the girls?" he asked.

She frowned and shrugged her shoulders. "I don't know. I guess I didn't feel like it. I must have needed my sleep."

"What did Aunt Karrie want? She asked for you when I let her in," TJ said.

Jessica's eyes widened as she glared holes in her sister. "Nothing important. She just stopped by to see how we were all doing."

Her little sister made a mocking face at Jessica as she bounced her shoulders, twisting left then right.

"La tee da. She didn't ask me how I was doing…but whatever."

Meagan saw Ryan's eyes focus in on his oldest daughter. He was watching her intently but didn't question her further.

The thought crossed Meagan's mind again. Should she say something? Deep within she felt it clearly…*say nothing.*

Conversation flowed as they finished off their dinner. When Helen asked if anyone wanted dessert, everyone passed.

The sun had taken a lot out of her today and she didn't need much of anything…except maybe a fan blowing in her face. "I think maybe I got a little more sun than I thought. Do I look sunburned?" she asked no one in particular.

TJ looked at her and grinned. When Rachelle's eyes rested upon Meagan, she gasped and covered her mouth with her hand. All Meagan saw was Rachelle's bright blue eyes staring at her.

"What?"

"Meagan. We have some crème you are going to want to use tonight. I have a feeling you will not be moving so freely tomorrow. Hopefully, for your sake, you will not have too many patients," the doctor said. "Are you finished with dinner?"

She sighed and rose from her chair as she said, "Yes. I am." The shirt on her back scraped her skin as she stood. She started to cry out but shut her mouth quickly.

"Yes. You definitely need the crème. And one of you girls will need to put it on her back for her. Come with me, Meagan, and I will get it for you."

She followed him up the stairs. This was Meagan's first time ever on the second floor. With each room they passed, she couldn't stop herself from glancing inside.

She could tell which room was TJ's, Rachelle's, and Jessica's. The rooms reflected their personalities.

This pleased Meagan. It was important when she and her siblings were growing up when their parents let them decorate their own rooms. Of course, back in her day, she and Shelly put posters up of the pop and rock 'n roll singers that were popular back then. It wasn't until Meagan had her own room that her tastes developed into other things.

Ryan stepped into a spacious bathroom with huge mirrors on the wall. Meagan was amazed. It was as big as one of the smaller bedrooms in her home. There was a large stained glass window as a backdrop to a tub one had to climb up and step down into. It had to be a Jacuzzi tub. To the left of it was a large muted glass stall of a walk-in shower. Inside, she could see spouts at two levels and seating areas protruding from the wall.

In the far left corner there were two chest high walls that she assumed sectioned off the commode. Small tile covered the counters around the two vanity sinks. Tiles similar but larger covered the floor. Huge plush rugs lay on the floor near the tub and shower. Matching decorative towels hung on the handlebars across the glass door that slid open to the shower.

The size and beauty of this room literally took her breath away. Her vision encompassed the whole room in a slow circular sweep. When she returned her focus to the doctor, she found he had opened a cupboard that connected the two mirrors over the vanity. He was rooting through and pulling out tubes and bottles.

"We have various things that will help. Let me see," he said as he pulled one more thing down.

Meagan took in the strength of his arms, the gentleness of his hands, as he searched the cupboard. Biting her bottom lip, she thought about how wonderful he was taking time to care for her. He made her feel special. Her gaze slipped back up his arm to his face. She found he was no longer rooting through the cupboard but was looking into the mirror.

She followed his gaze and found it was locked on her reflection. Surprise touched her, and then complete horror followed. "Oh my gosh!" The red of her face matched the red in a flag of the US. What a shock!

The doctor laughed. "It will be okay. Right now, you are starting to resemble a cooked lobster. I hope it is not as painful as it looks, and I guarantee you some of these crèmes and sprays I've pulled down will help ease your pain."

"Oh, Dr. Richardson, thank you so much. You are too kind." Touching her face with her fingertips, she felt the heat that exuded from her body.

"Did you wear any sunscreen today? And please, at home call me Ryan."

Warmth burned hotter in her cheeks at the thought of calling him by his given name, but because of the sunburn, she felt certain it wasn't noticeable. "Oh, ah. Thank you, sir…I mean, Ryan. I'll try." She had started thinking of him as Ryan for a short while now so it shouldn't be too hard, but she didn't dare tell him that. "Sorry to say, I didn't put anything on. I've never truly laid out to get sun. I've avoided it most of my life."

A deep grin covered his face. "I can tell. You have such lovely… or should I say *had* such lovely ivory skin…Still lovely but now red. Young lady, you must wear sunscreen every time you go outdoors. Here is a tube of sunscreen for your face," he said as he set it to the side. "And this is a spray bottle of SPF thirty sunscreen for your arms, legs, and back. In fact, we have a few of those, each a different amount, so you take all of them. The spray will help you take care of yourself. If the girls are with you, use this." He set a black tube next to the bottles of spray. "This one works the best, but someone has to put it on your back. And the water will not wash it away. And be sure to put some on your nose and cheeks before you get out in the sun."

"Thank you. I appreciate it."

"Here is the crème I was telling you about to help ease the pain." He opened the larger tube and squirted some in his hand. "Here, look at me."

She turned her face up toward Ryan's, and he started applying the crème gently. His touch was so tender. She found herself closing her eyes and enjoying the feel of his fingertips tracing circle patterns on her cheeks. As the medicine covered her skin, the sting of the burn eased and her face started feeling the comfort. She didn't know what felt better, the ease of the pain from the crème or the touch of his fingertips. When he stopped the motion, she opened her eyes. The doctor was looking down at her, just watching. Her breath suspended as her heart raced. His blue eyes caressed her…or at least she felt like they did.

He swallowed and opened his mouth as if to speak when she heard someone clear their throat loudly.

Both turned toward the doorway in an instant. *Oh no!* They were like two kids caught with their hands in the cookie jar. Guilt consumed her although nothing had happened.

"Daddy, Aunt Karrie is here and wants to talk to you," said Jessica.

Meagan heard him draw in a long slow breath and felt the tension in the air rise. "Jessica, tell her I'll be down in a minute. She can wait in my study."

"Yes, sir." Jessica spoke to her dad, but her eyes glared at Meagan. This girl truly did not care for her, Meagan felt certain. Jessica then turned on her heel and stormed away. Meagan heard her as she ran down the stairs. How did they not hear her come up?

"Back to you and your need."

She turned and found him looking at her. The softness was back on his face and the tenderness in his tone.

"You go see Karrie. I don't want to keep you."

"Nonsense. She can wait."

He didn't seem too concerned so she left it alone.

"Here is a bottle of ibuprofen. I have a feeling when you try to sleep tonight, you are not going to find much comfort if the rest of your body looks like your legs and face." If you feel you need something stronger, I can write you a prescription."

"This should be enough," Meagan said as she looked down. "I can't believe it; even my feet are burned."

A half grin touched his lips as he said, "Your skin was like a baby's…never been touched by the sun, and you allowed what… two? Three? Or was it four hours to do its worst to you?"

She looked down, embarrassed. A smart person would have thought before going out in the sun for that long.

"Hey. Cheer up. I am picking at you. Everyone does it at one time or another. But most learn from their first experience. I just hope…." He paused as he reached down and touched her cheek. "I hope your skin does not blister. If it does, let me know right away and we will get something stronger for you and for your skin."

Turning back to the products on the counter, he picked up the various tubes, the spray bottles, and the bottle of pills. "Let me carry this for you."

"I can get it."

"I have it. Come on. We will stop in the kitchen and see if Helen has a little bag or something you can put all of this in to bring back to your apartment. You might want to go ahead and take one of those pills when we get to the kitchen. Come on." He led the way out of the room and down the stairs.

She followed him as he detoured them through the kitchen. Helen was in there digging in a drawer. She looked up as they entered. "Glory be, child. What have you done?"

"That obvious, huh? Too bad I didn't use my brain this afternoon and I could have avoided all of this fuss."

"We need a bag, Helen. I found her everything she will need to get through the night and keep it from happening again. Right, Meagan?"

"So right, Ryan. I'm a quick learner!" She laughed as did he. Meagan grabbed a glass out of the cupboard and poured herself some water. Ryan stepped closer to her so Meagan could take the bottle of pills from his hand. She opened the cap and took one. *The sooner the better,* she thought as her clothing scratched against her back again.

Helen opened the drawer next to the one she was digging in and pulled out a plastic bag. "We have plenty. They mount up from the grocery store. I save most of them, 'cause we use them when the girls take things down to the beach. Plastic protects it some." She handed it to Meagan and Meagan dropped the pill bottle in first.

After that she took one item at a time out of the doctor's arms and stuck it into the bag. When there was only one item left, he reached over, covering her hand with his empty one and put the last tube in the bag she was holding. He caught her gaze with his and they locked on one another. In almost a whisper, he said, "Take care of yourself from now on…all right?"

"You got it." She smiled at him, and he smiled back.

Meagan felt the tenderness in his touch as he squeezed the hand he had covered with his own. "Now let's go watch a movie or something. You too, Helen. Come join us."

"I'll do that. In just one minute, sir. I'm trying to find my recipe for heavenly hash cake. I haven't made it in a while, but my recipe card isn't in my box of recipes."

The doctor looked at her. A serious look crossed his face as he said, "Well I for one hope you find it. I remember…it was delicious. But it can wait. Come join us in the den. Come on, Meagan."

As Meagan followed him out of the kitchen, she said, "Don't forget, Karrie is in the study."

He stopped in mid-step, his hands balled into fists. "I had forgotten all about her. What does she want this time? I am sure it is something to do with Jessica. You go on to the den. I'll get rid of her."

Meagan looked up at Ryan and wanted to warn him, tell him what she had overheard, but she didn't want to interfere. It was none of her business. "I'll tell the girls to pick out a movie and let them know you'll be watching it with us."

"Sounds good." He strode off in the opposite direction.

She watched as he stopped at the door, straightened himself standing taller, then opened the door and entered. Meagan noticed he didn't bother to close it behind him. A small grin tipped her lips. She found she liked the doctor more and more every day. Deep inside, she believed he knew what Karrie was up to…more than just meddling in Jessica's life. She hoped he wasn't blind to the advances that woman made toward him.

Meagan made her way to the den where the girls were still sitting around talking. Jessica wasn't listening to them. Her eyes were glued to the doorway. When she saw Meagan enter the room without her dad, the look on her face said, "It's about time." But the girl was smart enough not to voice it, Meagan thought.

"Hey, girls. Your daddy said pick out a movie. He said he'd join us in a few minutes and watch a DVD with us."

TJ squealed as she jumped up from her chair and ran to the bookshelf displaying their many movies. "Which one, Rachelle? What do you think Daddy would like?"

"Don't be silly," Jessica said. "He's not going to watch a movie with us. Aunt Karrie is here. He's with her now in the study."

Meagan knew better than to correct Jessica, but if the tension that woman brought to Ryan was any sign of how much he did not want to spend time with her, it was clear he would be with them very soon.

Rachelle chose to believe what her daddy said via Meagan and joined TJ in a movie search. "How about that one with Mel Gibson?

You know Daddy likes his movies…the one where he could read women's thoughts."

"Oh yeah. That's perfect. I remember the last time we watched that, he laughed a lot and said he wished he had that power. I remember because I loved hearing Daddy laugh. He doesn't do it much…or should I say he *didn't* do it much. But he has a lot lately. Have you noticed?" TJ looked to Rachelle when she was speaking.

Jessica grunted and rolled her eyes as Rachelle agreed with her little sister.

Meagan put her bag down and sat down at one end of the sofa. The back of her legs and her back sizzled as the material from the couch touched her burn. The pain was like skimming across the sidewalk on her bare back, but she would make it through the movie.

As the girls were getting the disc in the player, voices rose from the hallway, and then, clear as a bell, they all heard Ryan say, "I don't know what game you think you are playing, but my daughter is not for sale. Jessica will not be flying off to Rome or anywhere else for that matter. Do I make myself clear?"

"Perfectly!" Karrie's voice was followed by the slamming of the front door.

No one moved. No one breathed…because no one knew what to expect.

In another moment, maybe two, Helen and Ryan walked into the den together. Helen wasn't smiling, but she wasn't frowning either. Ryan, however, had a big smile on his face as he said, "What movie did you girls pick? I hope it's a comedy because I want to laugh!"

The two girls looked at one another and then their father as the smiles returned to their faces. In unison they said, "You're gonna love it, Daddy."

Chapter 21

Meagan fell asleep before the movie ended...not that it wasn't entertaining. What she saw of it, she laughed a good part of the time, but her eyelids fought to close more and more. She forced them back open most of the time. The medicine must have made her very drowsy, and she finally gave way to letting them rest. The next thing she remembered was voices whispering all around her.

"Don't worry. I will get her to her room. You girls go on to bed. It is pretty late for a weeknight. I don't know how I let you talk me into these things."

"I'll clean up our popcorn mess. Sleep tight, everyone," Helen said as she gathered up the bowls and started out of the room.

Struggling to open her eyes, Meagan caught a glimpse of TJ hugging her dad as Rachelle let go of him. In the back of her mind, she remembered Jessica hadn't stayed. Minutes after the movie started she had said she was bored and left the room.

"If she wakes up, Daddy, tell Meagan I said goodnight," TJ whispered.

She forced her eyes open. "I'm not sleeping, guys. I was just—" A yawn interrupted her words. "I think the medicine is working." Slowly she sat up. "This couch is so comfortable. I was resting my eyes, I think."

Everyone laughed. "Sure you were. Night, Meagan. Sleep well. I hope your sunburn feels better tomorrow," TJ said.

Rachelle had started out of the room but stuck her head back in and said, "Me too. Sorry we didn't think to tell you to wear sun protection. We've done it all of our lives, so we probably assumed you did, too. Goodnight."

She smiled at the girls as she slowly rose to her feet. Her eyes were still very heavy but she kept forcing them back open every time they closed.

Meagan reached out to grab the bag of ointments and such, but Ryan scooped it up.

"I've got it. I'm going to help you to your room." Ryan gently caught hold under Meagan's left arm.

About to pull away, she stopped herself. Right now, if she tried to make it to her apartment by herself, she'd either fall on her face or run into a wall or two. Quickly, she decided to do the smart thing and let the doctor walk her home. No big deal.

He guided her through the room and then down the halls that led to her wing of the manor. As they passed the workout room he said, "I hope you know to make yourself at home here. Anything we have, treat it as yours while you are here…like the exercise room, the pool, whatever."

Her senses were waking up, or the medicine was wearing off. She wasn't sure which it was. The tingles that spread where he touched she believed had a lot to do with it. "I already do. Thank you."

"Great."

"You do remember my mom is coming to stay a week here? How more at ease can a person feel?" She chuckled slightly.

"No problem." He nodded and stopped at her doorway. It was

wide open. "You must feel pretty comfortable, if you don't keep the door separating us closed." He loosened his hold on her arm and looked down at her. "Can you make it the rest of the way? You seem to have awakened."

"I don't close it when I'm on your side of the house. I hope that's okay."

"Of course it is. I just said I want you to make yourself at home."

More than her eyes had woken up...her senses were running wild, but she didn't dare tell him that. These thoughts or emotions she was having when the doctor was around, she needed to stop.

She'd work on that. In the meantime she needed to put some space between them. Meagan needed to walk away. "I'll be fine. Thanks," she said as she reached out for the bag he was holding.

"I am looking forward to meeting your mother." His gaze locked on hers, and she couldn't break away as he said, "She has raised a wonderful daughter, and I am so glad to have you here...helping the girls I mean. You have done wonders with TJ and Rachelle. I am very pleased. I only hope you get through to Jessica. I may have waited too long to try and get help for her."

The concern in his eyes tugged on Meagan. She reached out and touched his arm gently. "It's never too late. She'll come around. I sense she's fighting it, but I see your family starting to bond deeper than when I first arrived. That's what she needs right now. You keep on doing what you're doing."

    ***

As a smile touched his lips, he covered her hand that was resting gently on his arm. "I have not done anything...other than what I should have been doing all along. Thank you for helping me to see that. When the girls needed me the most, I withdrew. I cannot explain, nor is there any excuse. I am not even sure I know why I withdrew for so long."

He sighed and closed his eyes for a moment. *What am I thinking? She's too young for me.* But he couldn't help but look.

"You were hurting…grieving. But let's not look back. Now you need to look forward so the girls can too." She squeezed his arm gently then pulled her hand away.

He stepped back at the same time. *Quit staring!"*

Nodding he said, "You're right. Thanks. I will let you get in so you can try to put that crème on your burn. Sorry the girls aren't here to help. Take some more medicine before you go to bed, and if you don't feel up to coming in tomorrow, just let me know in the morning. I will square things at work." He paused for a moment and grinned as he raised his brow. "I have connections, you know."

A smile crinkled her nose. "Thanks. I'm sure I'll be there tomorrow, but I'll keep your connections in mind. Night." She turned and went into her apartment closing the door behind her.

Looking at the closed door, Ryan sighed.

Good thing her mother is coming. Too many family nights might have me believing she is a part of this family. Her mother will keep things right. That girl is ten years younger than I am. To her I am probably an old man. Why am I even having these thoughts? Jennifer has been gone for seven years. No one has caught my attention all this time. Why now? Why her?

Sighing, he raked his fingers through his hair, and then turned and strode away.

***

On the other side of the door, Meagan held her breath, waiting to hear him leave.

He was still out there. What was keeping him?

Part of her wanted to open the door back up and offer to make a pot of coffee or something. She had better not. Meagan quickly reminded herself she was there for the girls...not for the father. Leaning closer to the door, she was pretty sure he was still standing on the other side, or he had moved so quietly she hadn't heard him.

Meagan wasn't sure. Maybe it was because her heart pounded so loudly, she couldn't hear a thing. But then she finally heard him as he walked away. The beat of her heart went into triple time. Taking in a large breath, she wondered again what could have possibly held him there so long.

Should she talk to Shelly about this? She would know. Meagan had two men in her life over the years, and although she felt drawn to them, due to the life she felt God had planned for her, she knew they weren't in the picture...at least at that time. Meagan hadn't had a lot of experience with men in general and didn't want to think things that couldn't possibly be true.

"There's your answer," she said to herself as she headed to her bedroom.

"He's a doctor...has three children...owns a hospital. What would he want with you?" Of course it was all in her mind, him being attracted to her. She was so glad she hadn't made a fool of herself and invited him into her apartment.

Putting the bag on the dresser, she started pulling out the various tubes and bottles. Afterward, she pulled out her sleep-shirt and started removing her clothes. Meagan felt the burn, the pain, the ache.

When down to her underclothes, she looked in the mirror. Her white skin was so red. "Oh my gosh!" She couldn't believe what she saw. She hoped it didn't blister.

Opening the tube, she squirted the crème out and applied it to her skin. First the shock of cold hit her. Against the heat, it felt wonderful.

Then the soothing effect took over. It made her want to purr like a kitten. The thought brought a smile to her face.

"The doctor knows what he is talking about. Ryan knows," she corrected herself as a smile rested on her lips.

"Back to the work at hand." She continued to cover her sun-burned areas…the part she could reach.

"This stuff is great." The crème covered her arms, legs, face, and chest. The only place she couldn't put it was her back. It would have to suffer the consequences. Maybe tomorrow Rachelle or TJ could put some on for her. For tonight she would try the stuff in the spray bottle.

It didn't work as well as the crème, but it cooled her back somewhat.

Tossing back the covers, she remembered something Ryan had said. "Take some more medicine before you go to bed." He was right. It would definitely help her sleep. She padded into the kitchen and fixed a small glass of water.

Once she was back in her bedroom, she took a pill out of the container and swallowed it, and then followed it with water.

"Now I can go to sleep. Hopefully without any dreams… especially the ones I don't need to have."

After setting the alarm on the clock, she climbed into the bed and covered up. The sheets were cool against her back. That should help her have a peaceful night. Her thoughts started out on the girls but slowly made their way to their daddy. About that time the pill lulled her off to sleep.

Chapter 22

The week passed quickly and so did the sunburn. Her pale white skin was starting to tan. This was a first. It never blistered, and she didn't miss a day's work because of it. She did, however, learn from her experience and used the spray bottle of sunscreen the next two times she went to the beach with the girls.

Her tan continued to darken nicely, which shocked the heck out of Meagan. She'd been as white as hospital sheets all her life. A lot of things had changed in Meagan's life over the past few months.

While sitting on the sofa, she gazed out the window taking in a panoramic view of the ocean. Her cell phone rang and she answered on the second ring. She had made a couple of friends at the hospital, but since she spent most of her time with the girls, she hadn't given her number out to any of her co-workers this time. That was another thing different about this job compared to others before. It was either her mom or her sister calling. The latter was correct.

"Hello," she said as she pushed the button.

"Just wanted to let you know, Mom's plane just took off. She's so excited and I'm jealous. I wish Kirk had been another year older so I could have come with her. I'd love to meet everyone and hang out on my own private beach." Shelly sighed.

"Maybe next year they'll ask me to come back. I doubt it, since the girls are making such headway. But you never know. The only one I haven't been able to help is Jessica, and that girl does not like me. Not one little bit." She lay out on the sofa with her feet on the arm of the other end. This was the short one, so even she could reach both sides lying lengthwise. Closing her eyes, she draped one of her arms across her forehead, giving her sister time to speak.

"Yeah, right. I'm sure she likes you. You're a nice person. She has other things working in her mind right now. Remember what it was like being a senior. You still might reach her. Don't give up. And just think, at least you're learning to like the beach. Maybe you'll take a job in the Bahamas or somewhere like that. We'll all come join you." Shelly tried to encourage her sister to think beyond the moment or at least see the humor in it.

Laughing Meagan said, "You got it, girl. I'll keep that in mind." In her heart though, she realized she didn't want to leave this place. She liked where she was and she loved the family. Her eyes popped open as she realized the thought that had just crossed her mind. She didn't need to be thinking those things.

Can't help what you feel. That thought sounded almost audible. She looked around for who said it.

"Did you hear me?" Shelly asked.

"Were you asking me something about how I feel?"

"No, silly. I said be prepared for Mom. She's going to check out the doctor. We hear it in your voice. You're falling for the guy."

"Don't be ridiculous!" Meagan sat up on the couch.

"I know. You won't admit it. Mom and I noticed how you try not to even talk about him to us…but we weren't born yesterday. Especially Mom. She reads us like a book. Always has. Always will."

Sucking in a deep breath, she fell against the back of the couch, in a sitting position this time, her back to the window. "Okay. So y'all figured me out. I hope she doesn't say anything. And more than that, I hope the girls haven't figured me out. That might be why Jessica hates me so. Maybe she senses that I've fallen for her father, and the young thing wants her aunt and dad to get together."

"Meagan, don't be ridiculous. There is no way she could tell. That girl doesn't even hang around you much. The other two are probably too young to notice."

Her hand tightened around the cell phone. "I hope you're right. And I hope Ryan hasn't noticed. Oh, Shelly. I don't want to make a fool of myself. I know he's not interested in me. He's older. He's a doctor who owns his own hospital. I don't know why I've even allowed myself to fall for him."

"You can't help who you love."

"I didn't say love!"

"Okay. Okay. You can't help who you fall for. Just keep your heart open. You never know. God sent you there for a reason... remember?" Shelly's voice was gentle.

"Of course I remember. And it was to help these girls. I need to pray harder and concentrate more on Jessica. Help me here. Okay?"

"I'll be praying for you...in many ways. Mandy just came in and she's calling for me. Gotta go. Talk to you soon. Don't forget to pick up Momma at the airport."

"Like I'd forget. Bye, Shel. Thanks."

Later the girls offered to ride with her to pick up her mom, but because she wanted to make sure her mom didn't say anything about what she and Shelly had figured out, she thought it would be best if she picked her up by herself.

It was Saturday and the traffic wasn't that bad. Meagan made good time to the airport.

Inside the terminal, she watched the many people coming in from their flight. It seemed like her mother would never get there.

Finally, a short woman wearing olive green and white came scurrying through the crowd.

Waving her hands in the air, Meagan hollered, "Over here, Mom. Over here."

Her mom caught sight of Meagan and headed her way. They greeted each other with a big bear hug.

"Hey, sweetie. You look so good. So tanned. If I didn't know better I would say you were here on a vacation yourself."

Dropping her arms from the hug, she backed away. "I've already been on the phone with Shelly. I know exactly what you think I've been here doing. Try not to push or say anything about what you two have been thinking, and we'll have a great time. The girls are excited about meeting you. They've planned a snorkeling trip for you. We're going to go out on a sailboat. I haven't done that yet. And believe it or not, I'm looking forward to it."

Her mom's face lit up. That was part of her dream for retirement…to move near a beach and to have their own sailboat. But it was her mom's dream, not Pop's. "That sounds like fun. I do believe I will love these girls as much as you do."

"Mom, you'd love them without the sailboat."

"That's what I mean. They just seem like they care about other people. They are looking out for you, and I think that makes them special."

Meagan slipped her arm around her mother's waist and headed them toward baggage claim. "They are special, Mom."

"There it is," Carol said as she pointed to the red suitcase.

"Only one?"

"I've learned over the past few years I never need as much as I bring, so I packed smart."

Meagan pulled it off the conveyor belt and rolled it behind them as they headed to the parking lot. In no time, they were in the car and on the road home.

"Momma. I really mean it about you not pushing anything or coaxing the doctor in any form or fashion. You know what I mean, right?"

She reached over and patted her daughter's shoulder. "Don't be silly. I wouldn't do that. Your life is your life. I try to stay out of it."

A tight-lipped smile stretched across Meagan's lips. "Right, Mom. You and Shelly both try to stay out of it. I'm serious now!"

"So am I, dear. Don't worry."

On the drive back to the mansion, Carol caught Meagan up on what Troy was doing now. She even had time to gloat on the grandkids some. Her mom always bragged about those two. Meagan wished she had found true love and given her mother grandchildren, but it wasn't meant to be. In the past, that bothered Meagan, but today, she no longer felt as if she missed out.

Crossing the bridge to the island, her mom commented on the beauty.

"I know. I love it. I never thought I could feel such excitement over an island, surrounded by water." She caught her mom's gaze as she looked at her daughter with a puzzled look on her face. "I know. That's the definition of an island, but you know what I mean. Me living with water all around me. Even more, the fact that there is sand everywhere and water and I've always hated both. Not today. Mom, you wouldn't believe the fun there is in shell searching and beach walking and bike riding...and even wave dodging."

Her mom laughed and in a slightly sarcastic tone said, "Of course I don't know. I was only born and raised in southern

California. Remember?"

Meagan blushed as she realized what she had said to her mom. "Sorry. Of course you know. And I know you've tried to show it to me over the years, but it took TJ and Rachelle to help me see the good side of living on a beach. It's wonderful, Mom. I love it here. And I love the girls…all three of them." And to herself, she said, *and I love their father.* Contentment settled deep within her heart as that thought settled in her mind.

The drive came naturally. Meagan didn't have to think of which street to turn on or where. She drove straight home. As she turned into the drive, her mom gasped. "Oh my word. It is big. This is where you live?"

"You ain't seen nothing yet, as they say."

Meagan wheeled the car around to her garage and pulled in. As the garage door was shutting, the two climbed out of the car. "You'll love my apartment. And you'll love Helen, the girls, and the doctor. Just you wait."

Inside, Meagan gave her mom a quick tour and then walked her out the back door to see everything. The smell of saltwater attacked Meagan's senses so she knew her mom felt like she had come home. It was the Atlantic instead of the Pacific, but what the heck.

"Oh, sweetie. This is beautiful! Magnificent! You were blessed…and now I am. Thanks for letting me stay with you."

"It's my pleasure. Now I promised to bring you in to meet the family right away. Jessica isn't here, but everyone else is. And I'm sure Helen has made a spectacular lunch. It will be light, but it will be great. And then of course dinner. She'll make that too. The whole time you're here, you won't have to cook a thing."

"Have I died and gone to heaven? Thank you." They laughed together as Meagan led the way back inside.

She directed her to the other side of the house, pointing out the exercise room in passing. "Feel free to use it. I know you walk on your treadmill every day. You won't have to give it up here. They have one…plus more."

Her mom peeped in and then caught up with Meagan saying, "This is great."

They made a couple more turns and then found everyone but Helen in the den. Ryan and the girls jumped to their feet as Meagan and her mom entered the room.

"Mom, this is TJ, Rachelle, and Ryan. Y'all, this is my mom." Meagan figured her mom would rush over and hug them, but instead she shook each one's hand as they offered it. Maybe she didn't want to push. Meagan hoped her mom would like them.

"Mrs. Phillips. Welcome to our home. We're all looking forward to your visit. Like I told Meagan the other day, you'd have to be a great woman to raise a daughter like Meagan."

A warm smile touched her lips as she said, "Thank you. And please, Doctor, call me Carol," she said as she shook his hand.

"And you call me Ryan," he insisted.

Her mother's smile told Meagan she liked the doctor already. Meagan stepped between the two girls and put her arms on their shoulders. "These are the two people you have to thank for teaching me to love the beach."

"I do. I do. Thank you very much. You both did something I was never able to do. We never understood her distaste for beaches and oceans. Meagan's brother and sister loved our summers in the sun. They took to the water like fish. Our Meagan took to the water like a cat and stayed far away. She always stayed inside or under the umbrella. It never made sense to us, but her dad and I quit trying to push it on her. She was her own girl from the day she was born."

"Oh, Mom. I wasn't that bad."

Her mom lifted her brows and looked up as she shrugged her shoulders, but didn't say a word.

The girls giggled.

Helen popped in at that very moment. "Great! You're here! Lunch is ready. Welcome, Mrs. Phillips."

"Carol, please."

"Well welcome, Carol. Your daughter has been a blessing. We all love her. I'll never forget the first day she came when she met the doctor—"

"Okay. Let's eat," Meagan said interrupting an embarrassing story. She pushed the girls out the door and dragged her mother behind her. "I'm starved."

Chapter 23

Sunday morning they all went to church together, but since the number grew by one, to be comfortable, they drove two cars. This time TJ and Rachelle rode with Meagan and her mom. Ryan's car carried him along with Jessica and Helen. The service was great. Her mom even commented on the pastor and his way with words.

"He is definitely anointed," Carol said.

As a surprise after church, Ryan took them all out to eat.

Helen was the only one who knew. That was the only way to keep her from starting something cooking before they left. That woman loved to cook.

The restaurant he chose had plenty of selections, from steak to chicken to seafood. They even had salad choices as well as sandwiches from the grill. Ryan chose well.

Everyone seemed pleased. Even Jessica had a slight joy about her that day, Meagan noticed. Maybe the message touched her heart. The food had been selected and ordered. Conversation flowed without a problem and then the food arrived.

About half way through the meal, another surprise arrived as Carol was talking about growing up in southern California.

"Well, darling. Isn't this cozy? If I had known it was a family outing, I would have come sooner. But no wait. I'm family and I wasn't invited. You brought your hired help out to eat with the girls. How quaint." Karrie didn't even give Ryan time to respond before she turned quickly on her heel and stormed away.

Meagan watched the doctor. His brow furrowed as his jaw clenched. The nerve jerked repeatedly. Ryan dropped his fork down in his plate and stood. "Excuse me for one moment please." Quietly, but intensely he left the table following not too far behind Karrie.

Glancing around the table, Meagan saw the horror-stricken look on her mom's face. Helen merely looked stunned for a moment, but not surprised. Rachelle and TJ looked a little angry, while Jessica looked smug.

No wonder she had been so joyful today. She knew her aunt was going to confront her dad. Probably not in this form, but she trusted her aunt. She figured if anyone could straighten out her father's thinking it would be Aunt Karrie.

How wrong could anyone be? At least, she hoped Jessica was wrong in her thoughts. The words she had spoken about him taking out the hired help were meant to hurt.

Truthfully, it stung a little. Meagan knew she had been hired by the doctor for the hospital and for the care of his girls. But a relationship had formed. No matter what Karrie said, Meagan knew God had wanted her there and nothing the aunt said would make her run away. God had used her to help the two youngest, and she felt sure He had plans to use her to help Jessica. Meagan had to stay as long as she was doing His work.

A good five minutes later, which seemed like thirty, Ryan returned to the table. After he was seated, he said, "I do apologize for my sister-in-law's behavior. Unfortunately there is no excuse for her…other than she has been spoiled all of her life getting her own way. And that was her parents' doing. But she is a grown woman now. You would think she would learn."

He shook his head.

"I hope she didn't ruin anyone's appetite. Please let us continue our meal and return to our pleasant conversation. Mrs. Phillips...I mean Carol, you were telling us about your childhood in southern California. Things you and your brothers and sisters did on the beach. We have never had a bonfire before." Glancing at his girls, he added, "That sounds like something we ought to try. I guess fires would be best in the fall."

"Summertime weenie roasts are great fun too. Sitting around the campfire in the fall is wonderful, though." Carol smiled as she spoke. It was like she was reliving her youth in her mind. "Singing around a campfire...and roasting weenies and marshmallows is so much fun...any time."

"It does sound like fun, Daddy," Rachelle said. "Let's plan one soon. We don't have to wait till next fall."

TJ agreed with Rachelle and added her own thoughts. "And we can invite some of our friends too. That would be fun. Maybe we can even do it this week, while Mrs. Phillips is here. If not, then we need to at least do it while Meagan is still here."

Jessica gave no input. In fact, her joyous mood disappeared completely, along with her appetite.

So much for hoping the message this morning had touched her heart. Meagan pushed those thoughts right out of her mind. She had to stay positive and believe she could get through to the oldest girl, too.

The next few days while Meagan was at work, her mom took time with the girls. Jessica still wouldn't be bothered to be a part of the outings, but TJ and Rachelle kept Meagan's mom entertained. They lived on the beach every day...so much so that by the time

Meagan got home, everyone was ready to do other things. They did a lot of shopping in the quaint little town on the island. Each showed Carol their favorite stores. They also took Carol sightseeing. Other evenings the four of them played doubles tennis.

The week was going by fast. Carol convinced Helen to let her and the girls help cook one of Carol's recipes. Seafood gumbo was the menu planned for Friday night. Sitting around the dinner table, Meagan enjoyed listening to them recall the cooking of the meal as Ryan and Meagan couldn't say enough about how much they enjoyed it.

"Carol, I hope Helen was paying close attention to the details of this recipe," he said as he shoved one more tasty bite in his mouth.

"I helped too, Daddy. I chopped all the onions while Rachelle cut up the red bell peppers." The excitement in her voice thrilled Meagan's heart.

"The girls were great. And don't give me all the credit here. Helen made the roux and that's the hardest part in any good gumbo."

The flavor of the crabmeat and shrimp was better than Meagan remembered all her days growing up in a home where gumbo was served as often as spaghetti was served in most homes.

"So Meagan, did you do any of it?" the doctor asked.

She slurped up another mouthful and swallowed quickly. Glancing at her mom and then back to Ryan she said, "I made the rice."

"The rice is good too," he smiled as he said it and then slipped another spoonful in his mouth.

"I'm just sorry Carol's got to go back so soon. She's fun to have around...even in my kitchen." Helen winked at Meagan's mom as she nodded her head while speaking.

The joy around the table was evident in everyone but Jessica, and at times, she laughed without meaning to. As quickly as she did, however, she covered her mouth and made the smile disappear.

That broke Meagan's heart. The girl wanted to be a part of it all, but her pride wouldn't allow it.

The night didn't stop at the table. They spent time in the music room listening to Rachelle entertain them, and then they all reclined in the den.

Talk went on for some time until Carol started to yawn. "I do believe it's well past my bedtime. I hate to be a party pooper, but I have to call it a night."

The doctor said, "We all should. We have a big day planned for tomorrow. Everyone try to get a good night's sleep."

Each went their separate ways; probably ready to fall asleep when their heads hit their pillows. Meagan wanted to ask her mom what she thought about the Richardson's but decided it could wait till the morning. She found she was as tired as her mom.

Chapter 24

Saturday was to be Carol's last full day there on vacation. "So what do you think of them, Mom?" Meagan asked as they sat at her kitchen table sipping coffee, still in their PJ's after breakfast had been eaten.

"Sweetheart, I can see a family you've been drawn into. The two youngest girls really like you and I know the feeling is reciprocated. I don't know personally what they were like when you first got here…only what you had told me. And I guarantee they are nothing like that now. Both seem so happy and fulfilled."

Meagan sipped on her coffee again as she thought for a moment. Warmth spread from within as a smile crossed her face.

Nodding, she said, "They have come a long way, Mom. And I'm so glad for that. There was no laughter in this house when I first got here. Sure, Helen. She's a joy. She has been since the beginning."

"Yes. She's nice. And you can see she loves the whole family."

"And they love her."

Her mom reached over and laid her hand on top of her daughter's. "I see a twinkle in your eye that I've never seen before."

Taking in a slow deep breath, Meagan leaned back in her chair and laid her head back too. She didn't want to say the wrong thing or give her mother a wrong impression, so she wanted to make sure her words were just right.

She decided not mention her feelings for the doctor, because that was a one-sided infatuation and definitely a waste of time…but she couldn't help being drawn to the doctor.

Letting the air out quickly, she sat up. Looking her mother straight in the eyes, she said, "I never believed coming here would be so great, Mom. I love these kids. Not just care about them…but love them like I do Mandy and Kirk…almost as if they were my own. I don't think that was part of God's plan, though. Sure, He wanted me to love them through Him, but I believe I would give my life for theirs, that's how much I've grown to love them in such a short time. Does that make sense?" The moisture gathered in her eyes but she blinked back the tears.

"It doesn't surprise me, dear. You have a big heart. And I know you always care deeply for your friends. But these girls are different. I couldn't help being drawn to them myself. I would adore being like a surrogate grandmother to them. But I know once you leave here, I'll probably never see them again. I'm sure you'll keep in contact with them, though. And God knows your heart, and He knew you would love them like you do. He knew before any of us. So it's a good thing."

Glancing up at the clock on the wall, Meagan said, "We've talked enough. Today is the day we're going sailing." Grabbing both of her mother's hands in her own, she squeezed. "I'm so excited, but so nervous." She shivered.

"Don't be, dear. It will be great fun."

"Let's go get ready!" They both rose. As her mom left to go to the back of the apartment and get dressed, Meagan took a few minutes and cleaned up the breakfast dishes. They had convinced Helen to go with them today also, and she didn't want Helen to use cleaning as an excuse to back out at the last minute.

Thirty minutes later, both women were in their swimsuits, covered with shorts, T-shirts, and plenty of sunscreen. Meagan took Ryan's warnings earlier to heart for the rest of her stay there. For sure being out on the ocean with the saltwater all around and the sun shining down it would be best to be covered with the lotion before going outdoors. She even had her mom put on some of the sunscreen lotion.

"I'm packing a bag, Mom. Anything special you want to bring. I've got the sunscreen and a couple of beach towels for us."

"I'm sure they'll have anything extra we may need."

Cutting through the house by the connecting doorway, Meagan and Carol met the girls in the family room. Everyone was going, including Jessica. That was a good thing, Meagan thought.

Seconds later, Ryan joined them in the family room carrying an ice chest, followed by Helen.

"If the weight of this thing is anything to go by, we won't go hungry!" Ryan said as he laughed, glancing Helen's way.

"All right!" TJ shouted. "This is going to be fun!"

"I'll help you, Ryan, if you'd like," Meagan said.

"I can help him. Here, Dad. Let me grab it by one side." Jessica grabbed at the ice chest quickly, not giving her dad a chance to say anything.

Ryan smiled at Meagan and then shrugged his shoulders. She nodded as if understanding his plea. The whole group of them filed out the back door and headed around the patio, past the garage and the tennis court onto the beach area.

They walked the wooden planked pathway to the pier where the boathouse was connected.

Setting the ice chest down at the far end over the water, he said,

"You all stay here and Jessica and I will get the boat and bring it around to pick you all up."

Meagan had never been in the boathouse so she had no idea what the sailboat looked like. But since a family outing was planned on it, she knew it had to be big enough to accommodate all of them. Plus the size of the boathouse seemed large just to dock a boat. In fact, it looked large enough to hold a couple of boats.

Several minutes later, a large boat, about forty to fifty feet long, slipped out of the boathouse, made a large complete circle in the water and stopped next to the pier.

Jessica jumped out with a rope and tied it up, and then her dad tossed another one to her and she did the same with it. Meagan was in shock. Never in her mind's eye had she imagined such a big sailboat, of course she hadn't seen any sails yet. At the moment it was apparently being operated by a motor of some sort.

"Wow!" was all she could say.

Her mom touched Meagan's shoulder. "I had no idea," she whispered to her daughter.

"Come on, Meagan. Climb aboard," TJ called as she climbed over onto the boat.

Yacht was a better term for the sailboat. Holding on to her little satchel, she eased over to the end of the pier. Ryan climbed out to retrieve the ice chest.

"Let me help you," he said to her as he took her hand and held it as she crossed over to the boat. He did the same for her mother and Helen.

After the ropes were loosened and all were on board, the doctor crossed over to the helm and took the wheel of the boat.

Standing there, he looked natural as he eased them out into the ocean. He gave the command to the girls and each one did their part of raising the sails as Meagan, Carol, and Helen only stood by and watched. In a short time, the sails were up and caught in the wind as Ryan cut the motor.

"Meagan, come over here. See what it feels like to direct a lady like this one." His face was beaming with joy.

Excitement raced through her veins as she realized he wanted to share this moment with her. But it also scared her to death. What if she turned the wheel wrong and flipped them over? As quick as that thought came, it disappeared. No way could she do something that major to a boat this size.

Her mom nudged her in his direction as Carol said, "Helen, have you been sailing before?"

The voices faded in the background as Meagan made her way to Ryan. The girls had done what was needed and now relaxed, enjoying the time. As Meagan stopped short of the doctor, he reached out and tried to take the bag from her, but her fingers held on tightly.

"You look a little frightened. Don't be. You'll be fine. I'm right here with you."

She looked down as he helped loosen her grip. "I…I…I'm not sure. It's so big. I had no idea. I've never sailed before, but I assumed it would be one of those smaller sailboats. Of course, I think I would be more frightened on one of them."

He laughed. "Relax," he said. "Try to enjoy it. It has been a while since we have all been out. I am glad the girls suggested it. We have always loved sailing. Come around here," he said as he directed her around to the side of the wheel where he stood. "Put your hands where mine are, so you can feel it." He slipped her between him and the wheel and then lifted her right hand showing her where to place it. She put her left hand next to his.

Holding the wheel in her hands, she knew what he was talking about. She could almost feel the power of the boat skirting across the water as the wind carried it.

Slowly he turned the wheel sending them farther out into the ocean.

Exhilaration raced through her. Her spirits soared as her back pressed against him while he showed her how to direct the boat. Meagan wasn't sure which excited her most, his nearness or the power of steering such a large vessel? Her vision swept the horizon taking in the beauty around her. Her gaze caught her mom watching and then smiling at her. She returned the smile, hoping her mother was having as much fun as she was.

They sailed for a while, but because of the wind and the thrill, time flew by. He even let go of the wheel for a while, but stood close. "This is fabulous. Where are we going?"

"Nowhere…everywhere. We're just going. But in a little while we'll head to our favorite deserted little island. We'll anchor *The Dreamer* and wade over to the island. I have a little raft to float the ice chest and some things over with us. The water is so clear usually. The girls love swimming and playing over there. We hope you and Carol enjoy it too. Helen only went once. She's not one for loving boats. She came with us for you and your mom. Otherwise, she would have chosen to stay home."

As the doctor slipped his hands back onto the wheel next to Meagan's, Jessica rushed over to them. "I want to steer now, Daddy. Can I? Please?"

He nodded to his daughter as he dropped his hold. Meagan followed suit and backed away. "We're heading to the island. We're already on course, so keep it steady. Come on, Meagan." He grabbed her by the hand and led her toward the front where Helen and Carol were seated.

When they reached them, he helped Meagan to the open seating next to her mom. "I hope you don't mind that I helped you. I didn't figure you had your sea legs yet." He laughed as he spoke. "So Carol, what do you think of her?"

Carol glanced at her daughter, but before she answered, he laughed again saying, "Not your daughter. I'm talking about *The Dreamer,* the boat. Have you sailed much?"

A grin spread over Carol's face as her eyes looked up toward the doctor. "Ryan, I couldn't have asked for a better vacation. Sure I've sailed. Growing up in California on the beach, we sailed a lot. But we had those little beach boats. Two people tops were on them gliding across the waters. But this…this is something out of a dream."

"That's what my wife said when we first got her. That's why we named her *The Dreamer.*"

"I'm loving it."

"Helen, how are you holding up? You're looking a little green around the gills, girl." He patted her shoulder. "Did you take some Dramamine before we left?"

"I'm okay, Doc. Thanks." She gave a little worried chuckle as she said to Carol, "See, he remembers the last time I came out. I told you I wasn't much of a sailor." The women laughed together.

"We'll be on the island in no time."

True to his word, they came to an area where he took back over on the controls and had the girls drop the sails.

That was something Meagan knew she would never be able to learn. Being this would be her only trip, she didn't bother to try. Let the pros do what they know how to do and she would just watch… and appreciate.

When it came time to go over the side, Meagan grew nervous. She had always had a fear of heights. It was okay as long as walls or rails and such surrounded her, but when it came time to descend she realized how high off the top of the water they were.

It didn't bother TJ or Rachelle. They jumped over the side and swam around in the water. Meagan felt her stomach flip-flop.

Her mother and Helen climbed over the ladder and eased down one step at a time. Surely, she could do that too.

As she made her way to the ladder, she couldn't make herself go over.

"What's the matter? Are you scared?" It was Jessica asking, and she seemed to enjoy Meagan's discomfort.

"No. I'll be fine. You go on. Don't worry about me."

"Like I would," she said with a deep sarcasm in her voice and a sneer on her face.

Turning away, she dropped the small raft over the side, and then calling to her father who was dropping the anchor, she said, "I'm going over. Lower the ice chest and I'll secure it."

He gave her a signal, saying he understood.

Meagan watched as Jessica slipped over the side without hesitation.

Oh how Meagan wished she could do the same. She didn't even dare look over to see if Jessica was okay. Of course she would be. Looking out toward the island, Meagan saw her mother and Helen almost there. The other two sisters were still splashing around not even trying to get near the land.

Okay, she thought. *I have to give it a try.* Taking a deep breath, she grabbed the curved handle of the ladder and gripped with all of her might. Closing her eyes, she was about to lift her leg over to the top step when she heard, "You need some help?"

Putting her foot back down, she eased her eyes open and found the doctor standing right beside her.

"Hold on a minute while I lower this ice chest and then I'll help you over the side."

She swallowed hard. Help her over the side. The thought of that scared her silly. The 'over the side' part, not him helping her.

She laughed as she realized what she was thinking. She must look like a fool to him. Why couldn't she be more like her sister, Shelly? Her sister would have dove off the side of the boat, knowing her. Nothing frightened Shelly.

The doctor turned back to Meagan and said, "You have a problem with heights, right?"

"Yes. You can tell?"

"I figured as much. Don't worry. I'll help you through it." He stepped over the side and was a couple of rungs down. "Come here. Closer."

She eased over to the side and was about to look down.

"Don't look down. Look at me. Keep your eyes on me and I will help you over and make sure your footing gets to the right step. Come on. You can do it."

He held onto her as she stepped over, never taking his eyes off her. She had to turn her head around far to keep her eyes on him, but he kept his face close so she couldn't see behind him or feel the need to look down below at her feet to help find the top step.

She was lost in the depth of those blue eyes and was thinking so much about them, she hadn't realized she was over the side until he whispered, "Okay, we're going to step down one step at a time."

By now she was facing the boat and the ladder. She couldn't see his eyes anymore, but her skin seared where his fingers touched. She closed her eyes and listened to his voice as he directed her down the ladder. He kept his hands over hers as they made it down the ladder one rung at a time. Ryan secured her hold with his hands over hers and around the handles. Suddenly, after a few steps down she felt the water on her toes. "Now, if you want, you can let go and fall back into the water with me. Ready?"

She nodded.

"Let go."

On his words, she let go and the two of them fell back into the water. He wrapped his arms around her as they went under and then he pulled them up to the surface.

"Now, swim in a little and then you'll be wading in. Are you okay?"

A small splatter of water splashed her face. She smiled at Ryan and then looked up at the boat. From down in the water, it still seemed like a far distance. Looking back at the doctor, she said, "Thanks. I've got it from here."

He smiled at her as he reached his hand out and touched the side of her face. "Great. Relax. You did it. You will make it back up too, but that is a few hours away. So don't even think about it now."

She bit her bottom lip. That thought, climbing back up, hadn't crossed her mind...not yet anyway. But now that he had mentioned it, a jolt of fear tried to overtake her. Instead she focused her thoughts on the gentleness of the doctor and how wonderful he was. They were going to have a great day today. She nodded, then turned in the water and swam toward the shore.

Chapter 25

While everyone shed their wet shorts and shirts and got down to their swimsuits, Ryan laid out a large blanket. The three girls were the first to go back out in the water to swim some more. Helen got busy with the ice chest pulling some things out. "Need any help? If not, we're going to go join the girls," Meagan said. She knew where her mother wanted to be…out in that water.

Helen waved them off as Ryan said, "I am right behind you two when I get the blanket anchored down."

Carol and Meagan went back in the water and were making their way out toward the girls. "Look, Momma. You can see the fish swimming around." She jumped as she said it, laughing. "You can feel them nibble at your legs, too."

"They won't hurt you. I promise." Lowering her voice some, Carol said, "I'm proud of you, Meagan. I know you've never liked the beach, but you are doing amazingly well for a beginner…if you know what I mean."

Inside she smiled. Yes, she was a beginner. All of this was new to her, because in the past she had always hated this environment. But things had changed. She found she loved the water and the sand…along with the fish and the sun and everything else. "I amaze myself, Mom."

"Well, I'm going to swim out deeper like the girls. If you want to join us, come on. I'll be there for you if you need any help." On that her mom turned away, dipped her head down in the water, and swam out to the deep.

The water was so clear. She watched as her mom swam making her way out farther from the land. Looking up into the heavens, she had to say, "God, this is beautiful. Thank you for giving me a whole new perspective." No sooner than those words were out of her mouth, she let out a scream as she jumped. She had felt something grab at her foot.

Turning around and looking down, thinking she would find an octopus, Ryan came up to the surface laughing. "Did I scare you?"

"Ha ha. You're funny. Yes, you scared me, but only for a second. There aren't any octopuses or sharks out here…right?"

He dove underwater and swam out a little farther. Coming up, he said, "Come on out. Nothing will bother you. I promise."

"I'm not a great swimmer. I get by…that's all."

"Give it a try." His smile was captivating. How could she refuse?

Slipping her face into the water, she kicked and paddled her way toward Ryan. When she reached him, she came up and started dog-paddling with all of her might.

"Relax. You do not have to work so hard to stay afloat. Watch."

She did. He was barely moving his hands and his legs. "How are you staying up so easily?"

"The key is to relax. Tell you what, just float on your back…like this." He lay back with ease. Ryan now looked as if he was stretched out on a bed. "See how easy," he said.

Meagan slowed her paddling down. Eventually, she was gliding her hands back and forth slowly in the water.

"Wow. It's working."

Next she tried her legs. As quick as she tensed up, she started to sink and started paddling and kicking with all of her might.

Ryan came up behind her easing her onto her back. "Relax," he said. "You will float. I promise. I am right here. I have you."

His hand lightly caressed her back as if he held her suspended on top of the water.

She quit flinging her hands around and let them float, and at the same time stopped kicking her feet. They too floated to the top.

Meagan closed her eyes and enjoyed the feeling of floating on air. "This is wonderful," she whispered. "But if you let go, I'll sink. I know it."

"Just take it easy. You are doing great. I am going to lay back and float too. I will keep my hand under your back, but I tell you, you are doing it on your own."

She smiled but doubted that very seriously. She remembered she was solid as a rock whenever she was a kid and would sink just as fast. Troy and Shelly floated everywhere, but Meagan had to fight to stay on top of the water.

"Look at the clouds. Floating…just like us."

"I see them. They make it look easy, just like you did."

"How do you like the sun on your face while the water keeps you cool? Isn't that nice?" As he was talking to her, he slipped his hand away from her back…but so slowly she hadn't noticed.

"This is heaven. I believe this is as close to paradise as we can get until we die and go to heaven. Thanks again for bringing us out here and sharing your island with us. I know Mom is having the time of her life. I say that, because I am too."

A voice in her ear whispered, "You have been on your own for a couple of minutes now, so stay relaxed. You've got it."

Ryan's voice in her ear alone almost made her jump ten feet, but because he spoke in a whisper she had stayed steady. He was right. She was floating…and she was on her own. "Momma. Look at me. I'm floating," Meagan called out not daring to look around for fear she would sink herself.

Ryan laughed. "This is a big deal to you. Isn't it?"

Before she could answer, Carol and the girls were all around them.

"I can't believe it, Meagan. You did it. How?"

Carol looked at Ryan and added, "She has never been able to float. The girl has fought the water all of her life. No one could make her believe by relaxing she could float. Meagan has always worked hard for everything in her life. She couldn't believe something could come so easily."

"Let's play tag," TJ shouted as she tapped her dad on the shoulder and added, "You're it!" And then she turned and swam away. Everyone took off, leaving Ryan by himself to react.

"Okay, guys. Look out. Here I come." He took off after the girls. He quickly caught up with Rachelle, and then she caught Carol. It went on for some time, until everyone wore themselves out.

Finally, they stopped horsing around and made their way to the shore. "Maybe after lunch and we rest a bit, we can get the snorkels out and do a little snorkeling. Ms. Carol, there is some beautiful coral farther down," TJ said as she pointed to their right.

"I'd love to go snorkeling. I haven't done that in years."

When they made it to the blanket that was spread, Helen had plates out. "Good. Are you all ready to eat? I brought sandwiches, and we had a couple of pieces of chicken left over from the other night. Also, I brought cheese and fruit, as well as cold drinks."

Meagan laid out her and her mom's towels near the blanket as each one grabbed their food, and then she took a plate and helped herself to a sandwich and some chips. "This is great, Helen, but you should have been out in the water with us. It's so clear and beautiful."

"Yeah, yeah, yeah. I know. I'm fine here on land. Not much the swimmer. I get by. That's all. Thanks anyway."

With everyone's mouth stuffed with food, very little small talk went on around the blanket. By the time bellies were full and the place cleaned up, everyone found themselves a spot and laid down.

Jessica even seemed to enjoy herself, once she got past giving Meagan a hard time. It was like the magic of the island took away her distaste for enjoying family life.

Time passed and when Meagan felt like she was about to doze off, she got up.

A walk around the island would be nice, she thought. Sleep she did not need. Grabbing the dry T-shirt out of her bag, she slipped it over her wet suit and strolled away quietly.

Everyone seemed to be taking an afternoon siesta. As she eased away, she decided to walk along the shoreline. That way, she wouldn't get lost. Meagan had no idea how big or small the island was in size.

After a couple of seconds of only the sound of the water lapping up on shore or an occasional seagull calling out, she heard, "Mind if I join you?"

She turned to find Ryan only a few feet away. "Of course not. This beauty is for all to see. I didn't want to fall asleep and miss anything. I thought I'd walk around the island or part way around it anyway. You've opened a new door in my life, and I thank you."

"It is nothing compared to what you have done in ours. I cannot begin to thank you enough for what you have done for my girls." As they walked, Ryan occasionally bent down and picked up a shell while speaking. "I wasn't too sure when I asked Techs Across America to find me a rad-tech with a few extra qualities, if I had lost my mind. With Karrie working so hard to turn Jessica into a duplicate of herself, I was at my wit's end. I knew I needed to spend more time with them. I had let my work consume me since Jennifer's death."

Meagan watched the doctor's movements...his long strides...his strength in his arms when he would toss a shell back out into the ocean...the crinkles around his eyes as he spoke with such emotion.

"I got picked. Do you know I almost turned this job down? It sounded like a glorified babysitter's job." Meagan shook her head as she spoke, "But Shelly used her brain and convinced me this was the job for me."

"Shelly. That's your sister, right?"

She nodded.

"Thank God for little sisters."

"Yes. Thank, God," she repeated his words.

"And speaking of Him...thank you for bringing my girls back into church. I was so angry with God I didn't want my girls to know any more about Him. How could someone who loves everyone do this to three young girls? Take their mom from them, I mean."

He let out a gush of air in anguish. "I was so mixed up and so angry." He stopped walking and stared into Meagan's eyes stopping her from going any farther. "I was a bad father. I thought of what I wanted or what I needed...or should I say, did not need." The pain etched across his face as a frown tilted his lips downward. "But He blessed me anyway." A smile touched Ryan's lips as he reached out and touched her cheek. "He sent me you...for the girls, I mean."

She swallowed hard. For a moment there she thought he was thinking God had sent her to him...for Ryan. How foolish could she be? She shook her head. "I know what you mean." She touched his hand that was caressing her face and then they continued walking around the island…hand in hand.

By the time they made it around the whole island, Ryan had told Meagan about the form of cancer Jennifer had died from and the steps his research lab at the hospital had taken to find a cure. One step forward and two back, he had said. It sounded like every time they had a breakthrough and thought they had the cure something else was caused from the treatment.

He knew one day, they would find it, but it was a process…slow and steady.

The thing Meagan had made him see was that it couldn't consume his life. He still had one to live with all three of his girls. So much of it he had already missed out on, but he swore to Meagan, he wasn't going to miss any more.

Meagan felt if her time there came to an end today, it was all worth it. Of course, she hoped her stay would never end. As that thought crossed her mind, she realized she had fallen deeply in love with the doctor. Not long ago she had acknowledged she was falling in love…but it was done now. Head over heels, no turning back, in love. She knew she loved the girls, but this was so much more. Was it right for her to love him this way? Should she fight it? Or just see what happens?

It didn't matter at the moment, for the girls and her mom were out snorkeling. Helen was sitting on a rock with her feet propped on a smaller one watching the girls from a distance. "So what did you think of the island, Meagan?" she asked.

"It is beautiful. I love it. Glad I got to see it."

"The girls are having fun with your mom. She will do just about anything, won't she?"

Meagan laughed. A flashback to when she was a kid, she could see her mom in the midst of all the fun and games. "Just about. My mom has the courage of a lion and shows no fear in anything…that I can recall."

"Like mother like daughter."

"Yeah. Shelly. Not me. Remember my fear of heights?"

He looked out at the boat and back at Meagan. Smiling, a pleased look crossed his face as he nodded and said, "I sure do. And it is almost time to climb back up."

Meagan felt a quick panic rise in her chest as she took in his warm smile. She would be all right. Ryan was there to see her through this. The fear slipped away. A quirky smile touched her lips as she said, "I'm going to get wet one more time before we leave. Helen, are you sure you don't want to wade out in the water with me?"

The housekeeper shook her head. "I'm fine right where I am."

As Meagan pulled the T-shirt off and stuffed it back in the bag, Ryan slipped over to her, swooped her up in his arms, and ran toward the water. "This will get you wet," he said as he tossed her in the air out into the ocean.

She laughed so hard as she was coming down; she got a mouth full of salty water. On top of that, as she tried to stand up on her own two feet, a wave rolled in and knocked her back down. Ryan and Helen were laughing too, so much so that neither tried to help her up as she choked and sputtered her way back on her feet again.

The afternoon was a success. Everyone had a blast…even Jessica. This was the first time Meagan had seen her laugh and not try to cover it up. It was great. Even the climb up the ladder back into the boat held a victory for Meagan. This would be a day to put down in a journal…if she kept one…so she could remember it forever. Meagan doubted she would have a hard time remembering though. So far, this had been the best day of her life.

Back at the mansion, after everyone had showered and changed, Ryan took them out to dinner one more time…even though Carol tried to talk him out of it. "I insist," he said. "You are leaving tomorrow. If you do not mind all of us crashing in on your last night together, we could make a night of it. Maybe even go see a movie, if you would like."

"How about we rent one and watch it on your TV in the family room? That's almost as big as a movie screen," Carol said with laughter in her voice. "I would be honored to spend my last night with you and your family. Everyone has made me feel right at home from the beginning and I thank you."

So they went to the pizza parlor near them, and then stopped at Redbox and rented a movie. Meagan didn't care what they got. She was just so thrilled to have this time to remember. To go with their outing today, the movie they picked was *Captain Ron.* Perfect.

Halfway through the movie, Helen popped some popcorn, and Meagan helped pass out bowls of it. She gave each of the girls their bowls. All three thanked her as she handed it to them.

To Meagan's delight, Jessica stayed with the family the whole time. Not one complaint came out of her mouth and she was a pleasure to be around.

As Captain Ron took off with yet another new boss in a boat out into the ocean and the movie came to an end, Carol said, "I hate to have fun and run, but I need to go pack my suitcase."

"After I help clean up, Mom, I'll come help you."

"The girls can help Helen. Carol, it has been a delight having you with us and I hope you come again soon. Maybe bring your husband next time. We have plenty of rooms." He was about to shake her hand, but she reached out and hugged him.

"It's been my pleasure. I've loved it. And girls, thank you for keeping me company all week. It's been fun."

TJ and Rachelle giggled, as they said. "We loved it, too," in unison. Then they grabbed a couple of bowls and their drinking glasses and caught up with Jessica heading toward the kitchen.

"Helen, your food was wonderful and so was your company. Thank you. If you ever come down my way, look me up." Helen hugged Carol and then grabbed the last of the bowls and empty glasses heading out to the kitchen.

As Carol and Meagan started to leave in the direction of Meagan's apartment, Ryan said, "Meagan. I know you are going to help your mom, but do you have a minute you could spare first?"

She glanced at her mom. Carol smiled an understanding smile. She said bye as she went on ahead.

Ryan moved over toward Meagan and said, "I just wanted to say how much I enjoyed today. And I hope we have more of them... even though your mom will not still be here. What I mean is I hope you and the girls and I can do more...while you are here."

Meagan felt herself blush. She would love to do more. They would be like a family. Is that what he was thinking? She shook those thoughts out of her head...Of course not.

"What? Are you saying no, you wouldn't want to spend time with us...I mean, if I am with them, you won't spend time with them."

She looked up into his eyes. He had moved directly in front of her. "I wasn't saying no. I can't explain. But yes. I would love to have more outings like today. Like I told you earlier, this was the best day of my life."

The doctor reached out and touched her chin. Lifting her face toward his, his gaze touched her lips. Her heart pounded as she started chewing her bottom lip.

"You do that every time I make you nervous. Please don't. I want to kiss you…if that is okay with you."

His fingertips were still under her chin. His warmth drew her to him.

She wanted the kiss. Oh how she wanted him to kiss her! As she started to nod, she heard a noise near the doorway. He dropped his hand and backed away.

"Daddy, I was going to say I had fun today…but I think I've changed my mind." On those words Jessica turned and flew out of the room.

What have we done?

Ryan turned back to Meagan. "I'm sorry," he said. A moment of silence hung in the air as his eyes held hers. "I see the moment is gone. But mark my words…it will be back," Ryan whispered. The corner of his lips rose slightly.

Meagan shrugged her shoulders and said, "Sorry. Today was great though. Thanks again." She too left the room and headed for her apartment. This was a day of mixed emotions. Something she needed to think long and hard on. Was this part of why she was here? Or had she gone too far?

Chapter 26

Meagan missed church with the family today, because she took her mom to catch the 10AM flight. She decided she needed some alone time. When lunchtime came TJ, Rachelle, and Ryan caught Meagan up on the message she had missed. Afterwards, she let them all know she'd be making an early night of it; eat light from her own kitchen and then an early shower. She needed some rest before returning to work the next day. The truth was she didn't think she could take the chance of being alone with Ryan, the time they usually shared after dinner. She knew her heart wanted to be with him, but she doubted he truly felt the same way.

That evening as the sun set she showered and slipped on her nightshirt before calling Shelly. "Mom's on her way home now. In fact, she should be landing in less than an hour. Are you picking her up at the airport?" Meagan asked as she slipped down on the loveseat with one foot under her. This was the best spot in her apartment. Over her short time there she had learned to love the view of the ocean. Meagan remembered her first day there thinking how much her mom would love it, and now it was her favorite spot to curl up in at night. The moon reflected across the water like a sprinkle of diamonds. They glistened as the waves rolled to shore. The view took her breath away night after night. She wondered how she never saw the beauty before with every summer spent with the family at some beach resort, but she saw it now loving every glimpse she was given.

"Dad's meeting her plane. So did she have fun? Mom didn't call the whole time she was there, so I'm figuring you kept her pretty busy. What all did you do?" The excitement in her sister's voice never surprised Meagan. The energy her sister abounded in was an everyday occurrence.

"I'll let Mom give you the details. She did a lot without me. TJ and Rachelle kept her pretty busy. There is something I'd like to get your take on...I mean opinion...ah, advice on."

"Spit it out, girl. What is it?"

Taking in a deep breath and then releasing it slowly she paused before speaking. Her heart raced. She wanted to tell her everything, but there really wasn't that much to tell...or was there? "Okay. Yesterday we had a wonderful day. We went out on their sailboat. Ryan told me it is a Formosa ketch. It is beautiful...big and beautiful. Mom had the time of her life. We sailed to an island that they apparently go to occasionally." *Get to the point,* she told herself, but procrastinated.

"It sounds great. So why do you sound like there is a problem? I don't get it?"

"Mom told me to take it one day at a time. Not to rush—"

"Take what one day at a time?" Shelly interrupted, sounding confused. "What are you talking about?"

"Oh, Shelly. Ryan almost kissed me. I don't know what's going on anymore. I know I'm here to help the girls. I've been here for them. TJ and Rachelle have connected with the Lord, with me, with their family, and with life. You know what I mean? And yesterday Jessica actually seemed like she was enjoying being with her family, Mom, Helen and me for the first time. But then after everyone had gone their way, Ryan asked me to stay a minute so we could talk. And in that short time, he sounded like he was glad I was there. He moved closer to me as he talked and before you know it…" Meagan stopped in mid-sentence recalling the moment. Her insides melted at just the memory.

"Come on, Meagan. Don't keep me in suspense!"

"I'm getting there. Anyway, he moved in close. Touched my face. He was looking down into my eyes and he was about to kiss me and Jessica walked back in the room. He backed away quickly. Maybe he had second thoughts of the way his mind was working at the moment. Maybe it was a good thing Jessica blasted in there and broke it up before it began."

"Don't be silly," her sister interjected. "So what happened? Did she stay and you left? Did her dad throw her out of the room? What? Tell me."

Meagan rested her chin on her arm that was stretched across the back of the loveseat and gazed up at the moon. "He told me we lost the moment, but it would come again."

"Oh! Wow! That's great! It sounds great anyway. So what are you confused about?"

"Mom saw it in my eyes when I came back to my apartment last night. She even said she had seen the way Ryan looked at me throughout the day. But she also said to take it slow and make sure this is what God has planned for me." Meagan turned slightly and laid her head back against the sofa with her eyes now looking at the ceiling. "I don't know what to do."

"You don't have to do anything, sister dear. Just do what Mom said and take it slow. Let the Lord lead you. If he is the one for you, it will happen. You'll know. Do say a prayer and then listen. It's what you've done all your life. Don't make it sound so hard."

Closing her eyes, she smiled. "You're right. I don't know why I'm acting so foolishly."

"You're not acting foolish. This is new to you. You've never been in love…well not never. I remember you loved Daniel. You loved him so much; you set him free, if you know what I mean. You encouraged him to do the right thing and that's because you let God lead you there. That was true love, but the timing was wrong. Maybe this will be your turn. Maybe this is what God has planned for you. Just live it out and listen to your Spirit-man."

Sitting up and then rising to her feet, she said, "I will. It's not difficult. It's one day at a time. Thanks, Shel. And when you talk to Mom, let her tell you. Don't let her know I called for advice. Okay?"

"Yeah. No problem. Love ya. Take care, Meagan…and keep in touch!"

"Will do. Love you too. Kiss the kids for me. Night." She closed her cell phone ending the conversation.

As much as she wanted to go right to sleep after her shower, she couldn't. Her mind relived those few moments in time, just as it did the night before. "But tomorrow, I have to go to work," she told herself. She tried forcing her mind to shut down, and then she tried counting sheep. Nothing helped. Finally, she got up, grabbed her Bible, and read scripture. She still wasn't sleepy, so she pulled out the latest mystery she was reading, another Dee Henderson novel. How she thought that would help her sleep, she had no idea. Once she started reading, usually she had to force herself to put it down or she would read all night long…but this time her eyes grew so heavy she had to stop in the middle of a chapter. That was surprising, but sleep came quickly.

The next day at work went well. She didn't run into Ryan, but of course Cat wanted all the details of the sailing trip. Meagan had told her Friday that they would be going out on the Richardson's boat. If her eyes weren't already green, Meagan would have sworn Cat was a little bit jealous. But Meagan did remind her; she was only working with the girls, helping them find their way. The doctor wasn't interested in Meagan…he was just part of the family.

Work passed, but then evening came. She played tennis with TJ as they did almost daily before her mom came to visit. Although TJ won every game, Meagan was improving with time.

"Before you know it, you're going to beat me," TJ said as they were walking back up to the house.

"Funny. Very funny. But you have to admit, I've gotten better."

"That's what I mean. You had me worried in that last game. I almost missed the last two returns. If I had, you would have won that game." TJ bumped Meagan with her shoulder, causing her to lose her step, and then took off running for the door. "I'll beat you."

Laughing, Meagan straightened her step and took off after her. "Of course. You cheated!" she shouted out loud between her laughter. As hard as she tried to catch up, she couldn't. TJ hit the door, and Meagan took three more strides to catch her.

"Too bad. I won." The smirk on TJ's face was full of fun. "Maybe one day you'll beat me there too. Ha-ha. I doubt it." The young girl was full of spunk today. "I'll get us a couple of waters while you rest your weary bones."

As she laughed and ran out toward the kitchen, Meagan collapsed on the floor in the den and lay stretched out on the carpet. "Young people will be the death of me yet." She laughed to herself as she breathed a deep sigh and closed her eyes, resting her weary bones as TJ so eloquently put it.

"I hope not."

Quickly, she sat up. Ryan was standing near her looking down.

"I heard the pounding of TJ's feet run through so I hoped you'd be close behind. Hope you don't mind." The doctor's warm blue eyes held steady on Meagan as he spoke.

"Hi." She rose to her feet, feeling a little out of breath. "You're home early."

He smiled. "Yes, I am."

"I mean, I'm just not used to seeing you already here when we come in from playing tennis."

"So you play every day?"

"Hey, Daddy. Is Meagan telling you how I beat her in tennis and then in a race to the house?" As she walked in, she brought a bottle of water to Meagan. "Here you go. I hope you've gotten your wind by now."

Meagan shook her finger at TJ as she couldn't stop the grin from spreading across her face. "You keep this up, and I am going to beat you! Out of spite, I might add! You're getting a little too cocky, if you know what I mean."

"Check this out, Daddy. I beat the girl every day. She's improved, I admit…but beat me? Hah. I doubt it."

Looking back at Meagan, she added, "But you keep on believing it and one day, it just might happen. What's that they say, miracles do happen now and then?" She lifted her water bottle as if in a toast to Meagan and then guzzled it down. "I'm going to go shower. I'll catch you at dinner. Bye, Daddy. See ya later."

Meagan sipped some of her water, knowing she should exit the room herself, but the doctor was in between her and the door.

"You enjoy Tamara, don't you?"

"You know I do. She's a sweetheart. And she's taught me a lot in tennis. I know I could never beat her, though."

"Or like she said," he said with amusement in his voice, "a miracle could happen."

She laughed.

"Have you thought any more about what I said the other night?"

His question surprised her. Of course she'd thought about it. Over and over again, she had thought about it. But she couldn't tell him that. She didn't want to sound desperate or needy. Meagan couldn't think of how to answer his question, so she started guzzling her water.

Something, anything to do but answer Ryan.

He stepped closer to her and in a soft voice he said, "That is okay. You don't have to answer. I can see it in your face. You have thought about it."

His voice grew softer as he said, "For the record, so have I. It is all I can think about. I don't know if that will help you or scare you right out of here, but I had to tell you." His lips turned up forming a crooked smile before saying, "I will see you at the dinner table." His eyes sparkled as his gaze held hers for a few seconds longer, and then he turned and left the room.

A gush of air rushed out of her as she slammed the bottle down on the end table. It was as if she had held her breath while he was talking, the air passed so quickly.

Was she that afraid to speak? Why? The doctor was a wonderful man. Meagan was attracted to him, but she wasn't sure if she should be. Their lives were worlds apart. Not that she was ever one to feel one person was better than another, but she had to be truthful…at least to herself. He was a doctor. She worked for him. He was a boss…a big man on campus so to speak. He was rolling in the dough, while she did well for herself. He was several years older than she was. What would she tell someone else who came to her asking advice?

This gave her pause to think. What would she say? She would say, *Don't look at the differences. See if the attraction was deeper than surface feelings. Pray. Ask for divine direction. And then follow God's direction.*

She was praying all right…every minute of every day…at least for the last couple of days. And so far, the only thing she had received was nothing. Was she not getting through? You can't hurry God…or was that you can't hurry love? Both, she told herself as she left to go shower.

At the dinner table, as usual everyone was talking except Jessica. She only watched.

Meagan felt those daggers flying her way but decided to ignore them. She had done nothing to the girl, and deep inside, she still wanted to help her find peace.

That would take time and patience. She had both, so she would wait it out and be ready when the time was right.

When the meal was over and everyone was about to go their separate ways, Ryan said, "Just want you all to know, we're going to go out on the boat again Saturday. So be prepared. And if you want to bring a friend, you can. One each."

"All right!" TJ shouted as she was walking out the door.

Rachelle was on the heels of TJ and said, "Great. I'll ask Stan."

Jessica, pulling up the rear, said nothing. Instead, she rolled her eyes as she walked out of the room making sure her father knew she was not interested in being a part of this so-called family outing.

He shook his head but looked determined not to let his daughter get him down.

Turning his attention on Meagan he said, "You don't mind, do you? I know you have a hard time with the heights, but you did well Saturday. Maybe, if we do it enough, you'll overcome your fear."

How right he was, she thought. Every day Meagan found her likes and dislikes flip-flopping. It amazed her.

TJ started it when she helped Meagan find a love for the beach. Since then, anything was possible. "I think it sounds wonderful. I'll be ready. Since I've come here, I have a new love."

The doctor looked at Meagan, his eyes opened wide as his face showed a mixture of shock and curiosity.

Chuckling, she smiled, raised her hands pointing toward the beach and explained. "The ocean...I love it. My whole life I've turned from it. But since I've come here, I find I don't mind the sand in my shoes or in my swimsuit. I don't even mind the heat of the sand and sun. Sunburns don't bother me anymore, now that I have your special lotion."

Ryan looked pleased. "Great. I'm glad. I admit living near the beach has a few drawbacks, but not many."

Her brow crinkled as she wondered what could possibly be a drawback about living near the beach.

A few weeks ago she could have rattled off at least ten reasons not wanting to live near the beach...but now, not one crossed her mind.

She didn't dare ask. Meagan didn't want to know. She liked her new love for the ocean.

Ryan told her anyway. "Hurricanes. The weather sometimes can be pretty destructive. In the years we've lived here, we've received some damage, but nothing we couldn't fix." Changing the subject, he said, "Would you join me in the study for some coffee? We could talk some more. Things have changed a lot in the past week around here, and I would love to talk to you about some of it."

"Sure." She said this so casually to him but inside she screamed to herself, *Are you nuts? You're asking for trouble and more questions and more confusion!*

Was she crazy? Her heart was pulling her toward the doctor, but her mind fought it all the way. The sensible thing would be to pass on quality time with the doctor. Go back to her apartment. Leave the family alone.

Today she let her heart win as she reminded herself, *One day at a time.*

Chapter 27

The rest of the week went by just like Monday. Ryan and Meagan set a new pattern of coffee and small talk in the study every evening. Usually they only spent a half hour in there and then joined the two girls in the den or the music room, whichever the girls found themselves drawn to.

Each night was pleasant, although Jessica would never be a part of their evenings. Sometimes at the dinner table, though, Jessica's eyes seemed to want to be a part of the family talk and laughter, but as quickly as Meagan would see the look, Jessica would see Meagan and the girl's eyes would ice over. This left Meagan wondering if she imagined the desire in Jessica's eyes because that was what she wanted the girl to feel.

TJ and Rachelle seemed to enjoy the family time a lot, not minding Meagan being a part of it at all. In fact, they appeared to like the addition of Meagan and seemed to look forward to it, expecting the time together.

Friday night came. Ryan told them that morning he would be doing a little extra work at the hospital so he could have the whole weekend without having to think about things undone. He said he'd grab a bite to eat from the hospital cafeteria. Helen was called to her sister's, who had injured her hip and couldn't get around on crutches well yet. Helen knew her sister needed her, even though Barbara wouldn't admit it. Meagan assured both Ryan and Helen that she and the girls would be fine. With the rain, they decided to stay in and order pizza. TJ and Rachelle wanted to watch movies tonight. Maybe they could even entice Jessica to join them. Meagan agreed.

After the pizza was ordered, Meagan and the two girls were rummaging through the movies, picking out the ones they would watch throughout the night.

Jessica dropped down on the couch and watched them.

"Why don't you pick out one of the movies?" Meagan said.

She sighed. Rolling her eyes, she said, "I won't be here that long. After the pizza comes, I'm going to eat and then scram. I have friends to see, things to do."

"Oh. Okay." Meagan turned her back on the young girl and continued glancing through the movies with TJ and Rachelle. They agreed three should get them through the night…if they could stay awake that long.

The doorbell rang and Meagan went to answer it. The pizza had arrived.

When she opened the door to pay the man and grab the food, the wind shoved the door open causing Meagan to lose her grip. The door slammed against the wall.

"My goodness! What is going on out here?" she asked the delivery boy as she staggered slightly and reached for the doorjamb to hold her steady.

"The storm is kicking," he said as he stepped in out of the rain.

Holding on with one hand, she dug the money out of her jeans pocket and paid him. "Keep the change," she said.

Glancing down at the money, his eyes grew wide. "Thanks. It

was worth bringing it to you in this storm. You were my last delivery. We shut down. You better close up tight. They say Tropical Storm Harriet may turn into a full-fledged hurricane before the night is through. You all aren't watching the weather on TV? Man. I thought everyone was tuned in to it or at least listening to their radio about it."

He waved his hand as if saying bye as he turned and ran back to his car. The wind and rain whipped across his body plastering his clothes and hair against him as he climbed into his pickup truck.

With pizza in one hand, she grabbed the door with the other and pushed it closed.

The wind wasn't as bad as it had been a few moments ago, but it was still pushing pretty hard. "Come and get it," she called out as she passed the opening to the den on her way to the dining room table. Earlier she had laid out the paper plates and napkins. "I'll get the sodas out of the fridge and y'all serve yourselves," she said to the girls as they all came in one after the other. While she was in the kitchen, she searched for a flashlight in the utility drawer. They needed to be prepared.

"What was that guy saying about a storm?" Jessica asked as she popped her head in the kitchen. "I'll take a coke. I'll get my own," she said as she opened the refrigerator door and grabbed a red can.

"Grab two. TJ will want the same," Meagan said glancing up from the drawer. "You might want to turn on the radio in the music room and turn it up where we can hear it. He said there is a storm brewing out in the ocean and it may become a hurricane."

"I'll take care of it." Jessica snatched a second drink and ran out as fast as she had come in.

Once Meagan found a flashlight, she grabbed two more sodas from the fridge and walked back into the dinning room. She stuck the light in her back pocket and held the drinks in each hand. Of course, she had to take the flashlight out of her pocket to sit down, but that wasn't a problem. She would keep it close by the rest of the night…just in case.

Jessica walked over to the speaker on the wall near the door. "We can turn it on here. I'll get it." She flipped a button that turned on the radio throughout the house, turned the dial setting the station, and then joined the others at the table. The box with the pizza in it was pushed up and down the table while everyone grabbed a slice or two.

By the time all had a couple of slices of pizza each, the weather man came on the station warning everyone who didn't need to get out in this weather to stay in.

Meagan watched the wide-eyed expression on Jessica's face slowly turn into downcast eyes and a frown on her lips. The girl didn't want to spend a whole evening at home with her sisters and Meagan…especially Meagan…but it looked like she was wise enough to know not to go out this evening…at least not right away.

"Sounds like I'm gonna be stuck with you guys for a while. What movies did you pick?" Jessica asked sounding disappointed but not totally angry over the situation.

That was a good sign, Meagan thought. Maybe this would be the night they could help her turn that corner.

TJ and Rachelle both responded with pleasure, spouting out the movies they had chosen. The three sisters, although different in age, did love one another deeply and seemed to get along better than a lot of brothers and sisters Meagan had known over the years. She was glad.

Jessica made a face at the names of the movies they had picked.

"I know which one picked the sad romance, Rachelle, and which one picked the action/adventure, TJ. You guys never change. Couldn't just once you guys have picked a sweet romance or a comedy? Never mind. I'm sure I won't stay but for one if the storm passes. If not, I'll go to my room and find something better to do."

"We said we would each pick one out, so Jessica, feel free to choose one," Meagan said. She was supposed to, but truly she didn't care which movie they watched. Meagan was glad at the aspect of Jessica joining the group.

"We'll see."

The mouths were stuffed as everyone consumed the pizza and listened to the weatherman talk.

When they were about through, Meagan said, "I think before we settle down with the movie, to be on the safe side, let's get some candles out. One flashlight won't be enough light if the power goes off."

"The light might go off?" TJ asked.

"Don't worry," Rachelle whispered.

"I'll check the water supply. I know Helen buys water by the bottle, and those by the case. So I'm pretty sure we'll be fine there. We can fill the tubs up with water too. I don't know how hurricanes do over here, but I know what happens down in southern Louisiana. You remember Hurricanes Katrina and Rita for that matter?"

"We heard. I remember. My homeroom class collected a lot of things to send down to New Orleans and the Gulf Coast area. It was sad...some of the stories we heard," Rachelle said.

"This one does not sound as if it would be as bad, but don't you think one of y'all should call your dad and make sure he's heard the weather warnings? You know how he gets when he's doing research," Meagan said. "I'll clean up our mess and set a stack of the water bottles out."

"I'll call Daddy," TJ said scraping her chair on the floor as she rose to her feet.

"Jessica and I can get the candles and the lighter," Rachelle offered.

"Great."

Everyone took off as Meagan picked up the paper plates and tossed them into the empty pizza box. After closing the box, she stacked the empty drink cans on top and carried everything into the kitchen. Dropping the cans in the sink to rinse out for the recycle bin and folding the box in half and tossing it into the garbage, she said, "That was an easy clean up if I ever saw one." She laughed to herself as she stepped back over to the sink and started rinsing out the cans.

It didn't take her long to finish that and find the available water bottles, in case they were needed. She also checked the cupboard and refrigerator for snacks during the movie.

As a kid, if the power went out, they would play games and eat junk food…like dip with chips and ice cream…so it wouldn't go bad. Besides, she knew the girls would be hollering for a treat. TJ would if no one else did.

Everyone gathered in the family room and found their place on the various sofas. Rachelle grabbed her movie first. While she was putting it in, Meagan asked, "TJ, did you get a hold of your dad?"

"No. But I left a message on his machine. He'll get it eventually. Like you said, once he gets caught up in his research, he kind of forgets everything else."

Meagan felt a flush to her cheeks as she remembered similar words spoken not too long ago. "He'll be all right. Let's watch the movie."

Rachelle pressed play and TJ turned off all but one light and then everyone settled once again in the place of their choosing. The movie was a love story. It was actually very good…but deep. *Catch and Release* was the title and of course it was one Meagan had never seen before. It was a little over halfway through when she saw lightning streaking across the sky behind the sheer curtains and then heard and felt the thunder shake the house almost immediately. TJ let out a yelp as Meagan felt herself jump a little. They were all so engrossed in the movie no one seemed to notice the weather had worsened outside.

That was so close. Rising to her feet, Meagan got up. "I'll be right back."

First, she stopped in the dining room, turned the sound of the radio back up and listened for a moment to the DJ. He was calling Harriet a hurricane now. Apparently it had been upgraded.

Next, she went toward the front of the house and peeked out of the side glass windows near the front door. The palm trees out front were practically bending over in half. The wind was massive. Litter bounced down the street and swooped up in the air and swirled around some before falling back to the ground. The weather was aggressively getting worse. The hurricane may even be a category three or four by now.

As she turned heading back to the den, there was another crackling sound and the house went black. The light TJ had left turned on went out, and the light in the entryway went dark at the same time. The one time she didn't have the flashlight right next to her! Of course.

"Meagan!" TJ screamed from the other room.

"I'm coming. I'm coming," she said as she made her way back to the den. "I'm right here. Y'all hold on. It'll be okay. We're going to move to the music room. There are no windows in that room. It will be safer." After finding her way back to the place she was sitting, she felt around and found the flashlight. Turning it on she said, "Where did y'all put the candles?"

"On the table in the entryway," Jessica said. Huddling close to one another, the four of them followed the beam of light into the entryway and each grabbed a couple of candles and the holders. Jessica picked up the lighter.

By the time they made it to the music room, set up candles, and lit them, it sounded like the storm had settled some. But it was only their location that made it seem that way. "Do any of you have a battery radio? I know those are kind of outdated with iPods and such, but it would sure come in handy right now."

"Dad has one," Jessica said. "If I could take the flashlight, I could go get it out of his study. I know where he keeps it."

"Good idea." Meagan handed her the flashlight.

Jessica returned minutes later rushing into the room, almost as if she were being chased. The young girl appeared to have been a little afraid in the other part of the house without anyone with her. But as grown up as she was, Meagan felt sure she would not admit it. "Honey, find a station that's a lot of talk, like the one you had put it on earlier in the dining room. We'll keep it on in the background, but we're not going to focus on it. Have y'all ever had a hurricane party?"

Jessica pursed her lips and narrowed her eyes as she asked, "A hurricane party?"

"That's what we're going to have. We'll play games and there are some snacks when we get hungry. We'll stay together in this room. If it gets late, we'll grab blankets and sleep in here if necessary. But we'll stay together and stay safe. Does that sound good to y'all?"

TJ squealed with delight, as Rachelle said, "Sounds good to me."

Jessica shrugged her shoulders and said, "Whatever. Like what kind of games can you play without a computer? And no electricity…you can't do much without electricity to turn something on."

"Have you ever heard of charades? That can pass some time. There are other games too, like Twenty Questions, and You Don't Say. These are games my mom and dad used to play with us when we'd lost electricity. It helped pass the time and kept our minds off what was going on outside. There is nothing we can do about it, but ride it out by staying safely indoors."

The next couple of hours flew by. Charades had been a hit, but after a couple of rounds everyone was ready for some snacks. TJ went with Meagan to grab some chips and dip, some water bottles, and a big bag of M&Ms. During Twenty Questions, they laughed and ate and laughed some more. It got very late and they found out the storm had been upgraded to a category three as she had thought earlier, so Meagan got Jessica to help her grab some blankets and pillows from upstairs, letting Jessica lead the way.

When everyone had found their spot to cozy down for the night, they started the game of You Don't Say, after Meagan explained the gist of the game.

During it, TJ nodded off and Rachelle said she was pretty tired and would like to rest her eyes for a minute or two. That meant she was right behind TJ in falling asleep.

It got quiet in the room with only Jessica and Meagan still wide-awake. "I'm glad you decided to stay in. I would hate it if you'd gone out and then this had turned into a hurricane. There is no telling where you would have been stranded. You showed good sense."

"I'm not an idiot," Jessica snapped.

"I didn't think you were. I just wanted to tell you that was a wise choice you made." Meagan had meant to uplift the girl not berate her.

"Whatever," she said quietly, and then added, "I wish Dad was here."

"Me too." Meagan didn't dare tell her she was a little worried about him and had been for some time.

The hospital had back-up generators and such. If he stayed there she knew he would be fine.

Meagan worried because she thought he might feel it necessary to jump in his car and rush home to protect his girls as soon as he realized there was a hurricane stirring. She was surprised he hadn't called.

The hospital was a little farther inland, so they may not have lost electricity and gone to back-up power. He may not have even realized the situation they were in. That was a good thing, in a way, she thought.

"I'm going to try and call him again. Can I have the flashlight back?"

"Sure." She handed the light to Jessica so she could go find a phone and call. There was no phone in the music room. Jessica came back within a minute. That surprised Meagan. It should have taken a little longer. "Did you get him?" she asked as the girl handed the flashlight back to Meagan.

"The line is dead."

Meagan could go get her cell, but that was back in her apartment.

She probably should. Her mom and Shelly had both probably

tried to call to make sure she was okay.

But it was a distance, and she didn't want to leave the girls in case they woke up in the dark.

She would call her family in the morning and let them know everything was fine. They would have to lean on their faith tonight. She felt sure her family would do just that.

"My phone is upstairs or I would just call him on my cell."

"Why don't you just settle back down? Your dad is a smart man. He'll know we're okay. Besides, TJ left him a message. If he hears that, for sure, he'll know we are going to do just fine."

"You're right." She settled back down on the sofa she had picked and pulled her blanket up to her chin. "Thanks," she whispered.

"No problem. If you're sleepy go ahead and take a nap. I'll keep watch of the candles. If the lights come back on, I'll blow them out. Or if you're not sleepy and feel like talking, talk to me. Tell me what your plans are? Like college and such?"

Meagan watched as Jessica twisted around in her blanket and then settled. As she did so, she actually started sharing her thoughts with Meagan.

"I'm not really sure what I want to do with myself. I know I want to go to college, but I have no idea what I want to be."

"Don't worry. A lot of people start college with no idea what they want to be. Do you know which college you want to attend?"

"I know I don't want anything to do with medicine. So I'm not going to the university where Dad went. I'm not musically inclined like Rachelle. When it comes to athletics, I'm a bust. TJ got the sports quota for the whole family. I have two left feet, if you know what I mean."

Meagan laughed. "I know exactly what you mean."

"Did you always plan to be an x-ray tech?"

A smile touched Meagan's lips as she recalled her college career.

"No indeed. I wanted to be a singer. In fact, I wanted to be Amy Grant's back-up singer. I never was one for the spotlight. My dream was to get a college education as a teacher. Move to Nashville teaching fulltime until I could get a gig as a back-up singer for someone, and then one day become one for Amy Grant. She was my idol. I loved contemporary Christian music as a young girl. Michael W. Smith. I don't even know if you know who I'm talking about, but they were my two favorites."

"So how in the world did you get into medicine if you were studying to be a teacher?"

She sighed. "I let my emotions or feelings cause me to drop out for about two years after I had three and half years under my belt. I was so close, but something a teacher said made me drop out. My mom told me not to worry. That everything happens for a reason. And shortly after that they had the Columbine High School massacre in Colorado. Innocent students and teachers died. That was when my mother said, 'God knew what He was doing getting you out of that field.'"

"Wow." Jessica really sounded sincere.

"Then I didn't know what I wanted to do. I was working for my aunt and uncle…had been all through high school and during summer vacations from college. So I had a good job, and I had time to think it through. I prayed about it and then one day God showed me what I was meant to do. And the rest is history…as they say."

"So I'm not so unusual, not knowing what I want to do?"

"No, sweetheart. You're not."

"Thanks," Jessica said softly. A wide yawn followed her word of appreciation. "I think I'll rest my eyes a bit now too."

"Good night."

Meagan didn't lie down because she didn't want to fall asleep with candles burning. She did, however, look around the room and saw a little light glowing a foot from each of the girls. They all seemed at peace with the world.

"Thank you, Lord." She knew, just like her mom had said many times before, everything happened for a reason. That storm turned into a hurricane, not by chance, and all at the right time…for a specific reason. Look at the connection that was made tonight. Jessica opened up to Meagan. She even appreciated the words Meagan had shared with her. What a headway!

Now if she only knew how Ryan was weathering the storm.

Chapter 28

Ryan was alone in the lab looking at results through the lens of his microscope. As he stared into the light, the room darkened around him. Glancing at his watch, he saw the time. "I told them I would be late. I'm sure they are doing fine without me."

The door to the lab swung open and Clark, his assistant, walked in. "Dr. Richardson. The storm has turned into a hurricane. I need to get home to my family before the bridge closes down."

"Is it that bad outside?"

"The island has reports of power outages. My wife is six months pregnant, and she called three times already for me to come home. I've finished inputting the results of the test we ran this afternoon. Saved it. Made a hard copy and filed it, so I'm calling it a day. You ought not stay too late yourself. You'll get trapped here."

He nodded. "No problem, Clark. Be on your way. I'll shut things down in here and put everything up before I take off. I need to make sure we are down to a skeleton crew working and that the generator is in working order before I take off. Thanks for your dedication."

As Clark walked out the door, Ryan's mind was on his girls and Meagan. He hoped they were okay. Maybe he should call them. After putting up the samples and putting things away in the lab, he went to his office to phone home. There he found the light flashing. "It is probably the girls. By now, I am sure they have called me a couple of times."

His mind thought this was exactly the thing Meagan was trying to help him see. He needed to pay more attention to life around him and his girls. Pressing the button to play the messages he said, "I probably lost the few points I might have made with Meagan this past week." He shrugged and sighed.

When he heard Tamara's voice on the machine calling to say they were okay…that Meagan had already made plans to keep them safe, his thoughts of winning or losing points with Meagan immediately flew right out of his head. Since that message was left, things had worsened. His stomach knotted as he feared for his girls…all four of them. "I need to get home."

He picked up the receiver and punched out his home phone number. In his ear he heard, "All circuits are busy. Try your call later." He tried two more times getting the same result so finally he hung up the phone. He wouldn't be able to check on them before he headed home. He would have to see them in person.

Shutting his office door, Ryan rushed to the elevator and took it down to the ground floor. Thomas was still there. "How are things?" Ryan asked.

"I've sent the majority home to be with their families. Everything is under control. Maintenance said the back-up generator is in good working order. We'll be able to ride this hurricane out fine, Dr. Richardson," Thomas said.

"Okay, Thomas. Since you have everything under control here, I am going to try and get across the bridge and get home to my family. You are in charge here. If anything happens, call me on my cell, or page me. You have the numbers. I will come right back, but, as I said, it sounds like you have got it all under control. Thanks." He kept his cell phone in his car, but his pager was in his pocket. He need only remember to take his cell in with him when he got home.

On those words, Ryan left the hospital to rush home. He hoped he found everyone and everything in good shape. It was pitch dark outside and the rain was coming down in buckets. He was drenched by the time he made it to his car. Starting the engine, he eased out of the parking spot and headed toward home. He didn't live far, but there was a bridge to cross.

Barricades were being put across the bridge entrance as he was approaching. Pressing a button to lower his window, he eased up to the worker. "I have to get across. My girls are at home and need me with them."

"I'm sorry, sir. We can't let anyone go onto the island. Only those leaving can cross the bridge and as the hurricane gets closer we'll even stop that. It's for safety." The wind pushed hard against the man as he explained to Ryan why he couldn't cross.

He had to get home. Ryan couldn't let this man keep him from getting to them. He should have gone home earlier. He should have been paying attention to the weather.

Ryan knew there had been a storm out in the Atlantic that morning. "But my girls are thirteen, fifteen, and seventeen. They need—"

Suddenly the worker's eyes flashed on the sticker in Ryan's window showing he was a doctor. "Go ahead, Doctor. Be careful."

Knowing that, seemed to change the man's mind. That was fine with Ryan…whatever it took.

The sky devoid of stars and light of any kind continued to pour rain down all around. As he drove with his wipers slapping back and forth, his car swayed with the push of the wind. Gripping the steering wheel tightly, he held the car on the road as the wind tried to whip it around. On the island, streetlights were out and the wind had them flopping around in the air holding tight to the wire. Why did he wait so long to leave? His heart raced as he wondered about his girls and Meagan. He wanted to pray for their safety, but all he could do was hope. He didn't think God would be listening to him after all these years.

Turning on his street, he saw lawn furniture strewn across the road. Garbage bins turned upside down. Trees bent in half. As long as the girls were inside, he knew they had to be okay.

Jessica, he thought. It was Friday night. She probably insisted on going out. Hopefully Meagan was able to talk her out of it.

He realized as he turned into his drive he was holding his breath. Easing toward the garage he pressed the button to open it. It wouldn't open. *Of course,* he thought. *The power is out on the island. How long have they been without power?*

Turning off the motor, he jumped out of his car and fought through the wind and rain to the back door. When he opened the door and rushed in, he heard nothing. Closing the door behind him, he slipped through the house trying to find them, listening for them. They weren't in the family room or the dining room. Coming around the corner he saw a glow coming from the music room. The tightness in his chest released.

Quietly, he slipped closer to the door and heard Jessica saying thank you.

His baby, all grown up. Listening to her, he was so proud. It wasn't that hard little teenager who has been running around here for the past six months fighting with everyone about everything.

It was his soft-spoken, sweet-natured little girl. But she wasn't a little girl anymore. She was seventeen…all grown up. This year she graduated high school and one day she'd go away to college…but he knew she wasn't ready. She was still too mad at the world. To listen to her voice now made him hope that just maybe she would be ready when the time came.

As he looked into the room, he saw TJ at one end of a couch sound asleep with Rachelle at the other end. Jessica was curled up on the love seat talking to Meagan. His daughter's eyes looked heavy. She was fighting it, and she was about to lose. As her eyes closed, his gaze slipped over to Meagan. She was sitting on the floor with her back against the wall watching his girls intently.

"Hi there," he whispered.

Meagan looked up and smiled. "Thank God, you made it home safely." Her voice, too, was in a soft whisper. Quietly, she rose to her feet, dropped the blanket to the floor and walked over to the door. "Has the hurricane passed yet?"

He liked that…her calling this home. It was home to him and his girls. It wouldn't be a bad thing if this were her home, too. She would fit right in. And she had done so much for his girls.

Looking down into her chocolate eyes, he realized he would like her to be one of his girls…and he didn't mean a daughter. He was drawn to her.

This was a first for him. His wife had been gone for over seven years and not once had he found himself attracted to another woman. But now—

"No," he said, interrupting his thoughts. "It is pounding the island pretty hard right now. It's a three, so we should be okay here on the island. You were smart moving everyone into the music room," he said keeping his voice low so as not to wake the girls.

"Remember. I *am* from Louisiana. I've been through a few

hurricanes myself. It was no problem. You shouldn't have come out in the hardest part of the storm though. We left word to let you know we were okay. We didn't want you to worry."

He couldn't help but smile at those bright eyes as they looked up at him.

"I heard the message. I even tried to call, but the lines were not getting through. The recording said something about all the lines were busy." Remembering their earlier conversation about the pros and cons of living on the island, he said, "That is one of those things we were talking about before…negative things about living on the island…on the beach. We lose power and phones go out here with the drop of a hat. But I had to come. I wanted to be here. Make sure everyone was okay."

"We're fine." In a soft, confiding tone she said, "I think I had a breakthrough with Jessica. She opened up to me tonight after the girls dozed off." A yawn escaped her mouth as the last word came out and her eyelids dropped a couple of times.

"You look like you are fighting to stay awake. It is almost midnight. Why don't you go lay down? I will find a flashlight and then grab me a pillow and blanket. And then I will come back in here with you all." Glancing at the candles, he added, "And I will blow the candles out when I get back. Don't worry. You just get comfortable and get some sleep. The eye of the hurricane will be here shortly and then in no time the rest will pass."

She smiled as she seemed to fight to keep her eyes opened. "Thank you. You talked me into it, but I have the flashlight. Let me get it for you." She went back, scooped it up, and then brought it back to him. Then she said, "Night."

Turning, she made her way back to her pillow and blanket one more time. This time she stretched out on the floor and covered up.

In seconds, her breathing was even, she was fast asleep.

Ryan took in a deep breath and glanced around the room one more time taking in the sight of his girls under the glow of the candles. When his eyes rested on Meagan, he thought, *it would be nice having her here all the time.*

A smile touched his lips and at the same time touched his heart.

Chapter 29

With power restored, they gathered in the kitchen, everyone helping to prepare a late breakfast. Meagan was thankful. It was one thing to whip up a couple of scrambled eggs and prepare a couple of slices of toast for one or two…but for five at once. That was a little more than she was prepared to do.

TJ was busy buttering toast as it popped up and putting more in the toaster, while Rachelle and her dad set the table. Jessica took out the gallon jug of milk, still cold thanks to their refrigerator's insulation. She poured five glasses while Meagan stirred the eggs constantly as she watched the bacon sizzle in the skillet.

"Team work. I like this. We are like a great operating room… everyone doing his, or should I say her, part." Ryan joked as he slipped back in the kitchen pulling silverware out of the drawer.

"I like the smell, Daddy. I bet the operating room doesn't smell like this," TJ said as she laughed and then breathed through her nose taking in the pleasant scents.

Rachelle didn't say a word, she just shook her head showing how silly she thought they were being as she pulled down the napkins and counted some out. Meagan loved seeing this family come together. They have made such a giant step from the first day she arrived. *Thank you, Lord.* She knew where the credit lay.

"Someone get me a bowl. The eggs are ready," Meagan called out as she flipped the bacon strips one more time. "And hand me a plate for the bacon, please. And a couple of napkins, please, Rachelle," she added.

Ryan swooped around, pulled out a bowl and a plate and was at Meagan's side in an instant. "Your wish is my command." He smiled and placed them down on the counter next to her.

Meagan felt herself blushing, as her cheeks grew hot.

"Someone help me carry these glasses in the dining room. I just don't see how Ms. H does it all and makes it look so effortless," Jessica said.

After the eggs were spooned into the bowl and the bacon was laid out on the paper napkin, Meagan scooped the dishes up with her hands and headed toward the dining room. Jessica and Rachelle slipped through ahead of her carrying the glasses of milk.

In no time everyone found a seat. Ryan dished out the food and then the plates were passed around. TJ walked past with a saucer stacked with buttered toast and each grabbed what they wanted.

After the blessing was said, they dug into their meals. Meagan was pleased to see everyone. They seemed to be enjoying the eggs she had scrambled. The bacon was cooked apparently as they liked.

No one complained. *Mom would be proud of me. And Shelly would have been amazed!* Meagan fought back the laughter that wanted to bubble over.

After several seconds of silence, probably because the mouths were full of food, Ryan broke the silence. "So how did you all do during this storm? You seemed to have done fine without me," he said and then he put a fork full of eggs into his mouth.

"We had fun, Daddy. Didn't we?" TJ asked both of her sisters as she was speaking. "Meagan taught us how to have a hurricane party. While we had power still we were watching movies and eating junk food."

Shaking his head and laughing at the same time, he said, "Tamara. You can stop there. Mention junk food and you're in heaven." They all laughed.

"No, really, Daddy. It was fun," Jessica said. "I was going to go out, but because of the weather, Meagan made me stay home. I'm glad she did. I had fun." She smiled at her father and then glanced at Meagan.

Meagan felt a warm glow spread within her. She didn't make her stay home, but that was okay by her. They had connected last night. Meagan was happy to hear Jessica speak this out loud, because as a teenager, she could have forgotten last night just as quickly. But she didn't. It kept. They really broke ground last night. When she met Jessica's gaze, she smiled at the young woman.

Jessica smiled back.

"I liked the time in the music room with the candles lit and we just talked…told stories. Not that I stayed awake long once we got in there," Rachelle admitted.

The plates were clearing quickly as the conversation flowed. Each talked about their favorite part of last night. When they were all finished, Ryan said, "My favorite part was coming home and finding you all safe and at peace at home. Thank you, Meagan. I hope next time I will be home with you all for the hurricane party."

"How often do y'all get them here? Hurricanes, I mean…not hurricane parties."

The girls glanced from one to another with looks of curiosity on each face as they tried to figure it out. Their dad came up with the answer. "It varies. Some years we don't have any great scares, and other times we may get two back to back…but not as bad as the ones you all suffered through a couple of years ago."

Everyone appeared to be through, so Meagan said, "I'll clean up the mess. Y'all go relax in the other room."

"Thanks, Meagan. That will give us time to check out the weather and see if we can still sail to the little island today."

TJ jumped up squealing with excitement. "Great. Of course we can go. Come on, Rachelle. Let's go get the weather channel on. The sooner he sees everything is fine, the sooner we get to go. We can still bring a friend, right, Dad?" TJ asked.

"If their parents will let them go," he said as he stood. "I can help you clear, if you would like," he said directing his words to Meagan.

She was stacking one plate on top of another. "No. I'll be fine. You go ahead and check out the weather."

Meagan took in a slow deep breath. "Sailing. Yes." Her mind thought about the height of the top of the sailboat off the water. Did she really want to try that again?

She made it the first time, but that was because Ryan had helped her. Would he be there for her this time too?

Touching the top of her hand gently with his hand, Ryan looked into her eyes and said, "You will do fine. Don't worry."

How did he know what I was thinking? Just the touch of his hand on hers filled her with such peace, such assuredness. She nodded her head as a crooked smile touched her lips. "Yes. I'll be fine. Thanks."

It didn't take long to clean up the mess in the kitchen, rinse the dirty dishes, and load them in the dishwasher.

By the time the dining room and kitchen were cleaned and she joined them in the family room, she found Jessica sitting on the arm of the overstuffed chair Ryan was sitting in and TJ at his feet.

Rachelle was on the phone.

It sounded like she was making sure her friend, Stan, was still coming with them.

So the trip was on. The family was making a verbal list of all they wanted to take, and Ryan was telling each what they would be responsible to bring. They had it all under control.

Inside, a thrill of what was to come coursed through her. If the island were anything like last weekend, she would love it. It had been the best time in her life. How could she beat that? If it even came close, Meagan would love it.

"So I guess now we go slip on our suits?" Meagan asked.

TJ jumped to her feet and took off for the stairs. Jessica was right behind her. It was so good seeing her wanting to be a part of the family. She couldn't praise the Lord enough for what He had accomplished in this family in just over four months. It was amazing. But all things are possible through Christ. She knew and believed that most assuredly.

Ryan rose and stepped near Meagan. As he ran his fingers through his wavy hair, he said, "You got it. Don't forget the sunscreen and your hat, of course."

Rachelle hung up the phone and said, "Stan's parents won't let him come. They said maybe next time." The frown on her face showed she was not too happy with the boy's parents' decision.

"We'll do it again, Rachelle. Maybe next weekend. Maybe we'll do this every weekend while the weather allows." Turning back to Meagan he said, "With the clouds still overcast, you may think you won't need the sunscreen, but don't let the clouds fool you. That is when the rays are at their worst…burning blisters, I mean."

She nodded. "I'll get both, don't worry." She grinned and then headed for her apartment.

The sail to the island went smoothly although the water wasn't as clear as it had been. The teamwork was still present in their working together to get the craft under sail.

Meagan thought after a hurricane the waves would be too rough, but it was the opposite. It wasn't like looking at the damage after hitting a town, with trees strewn across the road and limbs everywhere. The Richardson's backyard backed up to the ocean and there were no trees out there. She did see some boats laid on their side and some up on the sand broken up. Those she saw as they sailed parallel with the shoreline. Once they turned east and headed out into the waters away from land, the water seemed murky with waves rolling and seaweed floating…but that was all.

The salty air and sea breeze was nice. Her hat was secured because it had a sash that she tied under her chin. She had managed to cover herself in sunscreen…at least her arms, legs, and face. She'd get TJ to do her back later. She was in heaven. Meagan wouldn't change her life for the world.

"Do you remember how to guide the sailboat?" Ryan asked her.

Smiling, she slipped between him and the wheel. With her hands securely holding the wheel, Ryan leaned back and appeared to watch her. She didn't see him doing this, but she felt his eyes on her and out of the corner of her eye, she could see him facing her way. "I'm doing this right…aren't I?" she asked.

"You're doing fine. You almost look like a natural. Did you put that lotion on you? I see you're not wearing a T-shirt over your suit."

She couldn't help but laugh aloud at him thinking she looked like a natural. "I know you heard this last time, but I have to say it again, I'm still amazed at how much I love the water…I mean being on this boat going to an island full of sand. It is so out of character for me." And then she shook her head no. "I'll get TJ or Rachelle to cover my back when we get to the island."

"Our character traits are forever growing, if we let them. Right?" he asked. "I'll put some on you while you hold us steady." He reached in a pocket near the wheel and pulled out a bottle. Squeezing some in his hand, he stepped behind her again and started covering her back with the lotion. His fingertips made small circles all over her back.

She thought for a moment about what he had asked...or at least tried to think. It was hard with him touching her. Concentrating hard, she thought, each one's character was strengthened in time if they were growing in their faith. Some people's characters worsened with time and some lay dormant.

She liked the thought of characters growing stronger, so she agreed. "Yes, they are." And then without thinking about it, she said, "I'm glad I took this unusual job. Your family has come to mean a lot to me. Thank you for giving me the opportunity to grow in character and in life."

When he dropped his hands and leaned against the side again, she closed her eyes for a second. She tasted the salt on her lips with the tip of her tongue before she continued. "At my age, you would think I would have already felt the joy of mothering, so to speak." She glanced his way and hoped she hadn't offended him.

"Please don't take me wrong," she said in a rush, not giving him time to respond. "I'm not trying to be their mother nor do I presume I could be a mother of three wonderful young ladies, but these past weeks I believe I have felt what other mothers have felt when they see their children grow."

She sighed. "I guess, knowing I'll never marry or have children, I thought my niece and nephew were the closest thing I would have as to my own children. But God allowed me to feel the joy of motherhood…in a small way…but one I'll be forever grateful for."

With brow furrowed, she looked at Ryan and asked, "Do you know what I mean?"

He pushed away from where he was leaning. Standing tall, he stepped close to her again.

She could feel the heat from his body he stood so near. Swallowing hard, she figured she had said too much or the wrong thing. Biting her bottom lip, she wondered what he was about to say.

"Meagan, in seven years, I have never once wanted another woman in my life. Jennifer was a great mom and wife. She made me happy and left me saddened with her death. But she also left me three wonderful daughters for which I will forever be grateful. I don't take offense by you talking about feeling like a mother to my girls.

"In fact, if I wasn't a man, I probably would have teared up when you said what you did. I am proud that you have grown close to my girls, so close that they were able to give that gift to you, the feel of motherhood."

Resting his hand on top of hers on the wheel, he said in a lower voice, "You have also made me think about the possibility of having another woman in my life."

She tensed, gripping the wheel tighter. Her heart pounded in her chest so hard, she thought it would explode. What should she say? She wanted to say something, and she wanted it to sound sophisticated. Instead, she heard her voice say, "Really?"

He squeezed her hand and said, "Yes. Really."

The last part of the sailing was done in beautiful silence. They stood, Meagan cocooned between Ryan and the wheel, where he kept his hands on top of hers helping guide the boat. She was so wrapped up in the moment that she didn't notice if the girls were aware of the emotion being exchanged between them or not.

When Ryan called the orders out to drop sail and the girls scurried around doing their part, Meagan believed they had just had a perfect moment in time. As the sailboat came to a near stop, the anchor was dropped and the girls stripped down to their suits. They stuffed their shorts and shirts in the bag. As TJ and Rachelle started to dive off the side, Jessica said, "Wait. Dad may need some help."

"You three go ahead. Meagan and I will get everything."

They didn't hesitate to go over the side. None of their friends were able to make it, but the three girls seemed to enjoy it anyway. That was the first thing Meagan had noticed in the first week she was there, the sisterly connection of TJ and Rachelle…and now Jessica. It was a tight bond of three. This warmed Meagan's heart.

She turned back to Ryan. "Okay. What can I do to help?"

"We did not bring as much with us this time. We were fewer in number, so we have a smaller ice-chest as well as less food. What we will do," he said as he pulled out the inflatable boat and pulled the string for it to expand, "is put everything inside this little boat and you and I will lower it over the side. Then I will help you over. Then the rest, as they say, is easy as pie. We will pull the boat to shore and do as we did last weekend."

It went well and Ryan helped her past her fear of heights as they went over the side backwards, together, and climbing down one rung after the other. In no time, they were in the water pulling the rubber boat to shore.

As the girls played, Ryan slid the boat across the sand to an area where they were going to make camp. It wasn't as clean as last time, but it was still okay. The two of them then laid out the blankets and secured them in the sand.

"All the pieces of wood on the island looked pretty wet. I don't think we will get to make a campfire this time," Ryan said.

"Do the girls eat cold hot dogs?" Then she laughed as she thought of the oxymoron she had just said. It sounded silly, but it was probably what they would have to do.

"No problem there. We have done it before. We have chips and dogs and sodas. The girls will be content. Let's go join them in the water."

The day turned into another wonderful day on the island. Everyone had a great time. As the girls wore themselves out and ran up and crashed on the blankets, Ryan took Meagan by the hand, "Come on. We will go around the island. This time, we will stay in the water."

Turning toward the shore he hollered, "Girls, I am going to take Meagan around the island by the water. We will be back shortly and then we will eat. Okay?"

No one seemed to mind. Each seemed content to lie in the warmth of the sun and soak it up.

The two started out wading through the water hand in hand, but eventually they dropped hands and swam and played in the water. It was fun. Even the ground under her feet that felt partially like muddy sand didn't seem to take away from the moment. Meagan and Ryan had a good time.

When they returned, the girls still lay quietly out on the blankets. They appeared to be sleeping. As Meagan and Ryan moved closer in, Ryan stopped between Jessica and Rachelle and then shook like a dog sprinkling water all over them.

Squealing and jumping to their feet the girls hollered all at the same time. "That's cold Daddy. Really. It's cold!" Then they all laughed.

"It woke you two lazy girls up, didn't it? I'm hungry. Let's eat."

TJ sat up when he said that about eating and yawned. Then as she stretched she said, "Good. I'm ready to eat, too."

The rest of the day was fun. The five of them built sandcastles, each trying to be better than the other one. This gave their food time to settle and then they all went back out in the water for more fun. Meagan joined them, after she applied some more lotion.

When they returned home, all safe and sound, the peace of the day came back to the house with them. As late as it had gotten, Ryan said, "We are all going to church tomorrow…right?" His eyes turned to Jessica apparently thinking she might be the only one to back out of going.

"I'll be ready, Dad," Jessica said.

"Us too, Daddy," TJ said as she turned and headed for the stairs. "I had fun. Thanks."

The room cleared as Ryan, while carrying the ice-chest, headed toward the kitchen, and Meagan followed him with the basket of leftover food and the bag of soiled towels. The blanket was left hanging over some chairs outside on the patio. In the kitchen, he went toward the sink while she headed to the laundry room. "I will do that," he called out to her.

"No problem. I can handle it. I'll put them on to wash and then after I've showered I'll put them in the dryer."

He placed the ice-chest in the sink. Opening the lid, he took out the drinks and hot dogs and put them in the refrigerator. Next he emptied the bag holding the chips, buns, and napkins. She noticed he finished about the same time she did, so they headed out of the kitchen together.

"I had a great time today. Thanks again for including me in your family outing. And I love seeing you and the girls so happy." She didn't want to hang around and push her desire to be near him. As much fun as they had, and those wonderful words he had spoken, she wasn't sure how the doctor felt about her. She had helped him see he was ready to find himself a woman, but she couldn't begin to believe she would be the one he would be looking at. And most of all, she didn't want him to think that was what she was thinking so she tried to hurry on past him.

He caught her by the hand. "I know you are tired and full of sand, so I am sure you are ready to go take your shower. But give me a chance to say thank you too. I had a wonderful day. And if I may be so bold, I would like one more thing."

She had been looking down at his hand holding hers, but his words drew her attention upward. Her face turned toward his, and her eyes couldn't help but soak in the beauty of his baby blues. Wetting her lips and wondering what that one more thing could be, she said, "And that is?"

"This." His face came down closer to hers, as his eyes never left them. He stopped only inches away, and then he closed his eyes pulling her to him and pressed his lips to hers. The kiss wasn't long…but long enough.

When he stopped kissing her and let go, she stood for a second or two with her face still turned upward and her eyes closed, letting what just happened soak in. Slowly she opened them. There his blue eyes stayed, looking down on her.

"See you in the morning." His voice was deep.

Scraping her bottom lip with her teeth, she smiled. "Yes. I'll see you in the morning," she said, sounding a little breathless.

Turning quickly, she headed down the hall toward her apartment. This moment she wanted to hold on to forever…but at the same time she wanted to pick up the phone and shout it out loud. She wanted to tell her sister, her mom, everyone, Ryan had kissed her, and oh what a kiss! She couldn't stop smiling as she ran back to her apartment. Not even the sand between her toes or the sand in her swimsuit could steal her attention. All she could think was what a wonderful kiss that was…and it was Ryan who kissed her.

Chapter 30

Meagan had a hard time going to sleep that night. She had shared her moment with her sister. Shelly, of course, was beside herself and ran on and on about how she knew this job was going to be different. Her sister also said she could tell by the way Meagan described the doctor to her in the beginning that she knew her sister was taken with him. The news about her sister's feeling for him hadn't surprised her one little bit…not even the kiss. Meagan made her sister promise not to say anything to her mom in case it was a one-time thing and it hadn't really meant anything special to him.

Coffee couldn't drip fast enough the next morning. Meagan wanted to see Ryan again. She needed to see if he would be looking at her in a different way, or if it would be things as usual. She didn't feel like things could ever be *as usual* again…at least not where she was concerned. Her heart was dancing, and she wanted to twirl around the floor. Life was more exciting than she had ever hoped it would be. God brought her there and introduced her to a ready-made family that she fell quickly in love with.

"Oh please, Lord, let this be what you intended. Please don't let me be running amuck. Let it be real and let it be Your plan."

With her cup filled, she sat down at the table and started reading her morning devotional. The scriptures were in Revelation chapter three. The verses that stood out most were seven and eight. It said the door He opened no one could close and the door He closed no one could open.

"Did You open this door to me? I know You led me here." After she spoke, she sat in silence. Then a peace came over her, and she smiled knowing, this was God.

"Thank you," she whispered. Finishing her coffee, she put her cup in the sink and then ran off to get ready for church.

It was different than before. Ryan sat next to her in the service. He did intentionally. She hadn't dreamed it. He showed his interest in his actions and in his speech. That day and the two weeks that followed were wonderful.

At work, she barely saw him, but when she did, Ryan would smile at her and say something like he hoped her day was going as well as his. He had even told her on one of the evenings when they were in the study sipping coffee after dinner how he felt he had a new reason for getting up every morning. He had a bounce in his step.

Helen even seemed to notice a difference in the household on her return. She had commented, "Maybe I need to go away more often. Everyone seems so happy." And then she winked at Meagan as if to say she noticed what was going on between her and the doctor, too.

"You've got less than two months to go. Do you think he'll ask you to marry him?" Shelly asked.

Meagan had called Shelly because she needed to talk to someone. "Shelly, I don't know what to do or to think. He hasn't kissed me again. But we have coffee every evening in his study and when we join the girls, he usually sits by me on the couch. No one seems to notice or think anything of it...but me. I think it means something. But what?"

"Don't worry about it. Remember, worry about nothing. Pray about everything. So simple, yet so hard. We tend to forget." Shelly's voice was sweet and tender. "You know you can't make things happen any faster than they are supposed to. All you can do is what you feel led to do. If you're supposed to say anything, you will. I know you pray about this, so trust God. Let Him lead you."

"I know. I know. You're right! It's just so hard. I've never really been in love before, except maybe Daniel. And I was what, twelve when I fell for him and twenty when we finally dated. I don't think I can wait eight years," she laughed as she said this to Shelly.

"You can wait however long you are supposed to. I know you."

"But Shel, I have never felt this way before. I think about him all the time. Just thinking about him makes me happy. I never knew love could be so wonderful!" Meagan played with the toss pillow on her lap as she sat curled up in the loveseat.

"You'll make it. Hang in there. One day at a time. Remember?"

When they hung up, Meagan showered, dressed, and climbed in bed. She spent the next hour praying and listening until finally she fell asleep. When her alarm went off the next morning, she didn't want to wake up. She had been dreaming, and she wanted to finish even though she couldn't remember what it had been about, but she believed she was about to know the answer. The problem was she didn't know for sure what the question was.

People at work treated her the same, so Meagan felt sure no one had noticed the sudden joy in her heart. They did say they liked seeing the doctor on the floor more often. He mingled with the other doctors and nurses. He even spent time with some of the patients. He hadn't done that in years.

That night after dinner when they retired to the study with their coffee and the girls went off their own way, Ryan sat on the couch beside her, instead of in the chair next to her.

"Meagan," he said, "what would you say to dinner Friday night…just the two of us?"

She sipped her coffee, almost choking on it, but keeping her composure. "I'd love to, if the girls don't mind."

"You spend all your spare time with them, except for this half hour we get alone in the study. I love our talks. Life has become more exciting in this past month or so because of you. I hope you know that. I am not sure what or where we go from here. I just know that I don't want the time to end."

Our talks. She smiled at him. *He loves the adult conversation. Of course.* That man had been cooped up in a lab for the last seven years. The only adults he saw before her were his lab assistants, talking tests, results, and possibilities, and Helen, his wonderful housekeeper and caretaker of his girls. Meagan felt a deep sigh that wanted to be released. It wasn't love on his part. He enjoyed their companionship.

Meagan was old enough to know she had let this get too far out of hand in her own mind. She had made more of it than it had really been. Down deep, she knew it was because she had fallen in love with him. But love had to be a two-way street or it would never work. Finally she said, "That's two nights from now. If nothing happens that would prevent it, I would love to go to dinner with you." She didn't want him to hear the eagerness in her voice. At least now she knew when her time was up she would be going home to life as usual so she better enjoy the last of her time there with the man she loved.

"Great!" he said. And as he put his arm around her and laid his other hand on her hand holding the cup, she turned to face him. He leaned in and kissed her for the second time. Now she was confused again. The moment she thought she had figured him out, he went and did something that turned everything upside down again.

"I have wanted to do that every night in here, but I didn't want to be too pushy and scare you away," Ryan said.

You confuse me, that's what you do. She didn't dare say that aloud and break the spell of the moment. Her heart pounded. She heard it in her ears, felt it pulsing in her neck. As loud as it beat, she felt sure everyone heard it…even the girls in the other room.

When she didn't say anything, he bent down to kiss her again and the door opened. Jumping slightly and turning toward the door her cup slipped out of her hands and fell to the carpet, spilling, making a mess.

"Jessica. What can I do for you?" her dad asked.

The young woman looked at her dad and then at Meagan and then glanced at the spilled coffee. When her eyes returned to her father, she said, "I was just going to let you know I need to run to Teri's. I won't be gone long." Her voice didn't sound so sure of what she was saying, but it made sense to her dad.

"Okay, sweetheart. But be careful and don't be too long. It is almost nine."

When the door closed, Meagan jumped to her feet. "Oh, Ryan. I'm so sorry. I made a mess of your carpet…and Jessica. She didn't seem too happy. Please forgive me. I have to go."

She started to leave, but he caught her by the hand and rose to his feet. "Don't run off. We have done nothing wrong. You have done nothing wrong. Coffee. It will clean up or it will stain. It's okay."

Meagan wished it were that simple. Jessica had come a long way these past few weeks and she didn't want to hurt her, but she saw the look on her face, the look in her eyes.

Ryan held her still, not letting her flee. He whispered, "Meagan."

She looked up at him.

"Please don't run away." His grip on her wrist tightened slightly then released.

"I'm not running."

He touched the side of her face and caressed her cheek. "You have brought us so much happiness. You have brought us peace. You have brought us back to the Lord. I forgot how happy a home is when it is centered on God. I cannot thank you enough for that. But you have brought more than that. Don't you know?" As his eyes searched hers, he waited for her to say something.

She knew he wanted her to say yes. She knew what he was talking about. But the girls were her number one reason for being there. Meagan could not forget that. Finally, she said, "I don't know. We'll see." Turning away one more time, she left the room.

In the family room, TJ and Rachelle were talking with the TV going in the background. "Hey you two. I have a headache, so I hope you don't mind if I call it an early night. I'll see you two tomorrow. Okay?"

They both nodded. "Do you want some Tylenol or Aleve? We have both. If you need something stronger, Daddy probably has that, too. I'll get it for you." TJ was on her feet ready to go fetch whatever Meagan wanted.

"No, sweetie. I think a long soak in a hot tub of water and then my little gel pack for my eyes will do the trick. It's probably sinuses. Thank you though."

"Hope you feel better," Rachelle said.

"Me too," TJ added.

"I will. See you tomorrow." She left before she cried in front of them. It was no sinus headache. It was heartache and nothing could fix it. She fell in love with the whole family, but she couldn't be a part of the family. It wasn't meant to be. Somehow she would have to get through the rest of her time here and not get any closer to anyone in the family. Of course she knew it was already too late. She couldn't get much closer than she already felt. Meagan also knew she could not be with Ryan, especially if Jessica was unhappy about her and Ryan's relationship…not that she was even sure what the doctor's intentions were.

She would go back to work tomorrow and get through one day at a time. There she would make sure no one was the wiser of how she fell head over heels in love with 'the doctor'. When her time was up, she would fly home and let them live happily ever after without her.

In her apartment, she debated calling Shelly to get words of encouragement. In the end she chose not to. Instead, she curled up in bed with the Dee Henderson book she had started several weeks ago. Maybe it would help keep her mind off of the matters at hand.

Thursday at work went by quickly. She didn't run into Ryan at all that day, and for that she was happy. Today, she would go to the house, play tennis with TJ, and visit with Rachelle and Jessica if they were around…and see if Jessica wanted to talk with her after last night. She changed her clothes and was coming down the hall, about to enter the family room when she overheard a conversation that stopped her in her tracks.

"Don't let it bother you, dear. She's just a glorified babysitter. Your daddy isn't dumb enough to get involved with the hired help. He loves you too much. I told you a long time ago; I would love to marry your dad when he got over my sister's death. It seems like he's finally gotten past it. So don't worry, darling, I'll make the moves and we'll work it out. We'll keep it in the family."

She heard Jessica sobbing and trying to speak at the same time. "I love Daddy. But I don't—"

Meagan didn't need to hear any more. She knew she was making a fool of herself. Who did she think she was? A doctor marrying an x-ray tech...a woman who cared for his girls? That wouldn't happen in a million years. Ryan was reaching out to her because for the first time in seven years he felt the resemblance of a home around him again and he loved that...not her.

Rushing down the hall, back to her apartment, she realized she couldn't stay. Tears were streaming down her cheeks as she opened the door. She had to get out of there, and she had to do it right away. She needed to call the airport and make a reservation. She would fly out tonight or in the morning, whichever she could get. And then she would tell Helen to explain it to the doctor.

The girls came to her mind immediately. Who would explain it to the girls? She had to. She couldn't just leave them. But what would she say? She couldn't lie to them, but she couldn't tell them the whole truth either.

Help me, Lord.

In her apartment, she looked up the phone number to the airline and made a reservation. They had a flight leaving out at eleven that same night. She could make that flight easily. Quickly, she pulled out her suitcase and started throwing her stuff in it.

With her bags packed, she sat down at the kitchen table and wrote a short note to Ryan. She apologized for leaving him and the hospital with no notice, but it was for the best. She told him she had to think of the girls, but also told him he was a wonderful father and she was glad she had gotten to know him. She prayed he would stay in church with his girls so they could keep their focus where it needed to be. She wanted to sign it "all my love," but didn't dare.

Instead, she said she would keep them all in her heart and for them to stay safe. Folding the letter, she sealed it. The letter she would give to Helen and have her pass it on to him in the morning.

"Do I write the girls a letter or go back and talk to them?" She didn't want to chance running into Ryan. Meagan couldn't handle it. She was too weak. Her heart would betray her.

With a clean piece of paper in front of her, she was about to write their names when she heard a tap at her door. Dare she answer it? What if it was one of the girls? Even worse, what if it was Ryan?

Taking a deep breath, she rose from the table and walked down the short hall to the door. Slowly, she opened the door and there stood TJ and Rachelle. "We hope you don't mind, but we wanted to check on you before we went to bed. You didn't seem yourself earlier. Can we come in?"

Meagan wanted to say no. Her suitcases were in the middle of the floor in the living room. They would see them and know she was leaving…besides, her eyes had to be a dead giveaway. But maybe it was for the best. This way she wouldn't have to write them a note. She could tell them…but tell them what?

"Come in. We need to talk."

The girls eased past her as she closed the door.

"Have a seat in the living room, please," she said as they were walking down the small hallway.

TJ took one step into the living room and froze. "Are you leaving?" She turned to face Meagan as questions rolled off of her tongue and tears rimmed her eyes. "Why? What did we do? You can't leave us! Meagan…please don't leave," she said as her breath sounded choppy. "I need you." Her face pinched as tears dripped from her eyes.

"What happened, Meagan? You've been like part of the family.

We love you," Rachelle said. "You've done so much for each of us. We don't want you to leave. Not now." She didn't cry, but her lids blinked repeatedly as if fighting back tears.

"Oh." Meagan didn't want to cry. She needed to be strong for the girls. But she loved them. She didn't want to leave them either. She rushed to them, her arms spread wide. Both girls flew into her arms, and she held them close. Tears streamed down her cheeks. She could not hold them back. "I don't want to go either, but I have to." The hard sobs coming from TJ shook them all as they embraced, and TJ's tears soaked Meagan's shirt. Rachelle's grip around her was almost like what she thought a boa constrictor would be like.

"We love you, Meagan. You've come to be like a…a…a mother to us," Rachelle said as her grip never lessened.

"I love you, too. All of you. It's because I love you that I have to go. You say I've become like a mother to you. Well it's the same with me."

She sniffed and tried to wipe away some of the tears. Not letting go of the girls to do this made it difficult.

"I'm not your mother, but I've begun to feel like a mother. That was something I never thought I would be blessed to do. I'm a little old for child bearing and I've never married, so I had resigned myself to be content to love other people's children.

"But with you three girls, I've come to love you more than I thought possible, and I don't think I was supposed to fall so deep." A ragged breath came between her words. "Please try to understand."

The three stood there in the middle of the living room holding onto each other tightly. This would be the last time she saw them. *Dear Lord, please help them keep a little piece of memory of me in their hearts.* "I'll never forget you, and I hope maybe in time, you'll forgive me for being so weak. But my heart was breaking at the thought of leaving here shortly, so I figured I better leave now or you'll never get rid of me." She tried to make a joke of it but couldn't laugh.

Kissing each girl's cheek, Meagan released her hold and pulled slightly away from them. Wiping the tears from her face with the back of one hand and reaching out to wipe the tears off of TJ's face, she said, "Try to understand. And above everything else, remember, God loves you. And I love you. Never forget that. I'm going to write my home and cell number down for y'all so if you need to talk about anything, feel free to call me…any time, night or day. I'm there for you. I just can't be here."

"I don't understand," said TJ as she grabbed Meagan's hand and wouldn't let go.

"Me either."

"Trust me that I'm doing the right thing. Please be there for Jessica. She has just started coming around. If I thought staying would help her, I would…but it wouldn't. If anything, it would make things harder for her. So you two have to be there for her. Okay?" Meagan loved these girls more than mere words could say, but how do you express that to teenagers? Leaving them was not a way to say I love you, but if she stayed she would hurt Jessica and Ryan's relationship and she could never do that. Besides, she would hurt herself, because Ryan didn't truly love her, he loved the memory of the joy he had with his wife. It wasn't the same thing. Meagan was doing the only thing she could.

TJ squeezed her hand and said, "I don't want to let go. You're the only mom I've ever known…other than a flash of a memory of playing tennis with my mom at four. But that memory is so dim. And Rachelle. She was like my mom for a lot of years, even though she was a kid." TJ looked at her sister and said, "No offense, sis. But you were and I love you for what you did for me."

Turning back to Meagan, she pleaded again, "But Meagan, you have helped me come alive. Before you came here none of us were living. You brought life back into this family. I don't want you to go. Please stay."

"I can't. But y'all will do fine. You have each other. And I'll only be a phone call away. With Internet and cell phones, it'll be like I'm right here. Y'all send me pictures and keep me posted…with your tennis, TJ…and your music, Rachelle. With your lives every day here. Okay?"

They hugged one more time, but then Meagan pulled away and went to the table. She picked up the envelope. "I was going to ask Helen to give this to your dad, but if y'all don't mind you can give it to him in the morning at breakfast. By that time, I'll be home. Hug Helen and Jessica for me and tell them thanks for everything and tell them I'll keep them in my prayers. Okay? And y'all stay in touch with me, if you will."

When they finally agreed to let her go, Meagan didn't hang around. Just in case the girls weakened and told their dad before morning, she couldn't be here if he came looking for her.

Meagan couldn't be as strong with him. She would have to admit that she loved him and couldn't bear to live there knowing he couldn't love her in the same way.

Leaving the key on the table, she put her luggage in the car and left the place she never thought she would love to stay. A place that was surrounded by sand and water and that she held in the middle of her heart with a family she wished was her own.

Chapter 31

It was ten o'clock Sunday morning. Her parents were at church and so were Shelly and her family. Troy had no idea what was going on so why bother him. Someone to talk to, she thought. He was a man…maybe he could help her understand things better. No. She didn't feel like pouring her heart out to anyone at this moment. Right now, Meagan wanted to curl up in a ball and retreat from everyone around her.

Ryan. That was an impossible dream. What made her think for a moment that the two of them could be happy together? They were from two separate worlds.

Hours passed and still she called no one. What could she say? Nothing. Her heart was broken, and it would never go back together. Her mother tried to warn her to take her time. Shelly even told her one-day at a time. But did she listen? No.

Her heart was so filled with love for those girls and for their father that she didn't even think far into the future. If she had, maybe she could have stopped the love before it started. Shaking her head, she knew that wasn't possible. God sent her there to help the girls.

"I thought You had opened the door to love for me, Lord. Apparently, I just wanted that. Forgive me. I was so content to be single and be used by You for Your glory. But I believed there was more there for me than You had intended. Please help my heart heal quickly so I can get back to doing what You want me to do. I truly was happy before. My life was full. Let me be happy and content again."

Sighing, she closed her eyes. And then she heard her back door open as a little voice said, "Let me, Mommy. Let me feed Gweny and the rest. Please?" The Kirkster was running on her hardwood floors, clomp, clomp, clomp. Quickly, she wiped the tears from her eyes.

And then she heard her sister call, "Meagan? Are you here?" She apparently saw the luggage Meagan left in the kitchen. Kirk didn't. He was focused on the fish.

Climbing out of bed, she glanced in the mirror and wiped at her face one more time. What little mascara she wore, was under her eyes. "I'm back here. I'm coming," she said as she headed toward the dining room where the fish tank was and where she knew she would find Kirk and his mom. Kirk would bring a smile to her face. She knew that without a doubt.

"Meagan," Shelly said as Meagan stepped into the dining room. "What happened? You look horrible."

"Gee thanks. Hey, Kirk. Come give Auntie Meggie a big hug." She leaned down, and Kirk took off running to her.

"Auntie Meggie," he squealed as he ran and leaped into her arms almost knocking her to the floor.

A smile touched her lips for a second and then tears started rolling down her cheeks.

"Auntie Meggie. Was sa matter? I make you cry? I sorry."

Hugging him, she said, "No, sweetheart. Thank you for your hugs and kisses. You make me feel better. I love you."

"Can I feed the fishes?"

The sisters laughed. "Help him feed them and I'll make us a pot of coffee. I'll call Brandon, so he won't worry. Mandy went to Mom and Dad's after church, so she won't even know I'm late getting home."

Within ten minutes or so, they were sitting in the living room and Kirk was watching a Scooby-Doo cartoon Meagan had for him at her house.

"Tell me, sister dear. What happened? Why did you come home so early? What did he do?"

Shaking her head, Meagan said, "Ryan didn't do anything. I did. I fell in love with a man I had no business falling in love with. He's a doctor. Who was I kidding?"

"He puts his pants on one leg at a time just like you. Don't put him up on a pedestal saying he's better than you just because he's a doctor. Look at what you do for people. You x-ray patient's broken bones, and you're gentle when you do it. You give them your kindness and your encouraging words as you do this. Your patients love you. Don't belittle what you do."

"I hear you, but it's more. My life is broken." Rubbing her eyes and shaking her head, Meagan didn't know how to explain her heart to Shelly. "As much as I love your two kids, I loved his three girls in another way and just as deeply. Do you understand what I'm saying? I felt like their mother, we'd become so close. And I fell in love with their dad. Two of them would have loved that, but the oldest wouldn't hear of it. Jessica was ready for a mom all right, just not me. She and I had become friendly in the last few weeks and I know I was being used by God to help her, but when she walked in on us right after he kissed me, I saw the look on her face. Shelly, as much as it hurt her to see that, it hurt me more to see her pain. Her dad didn't love me, so it wasn't worth hanging around hurting her for nothing, if you know what I mean."

Shelly put her arms around her sister and hugged her. "It'll be okay. I know it will. If it was meant for you and Ryan to be together, it will happen, but if not, you will heal and you will move on. Live in the moment. Although we have to be secure in our afterlife by making the right choice of serving God, we have to stay in the moment and enjoy where we are planted. Thank God for even this pain you are feeling right now. Look what you did for those girls. God used you in a big way. Be thankful! Find peace in that! And above all, don't worry or dwell on the pain. Remember the months you were there. Remember the good times and look forward to your future, but live in the now."

Holding Shelly tightly, Meagan whispered, "I know you're right. Help me, Shel. Help me."

Pulling back and grabbing Meagan by the arms, Shelly said, "And remember, if nothing else came out of this experience, think how you have come to love the water and the beaches. We can go on summer vacations again to the beach and you'll be a part of it. Yeah! My kids will love it!"

"And those girls showed me so much more than we've ever seen at a beach. I'll share that with you and the rug-rats…and Mom of course."

They laughed. It wasn't a hardy laugh, but it was a start.

"So wash your face and change your clothes. You look like you slept in them."

Smiling, Meagan said, "I did…well not really, because I haven't slept."

"Doesn't matter. We'll go to Mom's. We'll play some silly game and laugh and have a good time. I'll tell Brandon to meet us over there. Maybe we can call Troy and we'll barbeque. Brandon loves to barbeque."

The next week dragged by. Meagan didn't call and put her name out for another job. She wasn't ready to move on. She was surprised when she received her next check. She was paid for the full week even though she didn't go in to work Friday, and she received the double bonus as if she had stayed the whole time. Sure she was supposed to get one of them. She completed the first three months. But doubled? She didn't deserve that. She would figure out whom to call and straighten it out…just not yet. She wasn't ready to talk to anyone over there. She was still homesick for everyone.

Saturday, after she finished passing the dust mop on her hardwood floors and was about to scrub bathroom fixtures, she heard her doorbell ringing. "Who in the world?" she wondered aloud as she went to the side door. Opening it, she said, "Shelly? Why did you ring the doorbell? Why didn't you just call, and I would have left it unlocked for you? It's not like you to show up on my door step."

"Momma called and told me to pick you up and bring you over."

"What's going on?"

"I have no idea. I just do what I'm told. You know me, whatever Momma wants I try to give it to her."

Meagan laughed. "Yeah, right. Okay. Let me brush my hair and wash my hands and face. Get some of this grime off of me. I've been cleaning house."

"Now I have to laugh. Ha-ha." The sisters looked at one another staring for a silent second or two and then both burst out into laughter.

"Okay, okay." Meagan laughed till tears touched her eyes. "Thanks. I needed that. I admit I haven't been cleaning, I've been crying. I still need to wash up." She went back to her bathroom and did as she said. When she rejoined her sister a terrible thought came to mind and she had to ask. "Is Momma okay? Pops? Is something wrong? Did something happen to Troy and you're not telling me? Brandon?"

Shaking her head, Shelly said loudly, "And I thought I was the drama queen. It's nothing like that. Just get your keys and come on. You're riding with me. Lock your doors. I'll be in my car waiting." She turned and left no time for Meagan to ask any more questions.

When they pulled up in their mom and dad's driveway, she saw her brother's car as well as some strange car. "Oh please tell me Troy is not trying to fix me up with one of his buddies. They are so young! I don't want to be fixed up! I'm going to get back to being content in being alone. Take me home."

"Sorry. I can't."

"Oh, Shelly. Don't do this to me. You love me, don't you? I don't want to be fixed up. I'm too old for these childhood games. It was okay in my twenties. But not now. Please." She begged and pleaded with her sister.

"I'll tell you what. You come in with me. Stay fifteen minutes. Be nice. And then, I'll drive you back home. Deal?" Shelly said.

Smiling, Meagan said, "Okay. Fifteen minutes! No more!" And she climbed out of the car.

Shelly walked ahead of Meagan. She knocked hard on the door before opening and shouting, "We're here!" Then she quickly moved around the other side of the door letting Meagan walk in on her own.

The first step in, she had her head down, not ready to meet some strange young friend of her brother. Putting a fake smile on her face, she looked up as she took the second step in and froze.

The fake smile became a true smile as her gaze darted around the room. There in the living room she saw her mother and brother, but instead of a guy, three young girls sat on the long couch. TJ was the first to jump to her feet and run to Meagan. She grabbed hold of Meagan and wouldn't let go. Automatically Meagan's arms wrapped around TJ and hugged back.

"What are y'all doing here?" Meagan asked. Tears came to her eyes as her gaze brushed over TJ and on to Rachelle. Jessica was with them. "How did y'all get here? I said call me whenever you want or need me." Wiping the tears as fast as she could caused the hugs to become squeezes. TJ kept hugging and Meagan's tears kept falling. "Why didn't you call and tell me you all were coming?" Suddenly a horrible thought crossed her mind. She grabbed TJ by the shoulders and shoved her back. Looking her straight in the eyes, she asked, "Is your daddy okay? Nothing's happened to him, has it?"

"Yes. Something has happened," Jessica answered as both the girls rose. Rachelle went over to Meagan and hugged her. "We missed you," she whispered. "It's good to see you."

"Oh, sweetie. I've missed all of you too…and it's great to see all of y'all." Hugging her, but shifting her eyes to Jessica, she said. "Tell me, sweetie. What's happened to your dad? What can I do?" She could barely see clearly with the puddles of liquid standing on the rim of her eyelids.

Jessica walked over to Meagan and her sisters.

"I want to say I'm sorry for what I did. My aunt and I planned for you to overhear that conversation, but as I was doing it, I knew it was wrong." Her brows cringed as a deep crease appeared between her brows. Jessica's eyes filled with tears that didn't fall as she looked into Meagan's eyes. "You were the best thing that ever happened to our family and as much as I was fighting you and my feelings for you, the rest of the family fell deeply in love with you." Squeezing her eyes closed pushed the tears out causing them to slide down her face. She opened them, blinking her eyes, and said, "I did too. But I fought it and hurt you and Dad in the process. Can you forgive me?"

Releasing TJ and Rachelle, Meagan reached out to Jessica. "Of course I can. You're forgiven. Oh, sweetie. Thank you. I love you, too. I love all three of you." They did a group hug, and Meagan closed her eyes as she held on tightly. She loved these girls so much. They had touched a chord in her heart that no one else had ever reached. Her time with them had been the happiest times of her life. They would never be able to understand that, but she hoped they at least felt her love.

"We love you too." All three were hugging her back and speaking at the same time.

"I just can't believe you came all the way here to tell me this." Her vision was blurred from all the tears. "I love you so much. This means so much to me."

"Is there room for one more?"

Meagan heard the question and knew the voice immediately. Her eyes popped open, and she looked over Jessica's shoulder.

There standing side by side with her pops was Ryan. The girls dropped their hold and moved away as Meagan stood speechless.

"I hope you don't mind, but when you left us, you left a hole as big as Texas in our hearts and in our family. Without you, we are not complete. You couldn't have meant to leave us broken. You told TJ and Rachelle you loved us all. Did you mean it?"

The fact he called his little girl TJ instead of Tamara didn't even click in Meagan's brain. She was still on the part about the hole she left them with. "If I'm dreaming, please don't anyone wake me," she said as she glanced around the room. Every eye was upon her. She stopped looking around when her eyes came back to rest on Ryan.

He opened his arms and took a step in her direction. The girls reached out and in unison gave Meagan a push. She rushed into his arms. Wrapping his arms around her, he said, "I hope you don't mind. I did the old fashioned thing and asked your dad for your hand in marriage and now I'm asking you. Will you marry me?" he said holding her tightly in his grip.

The room fell silent, as everyone seemed to hold their breath waiting for Meagan's response.

"In a heartbeat," she whispered and then slipped her arms around his neck. Pulling his face down closer to her, she kissed him like there was no tomorrow.

As the kiss continued, deep within her she heard, *All in God's time, child.*

Acknowledgments

All in God's Time was given to me in a dream. I woke up on my daughter Rachael's thirty-third birthday telling her God just showed me her future or my next book…or both. She was an x-ray tech. She helped me with the details of the job. Thanks Rachael.

So thank You, God for the dream as well.

Again, I'd like to thank Melissa and Buddy Stockwell of Indigo Moon for answering sailing questions for me. This couple sailed all over the world and shared their journeys with friends via the Internet. I thank them for their time, and if I misrepresented anything about sailing, it was my fault, not theirs.

I have so many people to thank on the re-revised version of *All in God's Time*; I'm not sure where to begin. First I'm thankful I got the rights back for all three of my first novels. Now I'm working to update them and re-release them. I chose *All in God's Time* for the first one to upgrade. This book was a bestselling romance. The story is full of love—love for family, love for friends, and the love between man and woman. My friend who helped me understand how to get it ready for ePublishing once the editing and updating was complete, I can't thank enough. The questions I asked, but she patiently guided me through the steps. I'd also like to thank my critique partners who read the novel one more time making sure I tightened it up as well as updated it. Also all my friends who keep me pushing forward in my writing career, I can't thank them enough.

I hope you who read the novel will love it as much as I did when writing it and re-writing it. I suggest you keep a box of Kleenex handy. Thank you. God bless you.

ALL IN GOD'S TIME is a wonderful story that made me laugh and made me cry. Proverbs 3:6 lived out loud. "In all thy ways acknowledge Him and He shall direct thy paths" (KJV).

—Rachael R. Craft RT(R)
Radiologic Technologist

Deborah Lynne's latest novel, *All in God's Time,* is a story so warm and so real you can smell the brownies or feel the dreamy relaxation of being on the ocean beach during the family outing. The familiar ease of the dialogue brings each page to life as you quickly learn to love this family as your own and rejoice as God works in their lives. What a wonderful reminder of the life-changing power of prayer and God's perfect timing!

—Maria Hyland

Deborah Lynne is a gifted storyteller with a talent to bring her characters to life so vividly that I feel like I know them. She weaves a strong family bond together with moral wholesomeness into a tender love story that will make you laugh, cry, and laugh again. I didn't want to put *All in God's Time* down!

—Emy White

Deborah Lynne's first book, *Grace, a Gift of Love,* was our #1 best selling fiction book for 2007 even though we did not get it until the last quarter of the year. It is with eager anticipation that we await her second book, *All in God's Time.* Having read the manuscript, I know it is as good as the first one, and without hesitation I recommend it. Deborah is a faithful servant of the Lord, and her writing is in obedience to His will and leading. Her books are also good for our business!

—Lucille Montgomery, Owner/Manager
Christian Book Store, Inc.
Baton Rouge, LA 70806

About The Author

Deborah Lynne is the author of several inspirational fiction novels. *Grace, a Gift of Love; All in God's Time; Passion from the Heart; Be Not Afraid* BK 1 SCM; *Testimony of Innocence* BK 2 SCM; *The Truth Revealed* BK 3 SCM; *Against Her Will* BK 4 SCM; *Crime in The Big Easy; After You're Gone; Hidden Secrets; Bayou Secrets* – a collection of Deborah Lynne novels. She writes romance, mystery, and suspense. 2017 releases her first Young Adult fiction series – *Chasing the Lights* a Cooper Parks' Adventures, as well as a non-fiction – daily devotional called *Guidance from The Light.* As she wrote it, she downloaded one month at a time onto her website. It is free for the taking.

Lynne loves sharing the Lord and she hopes you'll check her books out. www.author-deborahlynne.com

Deborah was widowed in 2014. She's the mother of 3 and grandmother of 4. She loves her life living in the south with warm weather **almost** year round and having her family close by. She resides in the home she and her husband settled in after they retired.

She hopes you enjoy her revised version of *All in God's Time*. She'd love to hear from you. Feel free to contact her. See below.

Facebook: http://www.facebook.com/author.deborahlynne
Email: deblynne8@gmail.com

Her books are also available in e-book form. Paperbacks are in your local library. Some are even in hardback. Enjoy the reads!

www.ingramcontent.com/pod-product-compliance
Lightning Source LLC
Chambersburg PA
CBHW071253170626
46809CB00001B/207